A LOVERS' QUARREL

Ginger Judson was one of the most graceful and attractive dancers in the troupe. She wore a loose-fitting black sweatshirt and black tights. Her eyes were red, her mascara smudged, her complexion pale and translucent. She took a chair and faced Lieutenant Harald.

"I heard Emmy and Eric quarrel," she said.

"What did they fight about?" Sigrid asked.

"I don't know." Ginger lowered her eyes.

"You must have heard something," the Lieutenant prodded.

"He was jealous," the dancer whispered. "He accused Emmy of sleeping with someone else."

"Who?"

"Me." She raised her eyes defiantly. "He said she was sleeping with me."

Bantam Books offers the finest in classic and modern American murder mysteries. Ask your bookseller for the books you have missed.

Stuart Palmer
Murder on the Blackboard

Craig Rice
The Lucky Stiff

Rex Stout
Broken Vase
Death of a Dude
Death Times Three
Fer-de-Lance
The Final Deduction
Gambit
The Rubber Band

Max Allan Collins
The Dark City

William Kienzle
The Rosary Murders

Joseph Louis
Madelaine
The Trouble with Stephanie

M.J. Adamson
Not Till a Hot February
A February Face
Remember March

Conrad Haynes
Bishop's Gambit, Declined
Perpetual Check

Barbara Paul
First Gravedigger
But He Was Already Dead When I Got There

P.M. Carlson
Murder Unrenovated
Rehearsal for Murder

Ross Macdonald
The Goodbye Look
Sleeping Beauty
The Name Is Archer
The Drowning Pool
The Underground Man

Margaret Maron
The Right Jack
Baby Doll Games

William Murray
When the Fat Man Sings

Robert Goldsborough
Murder in E Minor
Death on Deadline

Sue Grafton
"A" Is for Alibi
"B" Is for Burglar
"C" Is for Corpse

R. D. Brown
Hazzard
Villa Head

A. E. Maxwell
Just Another Day in Paradise
The Frog and the Scorpion

Rob Kantner
Back-Door Man
The Harder They Hit

Joseph Telushkin
The Unorthodox Murder of Rabbi Wahl

Richard Hilary
Snake in the Grasses
Pieces of Cream
Pillow of the Community

Carolyn G. Hart
Design for Murder
Death on Demand

Lia Matera
Where Lawyers Fear to Tread
A Radical Departure

Robert Crain
The Monkey's Raincoat

Keith Peterson
The Trapdoor

Jim Stinson
Double Exposure

Carolyn Wheat
Where Nobody Dies

BABY DOLL GAMES

Margaret Maron

BANTAM BOOKS
TORONTO · NEW YORK · LONDON · SYDNEY · AUCKLAND

BABY DOLL GAMES

A Bantam Book / May 1988

ISBN 0-553-27281-0

Published simultaneously in the United States and Canada

Bantam Books are published by Bantam Books, a division of
Bantam Doubleday Dell Publishing Group, Inc. Its trademark,
consisting of the words "Bantam Books" and the portrayal of a
rooster, is Registered in U.S. Patent and Trademark Office and
in other countries. Marca Registrada. Bantam Books, 666 Fifth
Avenue, New York, New York 10103.

My thanks to Dr. Martha Wingfield of Chapel Hill, NC for her helpful comments on certain psychiatric technicalities.

Prologue

July

In Darlene Makaroff's shabby apartment on the Lower East Side, the ancient window air-conditioning unit wheezed into silence shortly after noon. By nightfall, a humid, almost suffocating heat had built up in the cramped rooms until Darlene was driven to a drunken search for a hammer and screwdriver with which to pry open windows that had been painted shut for years.

Bourbon usually made the seductive young woman cheerfully affectionate, but tonight she was sweaty and irritable. It didn't help that four-year-old Corrie kept whining about being hungry even though Darlene had sent Tanya down to the deli for heroes and a bag of potato chips only a couple of hours earlier.

"Why don't you let 'em get an ice cream?" asked Ray Thorpe, pouring himself another two inches of amber liquid.

From *her* bottle, Darlene noted resentfully.

"You so loaded with money, Mr. Gotrocks, *you* put out for ice cream."

Her daughters looked at the big man hopefully. Still something of a kid himself, the twenty-year-old construction worker was occasionally made generous by alcohol. Once he'd given Tanya a ten-dollar bill and told her to buy all the chocolate she and Corrie could eat.

But that was when he first started coming around, when he wanted to be alone with Darlene and was embarrassed by two little wide-awake girls there in the apartment. Now their presence no longer bothered him.

He just pulled Darlene into the bedroom and shut the door.

He wanted to go into the bedroom now, but Darlene was in a contrary mood and petulantly eluded his caresses. She kept mouthing about what a steam bath the place was while Corrie whimpered ever more fretfully. The younger child was tired and sleepy but so hot that her short brown hair was curled into tight ringlets by perspiration.

Finally nine-year-old Tanya went out to the kitchen, rummaged around under the sink filled with dirty dishes, and came back with the tools her mother wanted.

"That's my good little honeybunch," crooned Darlene, giving the child a sweaty hug. She wasn't wearing a bra and the thin cotton shirt clung to her ripe curves.

"I'll do it," said Ray, eyeing her hungrily.

"Over my dead body. This is my house and I'll open my own goddamned windows."

Darlene drained her glass and moved unsteadily to the nearest window. Carefully placing the screwdriver where the window sash met the sill, she began to tap the handle with her hammer. It took her several minutes to chip around the entire window, then she gave a strong shove but it wouldn't budge.

"No woman knows how to use a hammer," Ray jeered, flexing bulging biceps. He wore jeans and a dark red cut-out tank top and as he held out his hand for the hammer, his muscles glistened in the light cast by bare bulbs from a broken fixture overhead. "Let a man do it, baby."

Instead of laughing as she usually did when Ray joked about what women were good for, Darlene snarled a curse and started hammering directly on the window sash, trying to break the seal.

Slender and small, with her long brown hair tied back in a bouncy ponytail, she looked younger than her twenty-four years and her bitchy stubbornness fueled the big man's machismo. He wrested the hammer from her hand and the tip of the screwdriver caught his arm, grazing a bloody red line from wrist to elbow.

His temper flared at that and he shoved Darlene aside and tried to use the screwdriver like a crowbar to lever the window open. The ancient wood creaked and splintered but refused to give. As Ray and Darlene cursed and shrieked at each other in the simmering, airless room, the little girls cowered together on the greasy, dilapidated couch, once again forgotten by the two adults who raged around them.

"Shut your stupid face!" Ray shouted with a threatening lift of his big fist.

He had punched her once or twice before, but when Darlene was drunk, she was fearless. Ray's incompetence with the window suddenly seemed a hilarious repetition of his shortcomings in bed early that morning and she pointed out the parallels in increasingly graphic language.

"Shut up!" cried Ray in a towering rage. "Shut up— *shut up*—SHUT UP!"

With every *shut up*, his fist came down on Darlene's head, but it wasn't until Corrie and Tanya started screaming and blood splashed on his bare arm that Ray realized he still had the hammer in his sweaty fist.

"Oh Jesus!" he moaned, and his eyes locked with little Tanya's in an instant of horrified awareness as Darlene slid to the floor. The hammer fell from his grip, unheard beneath Corrie's wails, and Ray fled from the apartment, banging the door locked behind him.

Chapter 1

In an improvisational dance theater on lower Eighth Avenue, children watched silently as the friendly yellow moonlight of the last scene faded to a cold blue-white and the pumpkin patch was transformed into a graveyard. Pale blue lights swirled like mist across the stage through a section of sharply spiked cast-iron fence and picked out a row of cardboard tombstones at the rear of the stage. As taped electronic music quickened its eerie tempo, a narrow white beam flitted around the sketchy cemetery. The spotlight mimicked the nervous staccato of woodblocks, skittered away at an unexpected clash of triangles, and settled at last on a slender white form as it pushed aside a cardboard slab and rose like a hesitant spirit uncurling from the grave.

In the audience, Dr. Christa Ferrell felt a tug on her sleeve and inclined her head.

"That's Emmy," whispered the five-year-old beside her on one of the low-backed wooden pews which served as seating in this shoestring theater.

Dr. Ferrell smiled at her nephew to show she'd heard and turned back to the stage with renewed interest. She had met the dancer but had never seen her perform. The famous Emmy Mion! Emmy Mion, who could run like the wind, turn endless cartwheels, leap tall buildings in a single bound, then walk on her hands and water, too, to hear Calder tell it.

Ruefully and somewhat clinically, Christa Ferrell acknowledged to herself the twinge of jealousy she'd felt when she realized that Emmy Mion was the object of young Calder's awakening sexual awareness. For five years the psychiatrist had shared a special closeness with her brother's son, and while she could intellectualize his sudden ardor for the dancer, she couldn't completely quash her own feelings of displacement aroused by his uncritical admiration for the woman.

In the opening scene of this Halloween dance fantasy for children, five dancers, identically clad in black tights and baggy black sweatshirts, had worn grotesque and comical jack-o'-lantern heads of papier-mâché with brown crepe paper streamers to suggest cornstalks. If Emmy Mion had been one of the pumpkins, Calder hadn't been able to distinguish her, and Christa rather doubted it since there hadn't been time for a change into the white leotard and tattered draperies she now wore as a wistful little ghost dancing (and dancing very beautifully, Christa generously admitted) through the deserted graveyard.

According to the mimeographed program, the movements in this solo scene were to be improvised. If so—and in Christa Ferrell's experience, improvisation was seldom as exciting as reasoned-out choreography—Emmy Mion possessed an imagination equal to her technical virtuosity as she danced loneliness and curiosity, now peering through the iron palings as if seeking company, now trying to entice to her outstretched hand an owl silhouetted among the bare branches of a stylized tree.

Not much taller than a slender child herself, the dancer wore her dark brown hair in a ragged, gamin cut which suited her rounded chin and wide-eyed look of wonder.

As the indeterminate electronic music slowed to isolated percussive plonks and pings, the young ghost was unexpectedly joined by one of the jack-o'-lanterns, who immediately set the children in the audience to giggling as he clumsily tried to imitate some of Emmy's intricate movements. Failing, he invited her to a dance which first parodied a cheek-to-cheek tango and then turned increasingly athletic as the music picked up tempo.

The jack-o'-lantern appeared to hide in the shadows, the ghost sought him out. They played hide-and-seek among the tombstones, then he fled to the tree, swung himself up into the bare branches, and the ghost followed. As the music built to a crescendo, the jack-o'-lantern clamped his leg around a craggy tree branch to anchor himself and invited the little ghost to fly into his arms for a soaring lift.

She was held aloft in his strong hands for a triumphant finale, high above the stage, the wispy tatters of her dress fluttering in the spotlight almost as if she were truly flying.

It was a magical moment and the audience had begun to clap in spontaneous delight when, with an abrupt and unexpected flip of the jack-o'-lantern's hands, the small ghost was hurled from her precarious perch and thrown with such brutal force that her body slammed into the sharp pointed spikes of the iron fence directly below.

For one horror-filled instant, the pure white spotlight followed her torn body, then the theater was plunged into utter darkness.

But not before everyone had seen the bright red fountains of blood jetting from the motionless white form.

Chapter 2

A commanding voice cut across the horror and bewilderment building among the spectators. "Everybody stay in your seats, please, till we can see what we're doing. I'm a police officer. Who's working the board? Could we get a little light down here, guy?"

A moment later, two ceiling fixtures at the back blazed on, and under their harsh brightness, the shabby theater was immediately stripped of any shadowy glamour invested by the stage lighting.

People blinked, disoriented by the sudden return to ordinary surroundings after that incredible scene onstage. A few parents frantically tried to distract their children, while the rest stood and craned for a better view of the darkened stage.

A confused babble arose as they tried to make sense of it.

"What happened?"

"Did she slip?"

"Dear God! He did it on *purpose*."

"No, she must have fallen."

"Look! She's not moving."

"He *did* throw her—I saw him!"

"Mother of Jesus! That poor kid!"

The stage lights were still doused and the jack-o'-lantern dancer had disappeared, but Emmy Mion's body remained impaled atop the fence. Her white dress was now drenched in red; blood pooled on the floor beneath her dangling feet.

Four horrified members of the dance troupe rushed out to the limp form and two of the men started to lift her down, but Officer Papaky, the off-duty policeman who'd spoken before, quickly moved to prevent them. "Everybody stay off the stage," he roared. "Nobody touch *nothing* and I mean it."

He hoisted himself to the edge of the proscenium and scanned the small crowd which gaped back at him, a stocky man with a receding hairline, who spoke with an authority that commanded temporary obedience. "I'm a police officer," he repeated. "Is there a doctor here?"

Christa Ferrell had already given her stunned nephew instructions to stay put and was pushing her way to the stage. "I am," she called.

Papaky cast a doubtful look at the very attractive blonde, then reached across the footlights to give her a hand up. "If there's any chance of saving her, Doctor, we'll get her down," he said in a low voice for her ears only, "but if she's already gone—"

"I understand."

Reassured by Dr. Ferrell's competent air, Papaky next directed his wife to find a phone. "Call the station. Tell them it's a possible homicide."

At the rear of the audience, he recognized a heavyset middle-aged black man who managed a nearby grocery store where the Papakys frequently shopped. Papaky asked him to guard the front entrance. No one was to enter or leave. The manager nodded and immediately stationed his bulk in front of the lobby door.

Behind Papaky, Christa Ferrell struggled to maintain a professional detachment as she examined the broken dancer in the dim light. It seemed unlikely that anyone could survive a spike through the carotid artery, but she went through the motions: no pulse in wrist or ankle, no reflexes from the open eyes, no indication of life at all.

Other members of the troupe had joined the five dancers who were still clad in their black leotards and loose sweatshirts. Like anxious shadows, they bunched in the wings to watch her. "Doctor?" pleaded a husky male voice.

"I'm sorry," Christa said, shaking her head gently.

"God, *no!*" The man shook off the others' restraining hands and started toward her, only to be driven back again by a determined Papaky.

"Right now, till we find out what really happened, this stage is off-limits, guy," he told the distraught dancer. "Nobody messes with it till the investigators get here."

He escorted Christa Ferrell down a short set of steps at the side of the stage and allowed her to rejoin her nephew, but requested that the rest of the company wait with him on the steps until the police experts arrived.

"Police *experts?*" asked one of the white-faced girls. "For an accident? Didn't Emmy slip?"

"Oh no," replied Ginger, her tall red-haired colleague. "I saw the whole thing. Eric threw her badly."

"What do you mean *Eric* threw her badly?" asked the youth who'd had to be restrained before. "This was supposed to be Emmy's solo scene. I was upstairs when it started."

The redhead looked puzzled. "Then who danced with Emmy? You, Cliff? Win?"

The two men seemed equally puzzled as each denied his involvement.

"I think," interposed Officer Papaky, "that it would be better if you people didn't talk about it right now."

Papaky was not surprised that none of the men owned

up to partnering Emmy Mion. That had been no accidental drop. In his mind there was no doubt that the girl had
been thrown deliberately.

Upon joining the force four years ago, Papaky had
formed the habit of carrying a pocket-size notebook even
when off duty. He pulled it out now while he waited for
backups to arrive. After entering the time and place and a
condensed version of what he'd observed, he took down the
names and addresses of the light and stage designer; the
composer; a plump and flashily dressed woman who said
she designed the costumes; and the five remaining dancers, two women and three men. One of the men had the
same last name and address as the designer. "Husband and
wife?"

The woman, whose plumpness made her appear older
than the man, nodded.

The theater was so small that the audience could hear
Papaky's questions and the company's replies; and most of
the adults, still stunned by what had happened, were
willing to sink back into their seats and watch quietly, as if
Papaky's actions were a continuation of the interrupted
performance. Several children questioned their parents in
fearful whispers and scattered among them were at least
six or eight, like little Calder Ferrell, who realized that
Emmy Mion would never dance with them again and who
now sat with tears streaming down their innocent faces.

After several minutes, one anxious mother with two
sobbing children raised her voice to ask how much longer
they had to wait and subject their kids to this. "Couldn't
you at least pull the curtain?"

Male rumbles supported her growing distress.

Fortunately, new movement at the rear of the theater
quelled the mutiny as uniformed men from the precinct
finally arrived. Those who claimed no personal connection
with Emmy Mion were allowed to leave after giving their
names and addresses and showing some proof of identity
to the officers who guarded the door.

More officers came in, plainclothes now, who spread
out across the stage, measuring, photographing, examining everything in minute detail. Among them, directing
their activity, was a woman with watchful gray eyes and

short dark hair. She wore a loose off-white corduroy jacket, badly tailored gray slacks, and a nondescript black shirt. Although there was nothing particularly prepossessing about her, she seemed to be the still, quiet center from which order radiated. Her cool voice was seldom raised, yet when she did speak, the others listened.

Dr. Christa Ferrell paused as she gave her name to the officer at the door. "Who's that woman up there on the stage?"

"The tall skinny one? Lieutenant Harald."

"*Sigrid* Harald?"

"Yeah. You know her?"

"It's been years," Christa replied. Her mind raced with the possibilities this chance meeting might produce. "Look, I'm the doctor who first examined the body of—"

Abruptly she became aware of Calder's stricken face. "I have to take my nephew home first," she said, "but I think I ought to come back and speak to the lieutenant."

"Sure, Dr. Ferrell," said the officer. He made a notation by her name. "Remind me when you get here and I'll pass you back in."

Up on the stage, Lieutenant Sigrid Harald and her team had quickly debriefed Officer Papaky. They listened to his account of the dance performance, his observations about Emmy Mion's fall, and what he'd heard the other dancers say. Then, while the others fanned out to process the scene in their usual routine, the lieutenant watched quietly as an assistant medical examiner completed his examination of the young dancer. Officer Guidry had already photographed the torn body from every angle and now pointed her cameras at potentially significant details turned up by the other detectives.

Lieutenant Harald's eyes swept over the stage, noting exits, the position of the curtains and lights, and the sketchy scenery, but she kept coming back to that iron fence and skeleton tree.

The ten-feet-long, six-feet-tall section of cast-iron railing ran parallel to the front of the stage and was bolted securely to the floor at both ends. Vertical stability had been increased by anchoring it to the "tree," a rectangle of open steel scaffolding four feet square and approximately eight feet tall, which had been transformed with cardboard limbs and twigs, then spray-painted black.

All the stage lights were on now and Detectives Lowry and Eberstadt had patiently begun dusting the steel scaffold. The matte black paint should yield usable fingerprints, but Sigrid pessimistically expected to learn that every dancer in the troupe had swarmed over those rungs today.

Unlike the tree, the iron fence seemed less a part of make-believe than something scavenged from a real turn-of-the-century graveyard. A narrow band of ornamental cast-iron flowers and ivy twined across the bottom and each paling was tipped with an exceedingly sharp point.

As she watched, Dr. Cohen turned to her. "If you've got all you need, Lieutenant, I'll take her now."

"Eberstadt?" she asked.

Matt Eberstadt, a tall, heavyset officer entering middle age, looked up from his task. "I already got her prints, Lieutenant."

"Guidry?"

"Right here," answered the young photographer, reappearing from the left wing of the stage with her cameras. She waited until Emmy Mion's body had been gently lifted down and placed on a stretcher, then took several close-ups of the wounds.

As ambulance attendants wheeled the sheeted form up the short aisle, Sigrid noted that the remaining members of the dance company had been dispersed in separated seats around the theater and that Detectives Bernie Peters and Elaine Albee had begun taking down preliminary statements. Most of the audience was gone, no very young children in view and only ten or twelve adults and adolescents.

Her attention was suddenly snagged by a bright orange-and-yellow ascot worn by one of those adults, a tall and softly corpulent figure with hooded eyes and a sheepish expression on his familiar face.

The last person Lieutenant Sigrid Harald expected to find at a homicide scene was the man with whom she shared an apartment, and she had to stop and rethink the probabilities raised by finding him here in this run-down theater. Ever since their first meeting back in early spring, Roman Tramegra had pestered her for background and "color" so that he could write an authentic-sounding thriller. For one perplexed moment, Sigrid wondered if he'd decided to gather information on his own and if so, how he'd arrived on the scene before she had.

Almost immediately, however, she recalled that near the end of the summer he'd occasionally spoken of writing a scenario for a semiprofessional dance troupe that had recently won some sort of grant. Since Tramegra supplemented his income from a small family trust with various oddball writing chores, she hadn't paid too much attention to his chatter. She now remembered thinking that he seemed disappointed when, in answer to his inquiry yesterday, she'd told him that she'd be working all weekend.

Sigrid again scanned the mimeographed program Officer Papaky had handed her when she first arrived and read that this afternoon's performance was the premiere of a dance commissioned by the 8th-AV-8 Dance Company with a grant from the National Endowment for the Arts. Music was composed by a Sergio Avril; the dances were scripted by Roman Tramegra and choreographed by Emmy Mion.

Accepting the inevitable, Sigrid stepped down from the stage and walked over to her friend, who stood up as she approached.

"My dear, *dear* Sigrid! I'm so *grateful* you're in charge of this horrid ordeal." Roman Tramegra possessed an extraordinarily deep bass voice but he usually spoke in italics with an accent that was half Midwest and half Piccadilly Circus. His flashy neck scarf was reined in by an English squire's discreet brown corduroy jacket, complete with leather arm patches, and softly pleated brown wool slacks which helped disguise his girth. The impression he gave was not of obesity so much as the boneless softness of an overindulged Persian cat.

As self-centered as a cat, too, but Sigrid knew he also possessed a feline curiosity that was as all-inclusive as it was instinctive. Surely Roman would have observed these people quite closely.

Yet not closely enough. To her quietly blunt, "Who was the jack-o'-lantern dancer, Roman?" he gave a helpless shrug. "My dear, I simply cannot say. It could have been any of them."

She motioned for him to sit and propped her foot on the wooden pew in front of him. "So this is where you've been spending so much time lately."

"A poor place, but our own," he intoned sonorously, carefully smoothing long strands of side hair up over the top of his bare head. As Sigrid expected, Roman had acquired the history of this three-story brick building on lower Eighth Avenue and was predictably pleased to instruct her.

"Not that I know every little peccadillo," he cautioned, "but I believe it began life as a neighborhood movie house, then a nightclub devoted to sexual arousal, a disco, and God knows what else before the troupe organized as the 8th-AV-8 and scraped together enough money for a lease. My dear, you can't *believe* what they ask for a place like this! As you see, the old plush movie seats must have been ripped out *years* ago."

"And the pews?"

"Left over from its days as The First Assembly of God Almighty," sniffed Roman, who was high Episcopalian.

Again Sigrid turned her steady gaze upon the small theater which, even with the pews packed, would barely accommodate more than a hundred fifty people. Officer Papaky had estimated today's attendance at around thirty-five adults and perhaps forty-five children—hardly Lincoln Center or even P.S. 122, but respectable for a low-budget operation which seemed to be held together with spit and string and the eternal optimism of youth.

"My first foray into the art of Terpsichore," mourned Roman, "and look what happens!"

"What did happen here this afternoon?" Sigrid asked abruptly.

"We called it *Ghosties and Ghouls.* I thought it should have been *Fantasia for All Hallows' Eve* and Sergio wanted *Scream Time,* so we compromised."

"Sergio is the Sergio Avril listed in the program?"

Tramegra gestured discreetly to a meek-looking skeletal man in thick gold-rimmed glasses, who leaned forward with his chin propped on his hands at the far end of the front pew absorbed by the action onstage. "A talented composer but *totally* unappreciated."

When conversing, Roman Tramegra liked to wander up and down hills and wallow in all the valleys. Sigrid usually preferred that he just skim across the peaks, but now she listened quietly.

"Sergio has occasionally provided music for the dancers gratis—exposure is the only way to get discovered, is it not?—and Emmy asked him to create something original for them."

"Emmy Mion ran things?"

Roman considered. "Let us say she was first among equals. It was supposed to be an egalitarian enterprise but, yes, hers was the moving spirit. She acted. The others usually reacted."

The company had received a rather large grant back in the spring for a children's project and for the first time, there was money not only to commission Sergio Avril but enough to cover a scenarist as well, hence Roman's presence.

"We decided to do this autumnal fantasy. Sergio is a *genius* at the synthesizer. Quite deliciously eerie sounds. Our talents meshed so *beautifully*. I could visualize the whole scene the *minute* he began to play: an overgrown, deserted garden. Silent. Ominous." Roman's bass deepened dramatically.

"A pale beam of moonlight moves down the aisle, picks its way through the cold iron fence while the music simply *tiptoes* along with the spotlight. A huge pile of pumpkins, then *Bling!* The spotlight widens, the music *explodes* and the pumpkin pile becomes a *riot* of dancing jack-o'-lanterns. *Wonderful!*"

"And then?" Sigrid prompted.

"Then they exit, and the pumpkin patch becomes a graveyard. Emmy was *quite* good at improvisation, so we merely left it that this was to be a change-of-mood piece that she could dance any way she wished. Sergio gave her some marvelously sepulchral music for this passage and I

sketched in some suggestions. She was supposed to be
dancing alone here, giving the others time to catch their
breath and get ready for the next scene with the stuffed
goblins."

"Those figures I saw in the wings?" asked Sigrid.
"How were they to be used?"

"Like big puppets. You see, Helen Delgado—she
designs the sets and the costumes and is, I might add, the
consort of Cliff Delgado—" He paused and Sigrid nodded
to show that she remembered reading the dancer's name
in the program.

"Helen, you see, stitched together some tights and
sweatshirts and stuffed them with excelsior, so they're
rather light but quite lifelike, especially with the masks.
You *must* see the dance. *Utterly* postmodern! Puppets and
people are dressed alike so that when everything is moving, you can scarcely tell which is which flying through the
air. Marvelous!"

Sigrid consulted the mimeographed program. "So
Emmy Mion was supposed to be dancing onstage alone.
Where would the others be then?"

"Around." Roman threw up his hands. "There's no
particular drill. I suppose they would remove those pumpkin heads and towel off—dancers sweat like *horses*, you
know. Perhaps get something to drink, then put on their
hoods and masks."

At Sigrid's questioning gaze, he elucidated. "In the
next scene, when they were to dance with the goblin
puppets. To further the similarity between illusion and
reality, everyone wears a black hood and a goblin mask,
those cheap plastic things from the dime store that children wear for trick or treat."

Black hoods and goblin masks. To go with baggy
sweatshirts and pumpkin heads and athletic women dancers who were probably as strong as the men. That's all we
needed, thought Sigrid, absently rubbing her left arm
where she'd been knifed two weeks earlier. It was healing
nicely and no longer required a sling, yet considerable
tenderness still lingered. "So you weren't exaggerating
when you said that the jack-o'-lantern could have been any
of them."

"Exaggerate? Dear child, *when* do I exaggerate?" Roman asked indignantly.

"A figure of speech, sorry. But any one of those five could have thrown her?" She peered again at the names of the dancers listed in her crumpled program. "Cliff Delgado, Ulrike Innes, Ginger Judson, Eric Kee, or Wingate West?"

"Well, no, not *any* of them," Tramegra admitted.

"But if they were all dressed identically in that first scene—"

"They were, they *were*! But you're forgetting *anatomy*."

Although Sigrid had given the five dancers only cursory glances thus far, she had immediately noticed their similarity in build. "In a group, you might spot small differences in height or thickness of legs, but dancing alone, Roman? With a bright orange pumpkin head?"

"While it is true that pumpkins and paper streamers and loose black sweatshirts form an effective disguise for the upper half of the torso, you are overlooking a fundamental fact," Roman said magisterially. "They were all wearing *tights*, my dear, and I do not exaggerate when I say they were quite, *quite* tight. The jack-o'-lantern who threw Emmy Mion onto those spikes was undeniably *male*."

Chapter 3

Backstage, lights had been turned on everywhere. The walls immediately abutting the stage were painted black, but beyond the audience's view, the bare brick walls had been inexpertly sloshed with white paint. Sergio Avril's sound equipment and Nate Richmond's electronic light board stood inside the front wing of stage left, partitioned from the rest of the backstage area by one of the threadbare maroon velour curtains, which, according to Roman Tramegra, had been purchased thirdhand from a cinema up in Harlem. A folding metal chair held one of

those eerie goblin puppets that looked strangely human in
their cheap plastic masks.

Curious, Lieutenant Harald lifted the mask and was
vaguely disconcerted to find only a featureless black
smoothness beneath.

Walking past the light board, she saw that one could
turn right, down a short flight of steps, and open a door to
the audience or step out into an alley; or one could turn
left where a spiral iron staircase led to dressing rooms on
the second floor. Beyond the stairs, a wide hall opened
onto several rooms behind the stage.

The backdrop for today's performance was a simple
canvas screen painted midnight blue to suggest a Halloween sky. At the rear of the stage was a brick fire wall and,
since the theater contained no other large practice space,
the stage side was lined with mirrors. A narrow passage-
way had been left between backdrop and mirrored wall
and, on the other side of the wall, a wider hallway held
storage rooms of various sorts, a three-cubicle unisex rest
room, and Helen Delgado's workshop.

The layout of stage right was similar to stage left
except that there was only a single door down to the
audience and a wider straight flight of steps comprised the
stairway.

The large corner office beyond the stairs belonged
primarily to Emmy Mion; and as soon as Lieutenant
Harald stepped inside, she immediately sensed a duality
in the dead woman's nature.

The left side served as the troupe's business office,
while the right side was apparently Emmy Mion's personal
work space, complete with a cluttered drawing table where
she had worked out the movements for music played on a
nearby tape deck. At least twenty tape cassettes were
heaped beside the player amid a rat's nest of papers
covered with the obscure hieroglyphics of choreography.
Towels were draped on a rusty radiator, along with jeans,
leotards, and rainbow-striped leg warmers; and the walls
were layered with pictures of the troupe and sensitive
pictures of small children, usually barefooted and in practice leotards. A jugful of autumn branches shed its leaves
among the notepads and pens on the work table, and an

adjacent bookcase was jammed higgledy-piggledy with paperback novels, bulging manila file folders, and a dozen or more tattered dance books.

On the end wall above the bookcase, surrounded by smaller pictures, was an unframed poster-sized black-and-white photograph of Emmy Mion and two of the dancers Sigrid had noticed before: the tall, redheaded girl and the Asian boy. All three were in midair crossing leaps and the photograph radiated a joyous delight in lithe movement.

In sum, it was a slapdash happy-go-lucky area which seemed to overflow with creative energy.

The office side of the room was painfully organized: a dented file cabinet, every drawer tightly closed, stood at either end of a bank of open steel shelves upon which office supplies were precisely aligned; a corner table held a covered electric typewriter, two accountant's ledgers, and an Out-basket with a neat packet of stamped envelopes; and the desk, while battered and scuffed, was completely bare except for a pencil jar, telephone, stapler, and tape dispenser. Even notes and snapshots and newspaper clippings had been thumbtacked to the wall above the book shelves in an orderly fashion.

Sigrid, who had an orderly mind herself, was drawn to that part of the room. "We'll set up here," she told Detective Cluett, pushing an extra chair over to the desk.

As she spoke, the telephone gave a low, almost inaudible ring, then the answering machine cut in with a taped message. Sigrid leaned across the desk and turned up the volume. A woman's lilting voice said, "Eighth-Avenue-Eight Dance Theater. Our two o'clock matinee performance is the world premiere of *Ghosties and Ghouls*. Repeat performance at eight tonight and Sunday at four. Tickets available at the door. Four dollars for adults, three for children under twelve. If you're calling about something else, leave your name and number at the sound of the tone and one of us will get back to you. I promise."

There was a beep and then another voice spoke with the deeper tone of an older woman. "Helen Delgado? This is Flashy Trash over on Seventh Avenue. You said to let you know when we had some cheap rhinestones. We got

in a new batch yesterday, so if you're still interested, drop
by. We're open till six-thirty."

Sigrid returned the volume to its original setting and
as she circled the desk, she saw that the bottom drawer
had been pulled out as far as it would go. On the other
side of the room, she wouldn't have given it a second
thought; on this side, it seemed out of character.

"Better get Eberstadt or Lowry in to print this," she
said to the older detective who had propped himself
against the door frame.

"Right," said Cluett and lumbered off to summon
help.

Detective Second Grade Michael Cluett, pushing
sixty if he were a day, had been specialled in from Brooklyn
to help cover her department's temporary depletion of
manpower. Among the missing was Detective Charles
Tildon, who'd been sidelined earlier in the month by a
near-fatal explosion and who wasn't expected back on
active duty before January. Sigrid would have preferred to
work alone till his return; but her boss, Captain McKinnon,
had saddled her with Mick Cluett with unusually brusque
orders that gave her no choice in the matter.

She hadn't realized how much she'd come to depend
on Tillie's cheerful and unobtrusive helpfulness until she
had to do without him. Although his weakness for giving
equal weight to every little detail in an investigation had
often irritated her, at least he wasn't lazy. In fact he was
almost like a terrier doubling back and forth across a case.
Cluett, on the other hand, reminded her of a sag-bellied
phlegmatic basset. If he'd ever possessed any detective
skills, they seemed to have receded with his hairline. He
was like the poet's old dog that barked backwards without
getting up. Oh, he did whatever he was asked to do
willingly enough and if he resented taking orders from a
younger woman, as did so many of the old-timers, he
didn't show it; it was just that he never anticipated a
request and seldom volunteered an action.

He reappeared, trailing Matt Eberstadt, and though
Eberstadt was in his late forties, the contrast between the
two men was more striking than their similarities. Both
had iron-gray hair, but Eberstadt's had retreated to the top

of his head where it stood up in tight wiry curls like a
steel-wool halo, while Cluett's lay flat; both were overweight but, unlike Cluett's flaccid girth, Eberstadt's extra
pounds seemed solid and he was still fighting a rearguard
action against adding more. More importantly, Matt
Eberstadt expected to earn his pay.

"Got something for me, Lieutenant?" he asked briskly.

"These drawers," said Sigrid, stepping back from
Emmy Mion's desk.

"Doesn't quite go with the rest of the desk, does it?"
Eberstadt asked, automatically comparing the strict order
of this corner to the rifled condition of the open bottom
drawer. He knelt heavily and began dusting the wooden
handle. Only vague smudges appeared, but he carefully
transferred them to a white card just in case. The other
two drawers were a repeat.

While he worked, the telephone rang twice more.
Each time the caller hung up as soon as the taped message
began.

Eberstadt removed the drawers and dusted the un-
dersides of the handles but with no more luck than before.
"Sorry, Lieutenant. The wood's just too rough to take a
good print. Want me to do any of the contents?"

The bottom drawer contained crumpled envelopes,
carbon paper, typewriter supplies, and other office odds
and ends that seemed to hold little significance and had
probably been handled by several in the company.

Sigrid shook her head. "Don't bother. Did you finish
with the scaffold?"

"Almost. Lowry's up doing the top round now."

"Fine. When you're through processing the stage,
take a look around the rest of the theater, you know the
drill. I understand the killer ran offstage on this side so see
if there's anything to indicate which way he went after
that."

As Eberstadt packed up his fingerprint kit and left the
room, Peters and Albee, the two officers who had handled
the preliminary interviews, passed him in the doorway.
Sigrid motioned them over. "What do you have so far?"
she asked, taking a pen and notepad from the deep

pockets of her shapeless white jacket and placing them on the neat desk top.

Mick Cluett was sent back to the auditorium to help keep the witnesses separated, Bernie Peters co-opted one of the wooden straight chairs and straddled it backwards with his arms resting atop the back, and Elaine Albee brought over the tall stool from the drawing table and perched on it with the two-inch heel of one calf-length boot hooked over the middle rung while they discussed the murder.

The younger detectives were both in their late twenties but Peters was already the father of two preschool daughters and a brand new baby boy, while Albee, a bright-eyed whiz kid with short blond curls, had kept herself unencumbered despite Detective Jim Lowry's best efforts.

They nodded agreement when Sigrid repeated Roman Tramegra's opinion of the killer's sex, so she leaned forward with her elbows on the desk, her slender fingers laced beneath her chin, and invited them to tell her more about the three male dancers.

"My money's on Cliff Delgado," said Albee.

"Wingate West," said Bernie Peters with equal certainty.

"That space cadet? Christ!"

Sigrid fixed Elaine Albee with her calm gray eyes. "Why Delgado?"

"I could say feminine intuition." Albee's flippant remark was aimed at Peters, who possessed a latent streak of chauvinism, which he usually tried to hide from Lieutenant Harald. "But of the three possibilities, Delgado seems the most intense and impulsive and this *does* look like murder done on impulse, doesn't it?"

"If it was murder," Sigrid answered mildly.

"*If?*" snorted Peters. "She didn't just fall, Lieutenant. Everybody we've talked to says she was thrown, no ifs, ands, or buts about it. Cold-blooded, deliberate murder's what I say, and Wingate West may look spaced-out, but I'll bet you he started planning this the day he found that fence."

"West is responsible for the fence?"

"They were tearing down an old house on West

Eighteenth between Eighth and Ninth last month and the wreckers gave it to West for a few bucks. He even got 'em to drop it off in the alley. The thing weighs a ton, but the eight of 'em managed to walk it onstage and bolt it down when they started rehearsing ten days ago."

"Nobody brings home a ten-foot-long iron fence for a murder weapon." Elaine Albee's blue eyes flashed scornfully. "And if West'd been planning to kill her that long in advance, why'd he wait till the spotlight was on her and they were in front of an audience?"

Bernie Peters shrugged. "Who knows? You're the one who keeps saying the guy's spacey."

"Well, look at him!" Albee bounced from the stool and plucked a photograph from the wall. It was a three-quarter profile of Wingate West with his forehead resting on a window pane while rain beat against the glass outside. His features were attractively regular and perhaps someday he would mature into a handsome man, but the photograph revealed something childlike and unfinished about his wide mouth and, as Elaine Albee carefully pointed out, it wasn't so much that his gaze was unfocused and dreamy. "There's nobody home behind those eyes."

Sigrid remembered seeing cud-chewing cows on her grandmother's farm with more presence in their mild brown eyes than appeared in West's, but she left the thought unvoiced.

"I can see this guy forgetting to catch her, but to throw her down deliberately? No way!" Albee left the photograph on the desk top, returned to the stool, and crossed shapely legs beneath a skirt of russet suede that matched her boots. "Believe me, Lieutenant, Delgado's got the temperament. Besides, Ginger Judson said if the jack-o'-lantern wasn't Eric Kee, it had to be Cliff Delgado."

"What's his motive?" asked Peters, his usually mild face betraying his exasperation. He tugged at the plain maroon wool tie he wore with a navy-and-maroon plaid shirt.

Seated, Bernie Peters appeared to have the build of a six-foot athlete, but when he stood, he was no taller than the lieutenant's five-ten, for his torso was long in proportion to his legs. He had no problem with jackets—the navy

corduroy he wore today, though off-the-rack, fit perfectly—
but he often grumbled about the cost of getting his
trousers altered. If they fit his trim waist, they were
always three inches too long, and his wife was too busy
with a full-time job, the kids, and the house to add
tailoring to her chores, no matter how pinched their budget.

"So what's West's motive?" Albee challenged.

Sigrid held up her hand to stop their not-quite-
amiable bickering. "What about the third man? Eric Kee?"

"They were lovers and he really seems torn up,"
Albee said positively, and Peters agreed.

"He's an actor as well as a dancer," Sigrid reminded
them crisply.

"That's no act," said Peters. "The guy's really hurting,
Lieutenant."

"So it's either West or Delgado?" asked Sigrid, tapping her pen against her blank notepad. "No possibility
that it could have been one of the others, the composer or
what's his name? The light designer?" She fished through
her pockets for that program she'd misplaced.

"Nate Richmond," said Peters. "Couldn't have been
him. Richmond was working the lights from a second-level
booth at the back of the house."

"And Sergio Avril might know how to dance," Albee
said, swinging one foot with a doubtful air, "but he was
supposed to be at the sound controls. He couldn't have
changed to street clothes and made it back with the others
by the time the lights came on."

Sigrid found the crumpled program, smoothed it out,
and read through the names again. "Nate Richmond had a
spotlight on the whole scene. I'll start with him," she decided.

Chapter 4

"I wish I could help, Lieutenant Harald, but it was
Emmy's dance. I kept the baby white on her, tight and

focused, and left him in a general blue." Nate Richmond
wore a thin gold wire ring in his left ear and throughout
his account of Emmy Mion's last performance, he lounged
on the straight wooden chair with his left elbow supported by his right arm so that he could turn the
dime-sized gold earring slowly, with a certain absent-
minded persistence, as if calmed by the repetitive circular motion of the smooth metal through the hole in his
earlobe.

"Weren't you surprised when one of the jack-o'-lanterns
returned to dance with her?" Sigrid asked.

Richmond's long thin fingers hesitated, then resumed
their treadmill monotony. "Not really. There's always a lot
of improv. Even if we rehearse it one way, they'll usually
do something different." A gentle smile crept across his
small pointed face as if he were remembering felicitous
variations.

"How old are you, Mr. Richmond?" Sigrid asked
curiously, for she was finding it difficult to get a fix on
him. Usually she could place a person within a couple
of years, but Nate Richmond was different. An inch
shorter than she, with a slender, childlike frame, he
wore the ordinary uniform of any young working artist:
jeans and leather vest over a dark shirt, two gold
chains, and sneakers. His frizzy brown hair was clipped
short on the top and sides, then allowed to cover the
nape of his neck in the back. There was only a hint of
crinkles around his sea-green eyes but they looked as if
they'd seen more years than his gnomish face would
indicate.

"I'm thirty-three and, yeah, I knew Emmy before we
came to New York, if that's what you mean. Out in
California. I worked lights for an improvisational theater
near the campus while she was finishing up her master's at
UCLA. She used to come backstage, ask a lot of questions.
We worked out some stuff together. When she was ready
to do her thesis dance, she asked me to light it for her and
I did. We had a lot of fun."

Sigrid caught the wistfulness in his tone. Beyond his
shoulder, she saw again that large photograph of Emmy
Mion, her whole being electric with delight as she poised

in midair. She wasn't really pretty—her eyes were small and too closely spaced, her chin too childishly round—but the radiance of her smile seemed to come from deep within and did not appear to be a surface accessory turned on and off for the camera.

And now that she looked, Sigrid saw the dancer's face in dozens of the photographs pinned around the room: Emmy Mion in various combinations with the other dancers of the company, alone or surrounded by young boys and girls, her tiny figure scarcely larger than theirs. In none of those pictures, however, did Sigrid immediately see one of Emmy and Nate Richmond together; yet in looking at that small vibrant form, she sensed that in their California days they might have played off each other like two children.

In and of themselves, though, the photographs interested her. Her mother was an award-winning photojournalist, so she recognized their quality. "These pictures are quite good. Who's the photographer?"

"I play around with cameras some," Richmond answered. "No big deal. The kids like them, though, and the parents like them enough to buy, so it brings us in a little extra money."

He looked around the walls with something like nostalgia. "The children change even as you look at them," he said wistfully. "They're so dawn-of-the-world, aren't they? God! This has been a happy place and Emmy was so gentle with the kids."

"Were you in love with her?" Sigrid asked.

Until that question, Nate Richmond had seemed dreamily detached from the then and there of reality. Suddenly he dropped both hands to his lap and his attention focused upon the police officers. "She was good. Damned good. She shouldn't have been killed."

"Who was it, Mr. Richmond?" Sigrid asked, leaning forward to study him intently.

For a moment Nate Richmond stared back just as intently, then the intensity ebbed away. He shrugged his thin shoulders once more and slumped back in the wooden chair to resume absently twisting the gold ring in his ear again. "I had the baby white on Emmy," he repeated. "It was her dance."

"But you've known these guys," Bernie Peters interrupted impatiently. He flipped through the notes he'd taken earlier. "You're an original member of the company, aren't you?"

"Yes."

"So you've been seeing them dance for the last two years," said Elaine Albee, sharing Peters's impatience.

"I was concentrating on Emmy," he repeated, a defensive edge in his voice.

"The killer was able to blend in with the others when you doused the lights, Mr. Richmond," Sigrid said. "Why did you do that?"

"Was it to give him time to get away?" asked Peters.

Richmond's bewildered eyes swung from one face to another and rested on Elaine Albee. "I had to turn them off," he told her plaintively. "The blood—it wasn't right to let everyone see her like that—so much blood."

Impulsively, Albee patted his hand. "We understand. But if you could just make a guess as to who—"

Richmond jerked his hand away and put it behind his back. "I can't guess. I *won't* guess!"

And from that they could not move him. So far as Nate Richmond was concerned, as least so far as he was willing to confide, 8th-AV-8 was a happy, thriving group with no internal animosities. Emmy Mion loved everybody and everybody, including the three male dancers, had loved her back—from the smallest child in the dance classes that helped eke out the rent, to the owner of a hardware store next door who gave them wholesale prices on hardware supplies in exchange for classes for his three grandchildren.

If anyone had a reason to kill her, Nate Richmond claimed to be completely unaware of it. After another pointless round of questions, they let him leave.

"Comments?" asked Sigrid as her pen filled several lines on her notepad.

"I bet he does know who the jack-o'-lantern was," said Bernie Peters, stretching his short legs straight out from the chair. He propped his own notepad on the chair

back. "Two years these people have worked together and
for him not to recognize somebody he's seen every day
practically—" He shook his head derisively.

"He struck me as just a little too much California
dreamin' to be real," said Elaine Albee, her pretty face
thoughtful. "Could he be on something?"

"In which case, his perceptions would be dulled?"
asked Sigrid.

That wasn't exactly the way Albee would have put it,
but she nodded. "If he was high this afternoon—I don't
know, maybe it would have looked to him as if she were
dancing with her shadow or something. Even if Richmond
had widened the spotlight when they were touching, he'd
be taking his cues from her and not really watching
what—"

The door was opened hesitantly and Detective Cluett
peered in. "Lieutenant, Dr. Ferrell's asking to see you."

"Who?"

"Dr. Ferrell. She was in the audience when it happened
and she's the one told Papaky there was no need to hurry
with an ambulance."

"What does she want, Cluett?"

"She didn't say." Evidently, Mick Cluett hadn't thought
to ask, either.

Sigrid looked to the others for information and received equally blank looks. Dr. Ferrell's name had not
arisen in their brief preliminary interviews with members
of the dance troupe.

"Ask her to wait, please, Cluett, and send in Ginger
Judson."

Leaving the door ajar, the stolid Cluett departed
silently, mimicking the silence of the telephone on the
desk before Sigrid. Lights occasionally flashed on one of
the four buttons at the bottom of the instrument, but an
extension was now being answered by a uniformed officer
in the theater's green room two doors down the hall and
no bells disturbed them here.

While they waited, Peters and Albee filled Sigrid in
on the few facts they had gathered about the red-haired
dancer.

"She's twenty-three, grew up in Miami, moved to

New York to study dance. Joined the troupe when it was formed year before last," Elaine Albee said briskly. "She's the youngest member."

"Seems like a nice kid," Bernie Peters observed. "Very forthcoming."

"Did she come forth with anything useful?" Sigrid asked dryly.

"Well, she's the only one to claim she watched the whole dance," said Peters, tearing a sheet from his notebook. "She sat down here with one of those goblin figures off to the side of the stage."

Jim Lowry, who was more skilled, would eventually draw a detailed rendering of the crime scene to scale, but in the meantime, Peters handed Sigrid the rough sketch he'd made of the stage for his own use. After some initial confusion, he'd realized that when the dancers referred to "stage right" or "stage left" they meant right or left as they faced the audience, so he'd marked each side of his sketch accordingly.

Two small rectangles just off stage left were labeled "lights and sound" and a wavy line separated them from a half-circle that represented Ginger Judson's chair. A similar wavy line lay between the chair and the back entrance to the stage and there were two identical lines in the wings of stage right. The four lines were angled down from the back of the stage.

"What are those?" asked Sigrid. "Curtains?"

"Side curtains, yeah. They're called maskers," Bernie said, but as he started to elaborate, the door was pushed wide by the youngest dancer.

The girl's long copper hair was braided into a single thick plait which bounced on her straight back as she crossed the room with that curiously graceful, splayfooted walk acquired by most dancers. Her eyes were red, her mascara smudged, and, across her nose, a few light freckles had popped through her stage makeup. For the most part, however, her complexion was of the pale translucence so often found in redheads and it was enhanced by the loose-fitting black sweatshirt and black tights.

She took the chair vacated by Nate Richmond and,

when Sigrid asked her to repeat her name and address for
the record, did so with a wobbly smile.

"You danced in the first scene?"

"That's right." The girl nodded earnestly, her copper
braid echoing each movement of her head. "All of us
except Emmy. She had the solo dance between our ensemble pieces."

To satisfy a point of personal curiosity, Sigrid asked,
"Didn't those pumpkin heads make dancing difficult?"

"Not really. They're very light and the neck's pretty
wide, so there's freedom to move." She touched an incon-
spicuous black band that had been sewn around the neckline of her sweatshirt like a fuzzy ribbon. "This Velcro
holds the head in place, yet I can take it off or put it on in
a flash. The goblin hoods, too, for that matter."

"I see. Now, Miss Judson, when that scene was over,
in which direction did you exit?"

"We all came off stage left."

Peters's rough sketch lay on the desk between them
and Ginger leaned forward to point to her position with a
stubby index finger. "Some of the others went directly up
the spiral staircase—that's where the dressing rooms are—
and one of them, I think it was Cliff, went down to the
watercooler at the end of the hall.

"I wanted to see Emmy's dance, so I'd left my goblin
hood on a chair here"—she touched the half-circle that
Bernie Peters had drawn for a chair—"and I came around
and put it on so I'd be ready, then sat there to watch."

"Did you see any of the others after that?"

"Just Sergio. I poked my head around the masker to
wave at him," said Ginger, waggling her fingers in demon-
stration, "but after I sat down, it was between us."

"Could he have been the jack-o'-lantern?" asked Bernie
Peters.

"Sergio doesn't dance," Ginger giggled, her grief
momentarily forgotten. "Have you seen him walk? He's so
skinny and clumsy he looks like a nearsighted stork."

Impulsively, she stood up, flexed her leg, and it was
as if her supple flesh-and-blood joints had suddenly been
replaced by rusty metal hinges. With elbows pointed
toward the ceiling and her head dipping stiffly forward

with each step, she did an impromptu and entirely convincing imitation of an awkward, myopic stork. Albee and Peters both laughed, but Sigrid watched without smiling or moving and the young redhead quickly resumed her seat like a child who expected to be scolded.

"I'm sorry. I keep forgetting Emmy's gone; that it's not a scary scene that'll soon be over. It really did happen, didn't it?"

Her bare feet were small and white and she placed them side by side flat on the floor before her.

"You were watching from stage left," Sigrid said quietly. "Are you sure you didn't see any of the other dancers?"

Ginger Judson shook her head and her long thick braid swung slowly from side to side. "None of them were in place when I sat down and the stage lights were so dim I didn't notice after Emmy started dancing."

"How did the jack-o'-lantern enter?"

"From stage right, directly across from me, where Eric was supposed to enter in the next dance. I think I saw him the same time Emmy did and I couldn't figure out why he'd come on early and still in his pumpkin head. It was supposed to be a solo improvisation and she was dancing so beautifully. But Emmy was wonderful. Never let anything throw her. She looked a little puzzled at first, then I saw her turn her head away from the audience like she was trying to keep from laughing out loud."

Ginger Judson seemed puzzled herself. "He made the children laugh, too, but he wasn't all that funny."

There was a hint of resentment in her voice which made Sigrid raise one eyebrow.

Haltingly, the girl described the duet, then faltered as she neared the climax. "I was watching Emmy mostly," she said in a tiny voice, "so I can't say who he was. That's what's important, isn't it?"

"Yes," said Sigrid.

"I thought it was an accident."

"Did you really, Miss Judson?"

"Yes! I—" Her voice faltered before the police officer's cool watchfulness. "No. You're right. It wasn't an accident. He did throw her."

"At first you thought the dancer was Eric Kee. Why?"

"Only when he first came on. I thought maybe it was Eric's way of making up."

"They had quarreled?"

The girl nodded. "He was really mad at her and she laughed at him. It drove him up the wall that she wouldn't fight back. She never did. Not with him, not with anybody."

"What did they fight about?"

Ginger Judson's pale face was suddenly suffused with red. "I don't know," she said. "All I know is that Eric was furious with her."

She tried to deny further knowledge, but Elaine Albee and Bernie Peters pelted her with questions until Sigrid held up a restraining hand and said, "You must have heard some of his words, Miss Judson."

"He was jealous," the girl whispered. "He accused her of sleeping with somebody else."

"Who?"

"Me." Her chin came up bravely but her face was now crimson.

"And was she?" Sigrid asked mildly.

"That's none of your business, is it?"

"In the normal course of events, no. But as a motive for murder, I'm afraid it is."

The younger woman tried to return Sigrid's dispassionate gaze, but a large fat tear slid down her freckled cheek. With as much dignity as she could muster, she said, "Eric Kee was premature in his accusations."

Chapter 5

"I didn't kill Emmy because of some freckle-faced baby dyke!" Eric Kee said angrily.

As Sigrid would later learn, Emmy Mion's lover was only one-quarter Chinese, and that quarter was evinced in his straight blue-black hair and high cheekbones. From an Irish grandmother, he had inherited shamrock-green eyes and a well-knit five-foot-ten frame. He had also inherited her blunt forthrightness.

"No one's accused you, Mr. Kee," Sigrid said mildly.

She had offered him the chair by the desk but Kee chose instead to perch with crossed legs and straight back in a semi-Yogic position upon a nearby table. He had discarded his sweatshirt and now sat impassively in his tight-fitting black leotard with a hand on each muscular thigh like a modern, streamlined Buddha. Only his lips and blazing green eyes moved.

"Ginger told you I was the other dancer, didn't she?"

"As I said before, Miss Judson merely claims to have overheard a quarrel between you and Emmy Mion prior to the performance this afternoon," Sigrid replied carefully.

"She didn't 'overhear' a goddamned thing; she was eavesdropping. Spying on us. Every time we turned around, there she was, mooning at Emmy with those bovine eyes. I was starting to feel I ought to check under the bed every time we made love."

"So you *did* quarrel?"

"Emmy was cool but I may have lost it for a minute there," he admitted. "It wasn't what Ginger thought, though. Emmy felt sorry for her and she gave the kid wrong ideas. I wanted her to quit letting Ginger take up so much of her time. Before it went too far."

Sigrid was skeptical. "Before what went too far, Mr. Kee? A simple friendship?"

"For Emmy, that's *all* it was. But Ginger—! She was like a goddamned alley cat in heat." As he spoke, the bronze melted away from Eric Kee's impassive Buddha and he became a lithe and sinuous feline who rolled and writhed and stroked herself across the long tabletop in a frantic sexual ecstasy that was almost indecent to watch.

"So *that's* what's wrong with Tinker Bell!" exclaimed Bernie Peters, who had suddenly recognized his daughters' pet in Kee's vicious pantomime.

Elaine Albee giggled and Sigrid repressed a sigh. These dancers were too clever by half. "If you're quite finished now, Mr. Kee."

"Right." He did a slow rollover from the far end of the

table and came up in a lotus position, all his angry emotions frozen in bronze again.

"When did you last speak to Miss Mion?"

"Twelve-thirty, maybe; a quarter to one. I ran up to that Italian restaurant on the corner for a couple of orders of pasta primavera. She was waiting for a phone call so we ate lunch in here." He nodded toward the wastebasket where they'd disposed of the empty take-out cartons.

"Was the call important?"

"Enough to wait for, I guess, though not enough to mention after I got back. The phone rang a few times, but it was about the performance, kids wanting to check the starting time, things like that."

"Was Miss Mion worried about anything?" Sigrid asked. "Had she quarreled with any of the others?"

"Emmy didn't *quarrel*," said Kee, and a rueful smile escaped the stolid facade he seemed intent on maintaining. "Not like you mean, anyhow. She gave her ideas, listened to yours, and if yours were better, she'd do it. If they weren't, you could argue till the Hudson ran dry and she just didn't hear you.

"As for being worried—" He paused, as if to analyze something he'd never actually given much thought to before. "Emmy didn't stew about things out loud, she'd just go away inside her head somewhere until she got it all worked out in her mind. And you know what?" Realization dawned in his voice. "She *did* have something on her mind today! Something more than—"

He stopped abruptly and began again. "I put it down to the performance, but it couldn't have been that because she never worried about performing; yet she didn't hear half what I said about Ginger. I guess that's why I got so uptight."

"Would you say her preoccupation stemmed from the professional side of her life or something more personal?"

Eric Kee's black hair gleamed with dull blue lights as his head moved almost imperceptibly. "Sorry, Lieutenant. I just don't know. Whatever it was, Emmy wouldn't talk about it until she had it straight in her own mind what she was going to do."

Too bad, thought Sigrid. "Did you see her again after that?"

"She was standing at the top of the stairs just before we went on. She blew me a kiss and told us to break a leg, but I was still too ticked off to answer." The stone face was back again.

"After the first dance, the five of you exited stage left. Where did you go from there?"

"Straight up those steps to the men's dressing room. Win was right behind me. I didn't feel like talking and I went on down the hall to the bathroom and put my head under the spigot. Then I remembered that I'd left my goblin hood here in the office so after I toweled off, I came downstairs and got it."

Using Bernie's sketchy floor plans, Sigrid could easily follow Kee's narrative. The rear wall of the stage rose the full two stories to leave a backstage area that was basically the same both upstairs and down, from the wall which formed one side of the wide hall to the row of rooms along the opposite side.

The men's dressing room was at the head of the spiral iron staircase, directly above the prop-storage room. Two doors down was another three-cubicle, two-basin rest room, identical to the one next to the office below. At the far end of the hall, the women's dressing room lay above the corner business office. The wide staircase that connected the floors at that corner must have made it convenient for Emmy Mion to run back and forth in her varied roles of dancer, choreographer, business director, and teacher.

Roman Tramegra had told Sigrid that the second dance was timed to run exactly six minutes; he'd estimated that the jack-o'-lantern had joined Emmy Mion some three or four minutes into her dance and had probably been onstage less than two minutes total, an estimation which agreed with Ginger Judson's account.

How long did it take, Sigrid wondered, to splash water over one's head, towel off, come downstairs, and locate a masked hood? Two minutes? Three?

"Was anyone here in the office when you came in?"

"No."

"Did you open any of the desk drawers?"

"Why would I do that?"

"Just answer the lieutenant's questions," rasped Bernie.

"No, I did not snoop through any drawers," said Kee with exaggerated patience.

"What did you do after you found the hood?" Sigrid asked.

"Put it on, of course, and went out to wait in the wing. It was almost time for our cue. I got there just as Emmy was following that bastard up on the scaffold."

"Was there anyone else in the wing when you arrived?"

Eric Kee continued to sit in his yoga position, but as the questions came down to Emmy Mion's last few minutes, the police officers saw his open hands clench into white-knuckled fists on his brawny thighs.

"I've been trying to remember, but I can't be sure. You know the way maskers are hung?"

Sigrid frowned at the sketch and Bernie Peters leaned over her shoulder to point out the squiggly lines that represented the angled curtains, two on each side of the stage, which kept the audience from seeing into the wings.

"The stage lights were dim blue except for the baby white following Emmy so it was pretty dark in the wings. We three men were supposed to enter from this side, the other two women from stage left. My place was in the middle between the two curtains. Win was upstage, Cliff down from me; Ginger was directly across and Ulrike was opposite Win."

"You actually saw them in their correct positions?" asked Sigrid.

"I didn't look," replied Kee, frustration in his voice. "I was so surprised to see someone on with Emmy that I didn't notice anything else. I sort of remember looking past Win to see Emmy when I passed his spot but—"

A startled expression swept Kee's face. "It must have been his dummy!" he exclaimed. "Win's never been early for a cue in his life."

Those goblin dummies were really going to be a problem, Sigrid thought. She'd noticed before that at least one had occupied each wing position, either hanging from a hook on the curtains or slumped on a chair. Unless one looked closely, the poor light would make it difficult to differentiate between a living goblin and a stuffed one, especially if all had their masked hoods in place.

"When Miss Mion fell—"

"When she was *thrown*," Eric Kee interjected bitterly.

"When she was thrown, then," said Sigrid impassively, "who did you think the other dancer was?"

"There really wasn't time for me to get a fix on him. He didn't quite move like Cliff but Win would never horn in on someone's solo."

"This is hardly a case of someone hogging the spotlight," Sigrid reminded him dryly. Kee stared back at her stonily as she straightened her notes on the desktop. "Now then, Mr. Kee: what did you do when the lights went out?"

"At first, nothing." The young man abruptly flexed his legs and then re-bent them so that he was sitting on his bare feet. "Everything had happened so fast I couldn't believe what I'd seen. The next thing I knew, I was rushing over to Emmy, the house lights came on, and that cop started yelling at us to keep away."

"Us who, Mr. Kee? Exactly whom did you see when the lights came on?"

"Sergio Avril and Ulrike Innes," he said promptly. "Cliff Delgado, Ginger, and then Win."

"Wingate West was the last to arrive?"

Kee nodded. "But that doesn't mean a damn thing. Win's always the last to arrive."

"Were they all wearing their hoods?"

"Just Win. I pulled mine off when the lights went out and I guess the others did, too."

Sigrid leaned back in her chair and nodded to Albee and Peters.

"Did you happen to notice if any of the others were breathing harder than usual?" asked Elaine Albee.

"No, but by then we were all pumping adrenaline."

"If it wasn't you or West or Delgado," said Bernie Peters, "could some other dancer from outside your troupe have slipped in?"

"Friends drop by all the time to watch us rehearse, but I don't think anybody could just walk right on unless—"

He hesitated and then shook his head. "No, he would never hurt Emmy."

"Who wouldn't?"

"David Orland. He and Emmy used to—well, they lived together for a while till Emmy moved in with me this spring. No hard feelings, though. They were still friends."

"Then why wasn't Mr. Orland part of the troupe?" asked Elaine, jotting down the name.

"He was working steady at the time. A revival of *West Side Story*. It closed last month, so he's been around more lately. But it's crazy to think he'd kill Emmy."

"Yet if this David Orland suddenly appeared onstage," said Sigrid, leaning forward to rejoin the interrogation, "would she have danced with him?"

"Oh sure," said Kee. "They were always terrific together."

He stood up on the table, put one foot on the bookcase against the wall, and bent to unpin a small black-and-white photograph, which he handed to Sigrid.

In it, Emmy Mion was being held high above the head by an unfamiliar but very well-muscled male dancer.

"That's David Orland," said Kee and, as he stood there balanced between tabletop and bookcase and looked around at the many images of Emmy Mion upon the walls, that impassive, deliberate mask dropped over his features again.

"I grabbed a drink of water, visited the john, then went immediately to my place between the front curtain and the first masker," said Cliff Delgado, pacing before the desk, too keyed up to sit in the chair they had offered him. "And no, I didn't see any of the others and I certainly didn't speak to them, okay? We screwed up at the end of the first dance. I was supposed to do a back roll over Ulrike and our timing was off. It was such a *stupid* mistake I could have killed her!"

His passionate words hung in the air. He flinched and added uncomfortably, "That's just a figure of speech, okay?

My God! If men were sent to the gallows every time they felt like strangling a clumsy bitch—"

"Sit down, Mr. Delgado," said Sigrid, in a cold voice that brooked no argument.

Delgado threw up his hands in exasperation, but did as he was told.

"Were you in place when the jack-o'-lantern appeared onstage?"

"Yes, yes, but don't ask me whether it was Eric or Wingate because I didn't give a damn who the showboater was. It was supposed to be a *solo*, for God's sake! A delicate, wistful interlude, okay? And that jackass was turning it into such a farce, I couldn't watch."

"That fence and scaffold's less than ten feet from where you were standing," snorted Bernie Peters. "You *had* to see him."

"And I tell you I *didn't!*" Delgado shrilled, springing from his chair to glare down at Peters.

Cliff Delgado had been Elaine Albee's first candidate for the role of murderer, and the young man did radiate a near-psychotic intensity and impulsiveness, thought Sigrid. His dark blue eyes shot sparks; his short, punk-clipped yellow hair stood on end as with static electricity; and his dancer's body seemed poised for motion even when he was standing rigidly defiant.

"Sit *down*, Mr. Delgado," she said patiently. "You must surely understand that the only way we can discover who killed Miss Mion is by a process of elimination and that—"

"Okay, *okay!*" he snapped and sat down with a long-suffering sigh. "Just no goddamned lectures, okay? Truth is, okay, yeah, it had to be Win or Eric. The moves were familiar and yet they weren't. I didn't catch on at first. I figured it was Eric, rubbing our noses in it. But then—I don't know—it was more like somebody *dancing* Eric, okay?"

"Copying his style, you mean?"

"Yeah. But what the hell? Eric's a smart-ass. He's capable of dancing somebody dancing himself, okay? So it probably was Eric because Win's brains are in his feet."

"What did you mean about Eric rubbing your noses

in it?" asked Sigrid, although she suspected she knew the answer.

"Just talk, okay?"

She leaned forward on her elbows, her strong chin resting again on her laced fingers, and waited. It was a test of wills which Cliff Delgado was too impatient to win.

"Okay, okay," he said sulkily when the silence stretched too uncomfortably. "Eric couldn't quit gloating that he was the only one in Emmy's bed these days."

"So according to you, he had no reason to kill her?"

"Who knows what goes through the inscrutable Oriental mind?" Delgado sneered.

"What about David Orland?" asked Elaine Albee.

Delgado raked her deliberately with those intensely blue eyes, but Albee had been mentally undressed by subtler men than he and did not rise to his bait by showing either embarrassment or irritation. If anything, she seemed openly amused and the dancer was left to stew in his own impotence.

"He's been in and out enough lately to know the moves," Delgado admitted at last. "And he probably hates Eric enough."

"Did he hate Emmy enough, though?" asked Bernie Peters. "That's the real question."

"Hate Emmy? Nobody hated Emmy, okay?" Delgado gave a sour laugh. "Except maybe my dear wife. And the only dance she can do is 'The Waltz of the Elephants' with our refrigerator."

Chapter 6

If Nate Richmond had been, as Elaine Albee suggested, a laid-back version of California dreamin', Wingate West was, by contrast, practically comatose. In fact, Mick Cluett, sent to fetch West, was on his way backstage to tell Lieutenant Harald that their third male dancer had skipped out on them when he spotted West dozing peacefully on one of the side pews.

Awakened and pointed toward the office, West appeared before Sigrid with tousled sandy hair, sleepy brown eyes, and a succession of such wide infectious yawns that Albee and Peters were soon unconsciously yawning along in unison.

Sigrid fought off her own subconscious tendency to make it a chorus and told Cluett to send out for coffee all around; but long before it arrived, she realized that Wingate West was not going to contribute much to their investigation.

Between yawns, the young man at first denied the existence of any tensions within the troupe. He did dredge up a memory of David Orland's dismay at being replaced by Eric in Emmy's affections last spring, and when pressed for information on current rivalries, sleepily admitted, "Yeah, I guess Cliff did have the hots for her."

"Ginger Judson, too?"

"Probably. Everybody liked Emmy."

Peters pointed out that like and lust were two differing emotions but West was yawning too deeply to answer.

He couldn't recall if Emmy had seemed preoccupied when he saw her that morning, he denied knowing that she and Eric had quarreled, and he professed complete ignorance as to why anyone should have wanted to kill her.

Sigrid was left with the impression that personal relationships passed right over West's head and that the actions of his colleagues probably registered very faintly unless they were choreographed to music. He didn't stop yawning until describing the first dance that afternoon and then told them more than they wanted to know about the dynamics of the scene, exactly how he'd covered when Cliff and Ulrike screwed up near the end and threw Ginger and Eric off, and how disappointing it was that they didn't get to perform the goblin dance. "Emmy and Rikki and I had an incredible passage near the end like you wouldn't believe."

"Rikki? Ulrike Innes?"

He nodded.

"Then you must have recognized the dancer who

killed Miss Mion," said Sigrid, momentarily encouraged
by such specific observations.

He shook his head regretfully. "Somebody'd been
messing with my things in the dressing room and I
couldn't find my mask at first so I didn't get downstairs till
the last eight bars of their piece. I got to my place just as
he lifted her and after that, everything happened too
damn fast. Before I got a handle on what was going down,
he slammed her onto those spikes; then the lights went
out and I felt somebody rush past me."

The three police officers took turns asking the same
questions in different words, but to no effect. Although
wide awake now and no longer yawning, Wingate West
claimed that he couldn't begin to guess who had rushed by
him or which direction that person had taken, once past.

They let him go as Cluett returned with their coffee
and West looked at the white foam cups disapprovingly as
he passed. "Caffeine's not good for you," he said, drawing
back from the cup which had been ordered for him.
"Causes breast cysts. I've got a box of herbal tea bags.
Want some?"

"We'll take our chances with the caffeine," muttered
Bernie, already kiting the snap-off lid of his steaming cup
toward the wastebasket.

Ulrike Innes, last on their list of 8th-AV-8 dancers,
was twenty-five, a tall slender Valkyrie with fair, almost
silver hair that fell to her shoulders and was held back
from her smooth forehead by a wide black elastic band.
Except that the tip of her thin nose was pink and her eyes
were red as from much crying, her long oval face and
delicately contoured features could have come straight out
of an early fifteenth-century Flemish altarpiece, thought
Sigrid, who was partial to late-Gothic art.

Like the other dancers in the troupe, Innes probably
had a trim, well-conditioned body, but she had pulled on a
pair of baggy gray warm-up pants while waiting her turn to
be questioned and they combined with the oversized black
sweatshirt to effectively disguise her form. She also wore

soft leather slippers on her bare feet, yet she still shivered as she took the chair opposite the desk.

"Emmy wondered if we ought to put the heat on," she told them tremulously, hunching within the loose folds of her sweatshirt, "but we thought we could get through the weekend without it since heating oil's so expensive."

Her words made the three police officers aware that the office had gradually cooled over the past two hours. Without the hot stage lights and a large number of warm bodies to maintain the temperature, the theater was indeed growing uncomfortably chilly.

"We shouldn't be much longer," Sigrid reassured the dancer.

In his earlier thumbnail descriptions of the company, Roman Tramegra had coupled the tall fair Ulrike Innes with short dark Nate Richmond. Joan of Arc meets Alberich, thought Sigrid, and then gave herself a mental shake. When tired, her subconscious sometimes drew stupid parallels where none existed. Even if he was an inch shorter than her own five-ten, Nate Richmond was nothing like the misshapen little dwarf in Wagner's *Ring* cycle, she told herself firmly, and fixed her attention on Innes's account of her last words with Emmy Mion.

"We had a quick run-through rehearsal at ten this morning. Nate wanted to check some of the light cues." Ulrike's voice softened unconsciously at his name. "Emmy had some new ideas about lighting the goblin scene and they started bouncing suggestions off each other the way they always did."

"Did Miss Mion seem preoccupied or upset about anything?"

The dancer shook her head. "No, no more than any other performance day. Everyone gets keyed up and a little excited. A little crazy, too, I guess."

"Crazy how?"

"Just silly things." Innes pushed herself far back in the chair, drew her feet up to the front edge of the seat, and clasped her jackknifed knees. "Win had misplaced his pumpkin head—he's always losing things—and Ginger accused Eric of taking hers, not that it mattered. All the heads were exactly alike. Then a couple of the kids showed up even though they *know* classes are always canceled on performance days. And Helen had decided Emmy's ghost dress needed more floating tatters so she was tearing around trying to get Emmy back to her workroom for a last-minute fitting."

"That's Helen Delgado, your costume designer?"

"And set designer and half a dozen other titles, if you're keeping track," said Innes, watching Sigrid's pen move across the notepad. "We all wear interchangeable hats."

"Did you see Miss Mion after rehearsal?"

"She was with Nate when I went in to tell him lunch was ready in the green room. Win had made a huge salad and Ginger'd brought in a loaf of her six-grain bread. There was enough for everybody, but Emmy said Eric had gone out for Italian and they planned to eat here in the office."

"I understand she was expecting a phone call. Did she discuss it?"

"No."

Sigrid made a note to question the others about it, then asked Innes to continue.

"We ate, then Ginger and I went upstairs to change," said the dancer, stretching her long legs straight out before her with her feet together. "I was putting on my pumpkin head when I noticed that Ginger hadn't closed the door. The stairwell acts like an echo chamber. If the office door is open, too, and someone speaks loudly down here, you can hear it upstairs."

"And what did you and Miss Judson hear?"

"It didn't mean anything," said Ulrike Innes, looking uncomfortable.

"Then it won't matter if you tell us," said Sigrid.

"His words weren't clear, but Ginger went out on the landing and left the door ajar so I could tell that Eric was yelling about something. In just a minute or so, Emmy came upstairs to change and I heard Eric call Ginger a couple of ugly names."

"Was Miss Mion angry or upset when she came in?"

"Not the way you'd think," Innes said slowly, as if trying to choose the exact words to describe her dead colleague. "She didn't get mad because Eric was trying to pick a fight with her, but she did tell him to bug off when she thought he was being unfair to Ginger."

"Was he being unfair?"

Ulrike Innes folded her arms across her chest and studied the tips of her slippers. "Maybe, maybe not. The point is that Emmy was almost neurotic about playing fair and doing the right thing—all that truth, justice, and American way of life they try to teach you in Girl Scouts. She actually believed in it. I know that probably sounds unreal because she didn't care what you did to yourself— *for* yourself—drugs, sex, stuff like that. That was your own private business as far as she was concerned. But the bedrock stuff that hurt somebody else—cheating, stealing, or hurting someone on purpose—she positively, absolutely wouldn't stand for it."

Her blue eyes filled with tears and she fumbled fruitlessly in her pocket for a handkerchief. "I don't know if we can hold together without Emmy."

There was a box of tissues on a nearby shelf and Bernie Peters handed it to Innes, who took one and blew her nose with a firmness that tried to deny the grief which threatened to overwhelm her. "We all help Helen paint flats and stitch costumes; we all help Nate hoist lights and string extension cords; and we all take turns at housekeeping chores, secretarial duties, or teaching the dance classes. That's the whole point of being in a repertory-slant-improv company—just like we all take turns dancing the lead."

"Emmy had the solo today, but she wasn't what you'd call the star of 8th-AV-8." Fresh tears glittered on her long mascaraed eyelashes and her voice trembled. "I think she was its heart, though."

Emotion and sentiment always made Sigrid awkward. She pushed back in her chair, mentally distancing herself from the unhappy dancer, and her voice became brusque as she inquired about the last hour of Emmy Mion's life.

According to Innes, she and Ginger Judson had finished dressing and, as they went downstairs to join the men, Emmy had followed them onto the landing and told them to break a leg. That was the last time Ulrike Innes heard her speak.

Their dance had lasted eight minutes and she saw Emmy standing at stage right, ready to slip into her place as soon as Nate killed all the stage lights and everyone exited stage left.

"Where did you go?"

"Up the spiral staircase and along the hall to the women's dressing room."

"Did you see any of the others?"

Innes sat up straight in the chair. "Ever since it happened, I've been trying to remember as clearly as possible; but it's weird. Things we did at rehearsal keep getting mixed in with what we did this afternoon." She looked at them anxiously. "I don't want to give any wrong impressions."

"We understand," Sigrid said in a neutral tone.

With her feet flat on the floor and her hands folded in her lap, almost as if she were testifying from a witness stand, Ulrike Innes said, "To the best of my knowledge, then, Eric and Win went up the stairs ahead of me. I don't know what Cliff did. Win went into the men's dressing room at the head of the stairs and Eric went on down to the bathroom."

"How did you know who was which?" Sigrid asked. "Weren't they still wearing those pumpkin heads?"

"Win took his off as he opened the dressing room door and—I don't know—there was something about the way he walked down the hall in front of me that made me assume it was Eric and not Cliff. Am I wrong? *Was* it Cliff?"

"No, Eric Kee's account agrees with yours about that."

Reassured, Innes described picking up her goblin hood, then how she'd come back down the other stairs to watch the end of Emmy's dance.

"Did you see any of the men between the time you left your dressing room and the time you took up your position at upper stage left?"

"No, but that doesn't mean anything because I walked between the wall and the stage screen. Win wasn't in his place yet when I passed by it, but I glanced across the stage and saw Sergio at the sound board, and Ginger was already in place with her goblin hood on. She liked to watch Emmy improvise, too."

The dancer's voice wobbled, then steadied again.

"I must have gotten there a few bars before the jack-o'-lantern came onstage because Emmy was dancing alone when I crossed behind the screen and I watched her a minute and then there was a brief instant while I put my hood on and got my mask in place because when I looked again, he was there and she was dancing with him."

Sigrid pushed Bernie Peters's sketch of the stage toward her. "From where you stood, Miss Innes, you should have been able to see all three of the men."

"But I couldn't," argued the dancer, pointing to Bernie's representation of the iron fence and scaffold tree. "These blocked my view of Cliff and Eric and I've already told you that Win wasn't there. He doesn't miss cues but he's never been a second early either."

"Then who was the other dancer?" Sigrid asked bluntly. "Which one of them wanted her dead? And why?"

"I don't know, I don't know, I don't *know!*" cried the young woman and her shaky composure dissolved into choked sobs.

Dismayed, Sigrid looked at her two assistants for help.

"I'll get her a glass of water," said Peters, cravenly fleeing for the door while Elaine Albee offered more tissues and soothing words.

The young woman was obviously too shattered to answer further questions at the moment, so Sigrid nodded when Albee suggested that they continue with Ulrike Innes another time.

Detective Cluett returned with Peters and as they escorted Innes from the office, Sigrid decided she could use an emotional break and called, "Send in Dr.—what was her name? Dr. Ferrell?"

Cluett paused in the doorway. "Oh, she left a half-hour ago, Lieutenant. Said she'd catch you later."

Resigned, Sigrid rubbed her aching arm and said,
"Very well. Let's have Helen Delgado, then."

Chapter 7

Out in the auditorium, as the number of witnesses
awaiting their turn to be questioned dwindled and the
temperature became increasingly chilly, Roman Tramegra
decided there was really no reason he should continue to
sit alone on a hard cold pew, especially as he fancied there
was warmth and company to be had elsewhere in the
theater. Accordingly, he eased his bulk along the row,
smiled encouragement at poor Sergio Avril, still huddled
uncomfortably on a front pew, and when challenged by a
uniformed officer stationed at the door which led backstage, said loftily, "It's quite all right, my good man.
Lieutenant Harald has already questioned me to her complete satisfaction."

Police activity on the stage was winding down as he
passed along behind the wing curtains. Such as it was
seemed to involve meticulous measurement with a tape
rule, the numbers repeated to a young detective busy
with a sketch pad.

Tramegra reached the rear hall just as a tearful Ulrike
Innes emerged from the corner office. "Oh, my dear
child!" he said and opened his arms to her.

At the sight of his familiar and sympathetic face,
Ulrike pulled away from Peters and collapsed upon his
broad chest, her sturdy body wrenched with sobs.

"There, there," he soothed, patting her back with one
hand while locating his handkerchief with the other. "I
shall take care of her," he told Peters and Cluett and,
murmuring reassurance, guided the distraught girl into

the bathroom where he washed her face and smoothed her silver-blond tresses.

She stood as docilely as a small child, an unexpected turn of character, thought Roman as he straightened her black headband. Ulrike Innes had previously struck him as the troupe's most mature and self-sufficient member, without an ounce of temperament in her makeup. Completely and utterly devoted to Nate Richmond, of course, but with a tranquil, almost maternal devotion which did not disrupt the company and keep it on edge the way Emmy Mion's artlessly bestowed affection had.

He soaked a paper towel in cold water, folded it in a long thin pad, and handed it to Ulrike. "Hold this across your eyes for a few minutes and the redness will soon go away."

Mutely, she followed his instructions.

"I never cry," she said from beneath the wet brown paper. "*Never.*" She took the towel from her face and leaned across the washbasin to inspect her eyes more closely. "All those questions. And that police lieutenant trying to make me say whether it was Eric or Cliff or Win who hurt Emmy—and suddenly it hit me like a twenty-pound sandbag that Emmy's *dead!*"

"I'm sure the lieutenant will understand," Roman comforted her in his deep bass voice. "Come along to the green room now and I shall make us both a nice pot of tea."

"Tea?" She looked into his hooded brown eyes and smiled gratefully. "That would be lovely."

Lovely was not the word for the theater's green room, however. For starters, the only things green were the door, which someone had enameled a bright kelly, and a dilapidated sleeper couch upholstered in a nubby emerald fabric so threadbare that the springs shone through in several places. Roman rather suspected that the couch, like the faded chairs and scarred tables which rounded out the furnishings, had been scavenged from a nearby sidewalk minutes before a garbage truck was due to haul it away.

Although Roman occasionally indulged in some discreet scavenging of his own, his taste was less democratic and he preferred to hunt along the Upper East Side where wealthy apartment owners threw out traditional oak and mahogany because they were switching to pickled pine and bleached chestnut, not because a spring had sprung or a leg had broken.

Happily, colorful cushions and photographs of the troupe framed in bright plastic strips made the big shabby room cheerful, and the corner devoted to culinary matters met Roman's approval. Its tiny stainless steel sink was immaculate, the two-burner hot plate functioned perfectly, and the full-size refrigerator was a nearly new donation from the mothers of the Saturday-morning dance classes, concerned that their children's juice and milk should stay fresh and cool.

As Roman had hoped, it was much warmer there than in the auditorium and fully inhabited. Wingate West, Cliff Delgado, and Ginger Judson sat with mismatched mugs before them at a long narrow table near the refrigerator, while Eric Kee paced moodily back and forth. Ginger's freckled face lit up as Roman and Ulrike entered and she swung her long legs down from the two chairs next to her to make room for them, but the other three barely acknowledged Roman's greeting.

The older man was undeterred. "Do my ears detect a fading whistle from the kettle? Excellent timing! Sit down, fair Ulrike. Tea will be ready in a trice."

He bustled over to the hot plate, turned the burner under the kettle to high, and was almost instantly rewarded with a stronger whistle.

Upon offering his services to the troupe, he had brought along his own china teapot and a tin of his favorite souchong. "Will anyone else join us?" he asked now, spooning the dark leaves into the pot.

Win West was drinking a concoction brewed from chamomile and rose hips, Cliff and Ginger were halfway through mugs of mulled cider, and Eric Kee shook his dark head impatiently. "I'm not thirsty."

"Tea for you, sir?" asked Roman, raising his deep voice to reach the police officer seated beneath a wall phone next to the door. The officer held up a can of root beer to show that he'd been taken care of. "Thanks anyhow."

Even as he spoke, the telephone rang. Everyone listened expectantly, but they soon deduced that it was police business and not for any of them.

Roman poured boiling water over the loose tea leaves and brought the pot to the table, where its warm smoky fragrance permeated the air.

"Where's Nate?" asked Ulrike, watching Roman fill her cup.

"Next door," said Ginger. "He said something about a roll of film. You okay?"

"Yes. Is Nate?"

"I'm fine, you're fine, he, she, it's fine!" snarled Eric Kee. "Everybody's fine but Emmy." He leaned across the table and glared into her pale oval face. "Who's your choice, Rikki? Which one of us killed her?"

"Aw, c'mon, Eric," said Win. "Knock it off."

"Don't try to bully me, Eric," Ulrike replied quietly. "I don't know who killed her."

Cliff Delgado pushed his mug aside. "Then at least tell us who didn't do it."

Ulrike looked at him blankly. "Excuse me?"

"Dammit all! I could see Ginger sitting mesmerized from where I stood, okay? But she says she only had eyes for Emmy. So what about you? You *must* have seen me."

"Sorry, Cliff. The fence and the tree were in the way." Her eyes met his unblinkingly. "I couldn't see you or Eric. You know how dim the lights were then. I didn't see Win either, for that matter, and he was supposed to be directly across from me."

Cliff's dark blue eyes narrowed and Roman could almost see the workings of his mind as he considered and then brushed aside the question of Win's whereabouts with an impatient shake of his head. (And why he'd ruined such attractive golden hair with that hideously chopped, neo-Nazi crew cut was more than Roman could fathom. All Delgado needed was a dueling scar to complement his frequent sneers and he could have walked out of a dozen B movies from the early fifties.)

"Quit worrying, Cliff," said Ginger, toying with the end of her thick braid. "If you were there, Sergio must have seen you."

"*If*—?" spluttered Cliff at the same instant as Eric's scornful, "Don't try to act more stupid than you are, Ginger. Everyone knows that Avril's blind as a bat behind those Coke-bottle glasses."

"Of course, Eric. How brilliant you are." The red-haired dancer looked up at him with a spiteful smile. "Everyone *does* know. And isn't that convenient for somebody?"

Ulrike pushed back from the table and rose abruptly. "I'm going to find Nate."

"But your tea—" protested Roman.

"Wait, Rikki," said Win. "We've got to decide about tonight."

She looked at him in disbelief. "Decide what? You don't think—?"

"Yes, folks, the show must go on," Cliff said in a heavily ironic tone.

"You're crazy! How can we dance with Emmy lying in a—"

"It's what she would have wanted," Eric interrupted. "You know how hard she worked for this theater. We can't let it go down the slop chute without trying to save it."

They had evidently discussed it before Ulrike and Roman came in and now they cajoled her with reasons and rationalizations.

"Tickets have been sold."

"Emmy would have wanted it like this."

"Do we lose what we've built up?"

"We can't disappoint the children."

"We'll dedicate the performance to Emmy."

"And the critics are *finally* coming."

This last from Ginger.

"We don't know that," said Ulrike slowly. "It's just a rumor."

"Okay, so even if it's a rumor," argued Cliff, shrugging, "what happens if someone from the *Times* or the *Voice* does show up and we've canceled? How long do you think it'll be before they ever come back again?"

A point well taken, thought Roman, but since his opinions were not solicited, he quietly stirred another spoonful of Wingate West's raw honey into his tea. He had liked Emmy Mion, admired her talents, and found her brutal murder appalling. Nevertheless, while sitting out in the auditorium, alone with his thoughts, he'd been surprised to find himself so keenly regretful that the dancer's death meant that his and Sergio's collaboration might never be performed in its entirety. The nobler part of his character was shamed by such admission, yet little tendrils of hope uncurled in his heart as he listened to the dancers argue and realized that Ulrike was weakening.

"We don't have time to restructure the dances," she said, "and none of us has the stamina to go from the first one into the solo."

Roman tucked his colorful ascot more firmly into the open neck of his safari shirt and cleared his throat. "What about young Orland? He's watched your rehearsals often enough, I should think, and I've seen him do parts of the goblin dance with Emmy. They gave the Wednesday class a perfectly charming little preview. While it's true he left early today—"

"David Orland was here today?" Eric Kee stopped pacing and an overhead light emphasized the pale golden tones of his face as the skin tightened over his high cheekbones. "When? And when did he leave?"

"Immediately after the performance began," answered Roman. "Most unexpected, but I assumed he must have remembered an urgent previous engagement, for no sooner were the five of you onstage for the first dance than I saw him tiptoe out."

As if they'd been waiting for that cue, Nate Richmond entered the room on the heels of an agitated young Hispanic who cried, "Nate just told me! My God! Who—?"

At the sight of him, Eric Kee seemed to go up in flames. As Roman was to tell Sigrid later, it was as if a kung fu movie had suddenly exploded around him. Without even a warning curse, Kee launched himself with a midair kick to David Orland's chest and knocked him heavily to the floor, then followed with a flying leap onto the newcomer's body to begin hammering him with iron-fisted blows.

"Stop it!" Ulrike shouted and tried to pull Eric off, but she was flung aside.

Though dazed, Orland recovered quickly and twisted his legs with enough leverage to flip Kee away so he could get in a few blows of his own. Chairs crashed and a small table was destroyed as they rolled and tumbled, each fiercely trying for the other's throat.

"Just a goddamned minute!" roared the startled policeman. He rushed forward and yanked Eric Kee from the floor while Cliff and Win held onto the enraged David Orland. "What the hell's got into you?" rasped the officer, shaking the younger man as if he were a rag doll.

Kee was in better shape physically, but the officer had the advantage of forty pounds and twenty years of police experience in breaking up street brawls and the dancer found himself held in an unbreakable grip.

"He killed Emmy," Kee gasped, his face flushed with rage.

"You filthy liar!" David Orland lunged for Kee, but the others restrained him.

The police officer looked from one to the other. "You," he said, nodding to David Orland. "Lieutenant Harald seen you yet?"

Chapter 8

Sigrid usually tried to approach each witness in a homicide case with as few preconceptions as possible, but by the time she was ready to question Helen Delgado, she knew that Emmy Mion had been a sexual magnet who seemed to draw every affection that wasn't firmly committed elsewhere. Apparently the costume designer's husband was included in that category. Cliff Delgado had smoldered with open jealousy of Eric Kee's late monopoly on Emmy and Sigrid doubted if he'd hidden it from his wife since he spoke of her with such scorn.

Accordingly, as she waited for Mick Cluett to bring Helen Delgado to her, Sigrid braced for a drab neglected wife and another trying, emotional outburst. The woman who entered, however, came swathed in queenly serenity and, although considerably overweight, she wore vivid makeup and a flattering scarlet caftan and she moved with unexpected lightness of foot.

When asked to give her version of the murder, she faced Sigrid squarely and told her, "I'm sorry, Lieutenant, but that's impossible. Your people separated us before I heard all the details and I never see a first performance if I can help it. Second performance, third—I'm right there watching from the back or in the wings. But never the first. I guess it's a mixture of superstition and stage fright."

Helen Delgado's skin glowed above the high neckline of the scarlet caftan. Her glossy black hair was brushed straight back on one side to cascade down the other in a dramatic contrast of dark curls against a flawless complexion as she tilted her head to consider Sigrid's questions.

"It doesn't really matter though. I couldn't begin to tell you why Eric did this horrible—to hurt Emmy like that. He's as temperamental as the others, of course, but still—" Her warm contralto voice trailed off as she shrugged her heavy shoulders in puzzlement. "So much for love, I guess."

"Why do you think Eric Kee did it?" asked Sigrid.

"Because Ginger said so." A single earring of red stones dangled from her exposed ear and glittered brightly as she looked from Sigrid to Elaine Albee to Bernie Peters. "Didn't she?"

"I'm told she did so initially," Sigrid admitted. "She now claims she's no longer sure and since Mr. Kee denies it, all three men are under equal suspicion."

"All of them? Why?"

"Each appears to have had equal opportunity, and none can prove he was elsewhere."

"Oh. So, does anyone know why Emmy was killed?"

"No," replied Sigrid. "Do you?"

The designer crossed surprisingly trim ankles. Light

flashed on her gold slippers and was reflected by the many rings on her plump fingers. "No. I couldn't believe that Eric had flipped out like that, but if he's not the one—no, I just can't figure it. Everyone was crazy about her."

"Nevertheless, she was killed," said Sigrid, who was getting a little tired of hearing how universally beloved the murdered dancer had been.

A look of inexpressible sadness crossed Delgado's plump face. She took a deep breath and said, "Not by Win. He doesn't have enough passion."

Sigrid let that pass for the moment. "And Eric Kee?"

"Eric has passion. And he was frustrated by coming so close to what he wanted."

"Which was?"

"To possess Emmy completely. She wouldn't let him. And she had already tired of his sulks."

"So that he might have killed her to keep from losing her to someone else?"

"It's happened."

"What about your husband?"

"Cliff?" Her eyes met Sigrid's, then settled on the toes of her golden slippers. "Yes, poor Cliff has enough passion, and he wanted Emmy so damn bad."

"That didn't bother you?" asked Sigrid.

Helen Delgado shrugged. "How could I expect him not to lust after her? She was so elfin and exquisite while I—" She flung out her arms. "This is hardly the body that launched a thousand ships and burnt the topless towers of Ilium."

Her voice was light, but Sigrid, who was currently caught up in emotional entanglements of her own, heard something darker underneath.

"Then you did mind?" she persisted.

"I am a Jew. If you cut me, will I not bleed?" the designer parried.

"A simple yes or no will do," Sigrid said quietly.

"Nothing's ever that simple, Lieutenant."

"Try."

Helen Delgado sat back in her chair with a quizzical smile. "Are you actually as bloodless as you try to look?"

She turned to Albee and Peters, her earring swinging. "I'll bet she's a real pisser to work for, isn't she?"

Bernie Peters choked on his coffee and Elaine Albee abruptly discovered something about her left boot that required her immediate, head-down attention.

Sigrid had hoped that Delgado would be as she'd originally appeared, a rational bystander who had somehow managed to stay above the tempestuous currents which swirled around her colleagues. Evidently that was not to be.

She turned her slate-gray eyes on Bernie Peters, who was red-faced and half-strangled, and coldly suggested that perhaps he should go get himself a drink of water. "And you might as well question that composer when you've recovered."

The three women watched the coughing detective leave.

"I'd love to see *him* in tights," murmured Helen Delgado.

Sigrid said patiently, "Any time you're ready to get serious, Mrs. Delgado."

The woman arranged the folds of her scarlet dress. "Very well, Lieutenant. Yes, if pushed far enough, my husband is probably quite capable of murder. But if he killed Emmy out of frustrated lust, he killed the wrong woman. *I* was the roadblock on his highway to paradise, not Emmy. Emmy would screw with anyone who asked nicely."

She settled her large body more comfortably in the chair. "You ask if I minded? Yes. I did mind. Less than you might think, but enough. And Emmy knew it. For such a thoroughgoing libertine, she was quite the born-again moralist at times. If I'd told her that the marriage was over, she'd have had Cliff on the green room couch ten minutes after I announced it; but until she knew for a fact that I didn't give a tinker's damn, she wouldn't let him touch her. And that wasn't just because I'm more valuable to the troupe than Cliff."

She caught the skeptical look that passed from Elaine Albee to the lieutenant. "Don't laugh, doll," she told Albee. "I am, you know."

It was a proud statement of fact.

"Cliff's a very good dancer. Good, not great. Any casting call would turn up a half-dozen dancers just as competent. On the other hand, costume designers of my caliber don't pop out of every box of Cracker Jacks. I'm a genius with a sewing machine but more than that, when it comes to stage design and making ten dollars' worth of nothing look like a thousand, Nate Richmond and I are pure unadulterated magic. We could work anywhere we wanted."

"Then why are you in this shoestring theater?" Albee asked curiously.

"Nate and *I* can work anywhere," she repeated. "Cliff can't. You'll have to ask Nate what holds him here; Cliff's my reason. We helped start this company because it gives him a chance to dance more often than he ever could anywhere else."

"Ulrike Innes appears to doubt that the company can survive without Emmy Mion," said Sigrid.

"She may be right," nodded Delgado. The glittering stones brushed her rounded cheek. "Emmy took care of most of the business end—licenses, insurance, the grant applications, billing the parents. The dance classes bring in a large chunk of our income and after that ghastly experience last winter, it was Emmy who—"

Sigrid held up a slender hand. "What ghastly experience?"

"Last February. One of our students was killed. So horrible. Her poor little body was stuffed in a snowbank near her apartment. It was nothing to do with us, except that she'd been on her way home from class when someone grabbed her, but mommies and daddies get real spooked real quick when something like that happens. I couldn't blame them, but if Emmy hadn't called a meeting and talked them around, 8th-AV-8 might have gone under then and there. God knows how they'll react to this."

"What was the child's name?" asked Sigrid.

"Amanda Gillespie. Mandy." With her loose caftan falling in graceful folds around her full body, Delgado moved over to the wall above the bookcase and began scanning the photographs tacked there. "You people still haven't found her killer."

The image of a child's body stuffed in a snowbank triggered faint memories and Sigrid glanced inquiringly at Albee.

"I think Hentz and Lambeth caught that one," Albee murmured, referring to the department's two most chauvinistic detectives. Competent police officers, but seldom interested in a woman's view on any of their cases.

"Here," said Helen Delgado, returning to her chair with four photographs which she spread on the desktop before Sigrid. "That's Mandy."

Her index finger with its large topaz ring located the little girl in two pictures of a clustered class and again in two pictures where she was one of three or four children.

In the photographs, Mandy Gillespie appeared to be an ordinary child—cute enough, as were most children in Sigrid's disinterested view, but nothing to make her an immediate standout among her peers. Her tentative smile hadn't quite caught up to those new front teeth, but she had nice eyes and, given the chance, would probably have grown up to be an attractive woman.

"Poor little kid," said Elaine, her eyes compassionate.

"Yeah," agreed Helen Delgado with a sigh. "We were really cut up about it at the time."

"Was she sexually molested?"

"Not that we heard. He strangled her with one of her own hair ribbons. It was rough on the other children, too. Some of them had crying spells and nightmares. We finally had a psychiatrist come talk to them. Dr. Ferrell."

"The same Dr. Ferrell who was here this afternoon?" asked Sigrid, surprised. She was under the impression that the woman was an internist, not a psychiatrist.

"Why, yes. She has a nephew in the Monday-afternoon class so she occasionally comes to pick him up. She even makes most of the recitals." Her eyes narrowed thoughtfully. "Maybe we can get her to talk to the children again."

Retaining one picture of the Gillespie child, Sigrid stood up, flexed her stiff neck and shoulder muscles, and returned the rest of the photographs to their former wall positions.

"When did you last see Emmy Mion?" she asked as she walked back to the desk and drew her notebook toward her. "Did she seem different in any way? Was something bothering her?"

The designer sent her dangling earring swinging again as she slowly shook her head, and it snagged on the scarlet fabric. "No," she said, removing the post from her ear and carefully untangling the sparkling bauble from the thread which had caught it. "Performance mornings are always hectic and today was no different. Emmy's little ghost dress wasn't quite right but she didn't want to take the time to let me fix it. I finally had to sit on her. Metaphorically speaking, of course."

A self-deprecating smile lit her face while her fingers played with the earring. "She and Nate were talking about the lights when I tracked her down and stitched on a few more cheesecloth tatters. She seemed the same as ever. Well, no, now that you mention it, maybe she *was* a little more preoccupied than usual, but Emmy could always hold two thoughts at the same time. I never knew a person more in touch with both sides of her brain."

She threw out her hands, dramatically gesturing to the room in which they sat. "I mean, look at this office: sloppy creative choreographer on one side, spastically neat administrator on this side. And both were valid parts. Sometimes she'd have trouble changing gears and we'd threaten to board her up in the executive board room. She'd hoot and mellow out again."

"We were told she was expecting a telephone call," said Sigrid. "Did she mention it?"

"I think someone—Rikki? or was that Ginger?—said that was why she and Eric ate lunch in here alone, but Emmy didn't say anything to me about any phone calls. As far as I'm concerned, that's why we bought an answering machine."

As the session drew to an end, Elaine Albee suddenly asked, "Did you like her?"

Delgado stopped playing with the sparkly earring. She looked at it blankly for a moment, almost as if she'd never seen it before, then said, "Good question, doll. I guess I liked the dancer part of her—maybe because *she* loved it so much. And I liked the bawdy, don't-give-a-damn-'bout-nothing side of her when she'd kick back and open a bottle of champagne."

She slipped the post of her earring through her earlobe and adjusted the bangle. "What I didn't like was her preacher side. This place used to be a church, you know, and sometimes I'd think we still had a pulpit out front and center on the stage."

"What did she preach about?" asked Sigrid.

"Oh Lord! I don't know if I can give you an example off the top of my head. It was never over anything really big." Delgado thought for a moment. "Okay, how's this: one of our friends—has anyone told you about David Orland? How he and Emmy were together before she moved in with Eric?"

Sigrid and Elaine nodded, so Helen Delgado continued, "This was last winter when they were still living together. David got us an incredible deal on some decent sound equipment and Emmy decided that the stuff had to've been stolen for that price. David said so what? He didn't steal it, she didn't steal it, so as long as they were clean, what difference did it make?

"He and Sergio finally had to wait till she was out, then they put a big dent on the console of the synthesizer and told her that was probably why it was so cheap—salvaged goods. Too late, though. I think that's why she dumped him."

"Not wanting to be a receiver of stolen goods is hardly a character flaw," Sigrid said stiffly.

"Maybe not to a cop," said Delgado with a throaty chuckle, "but when you're trying to put together a dance theater on nothing, you can't afford to be too picky about bargains. Maybe that was a bad example. Try this: it was Ginger's turn to come down one Saturday morning last winter and put up the heat before the kids got here for the first class and she overslept. If she'd just *said* she'd overslept, Emmy would have bitched a little and that would've been the end of it. Instead, Ginger made up some cock-and-bull story about why she was late, and then forgot and let it slip that her clock hadn't gone off. Emmy went right up in smoke and started preaching about liars and duty and obligations to the company and to the children. How Ginger's negligence left the children shivering in their little leotards. Big deal. So they had to warm up a few minutes longer. It wasn't all that cold inside and—"

She broke off as the door opened and the police officer who'd been stationed in the green room bustled in with a youth who held a cold wet towel to his face. There were cuts on his jaw and a bruise was already darkening around his swollen eye.

"David Orland," the officer told Sigrid. "They're saying he's the one killed that girl."

Chapter 9

The minor cuts on David Orland's cheek had stopped bleeding and the swelling around his eye seemed to have peaked but the cut on his chin still needed the ice cube someone had provided.

"I want a doctor and I want a lawyer," demanded the battered youth. His stubby fingers gingerly probed his square-jawed face for additional damages.

"That's certainly your right," said Sigrid. "Albee, get Peters to help you escort the witness over for questioning."

"Witness?" yelped Orland. "What witness? I wasn't even here. Listen, I left before the first scene was over—"

"Mr. Orland," Sigrid said firmly, "you have the right to a lawyer when you're questioned, but if you choose to give up that right—"

"I'm not giving up nothing," he said, thrusting out a belligerent jaw.

"Fine. Detective Albee?"

Elaine Albee slid her notes into her calfskin bag and slung it over her shoulder. "Okay, Orland, let's go."

He started to rise, then slumped back into the chair with a fatalistic, "Aw, what the hell?"

"Does this mean you forego the lawyer?" Sigrid asked, wanting his waiver on the record.

"Yeah, yeah, ask your questions. I got nothing to hide." He took the cloth-wrapped ice cube from his chin and examined it for fresh blood.

In assessing this fourth male dancer, Sigrid decided that David Orland was probably a stage name. The young man had a wiry and well-muscled body and his pugnacious attitude proclaimed him a street-smart Hispanic. Late twenties in age, about five-eleven in height, he had black hair and smoldering dark eyes, with light olive skin. He wore jeans and a denim jacket, but visible through the holes in his fashionably ragged white sweatshirt was a black tank top. Glancing down at his sneakers, Sigrid saw that his feet were sockless except for the stirrups on the black tights he wore beneath his jeans.

"Begin with your movements today, please," she said. "Why you came here, when you left, who you saw."

"You want it from this morning?" He pulled a worn address book from his back pocket and read them the precise address of the dance class he had attended up near Lincoln Center. "Class breaks before one and it's a nice day, sun shining and everything, so I tell myself I'll walk down Eighth Avenue to the Village. Listen, I wasn't even coming here, believe me. But I don't know—somehow I wind up getting here a couple minutes to two and I think what the hell? Might as well stick my head in, right? Count the house, see how they're shaking down. The kid on the door knows me so I walk in and sit near the back."

"You didn't stay long," Sigrid observed.

"I've seen them rehearse for the last three weeks and besides, all of a sudden, I remember a phone call I gotta make."

"Whom did you call and what telephone did you use?" Sigrid asked, her pen poised.

"Two booths down the corner," Orland answered promptly. He shifted the cold compress from his swollen eye back to his cut chin, but even bruised and battered he couldn't resist turning straight narrative into animated pantomime with broad hand gestures. "One's out of order, see? And three people's waiting for the other one so I go in the deli there and get a pastrami till this fat lady quits yakking, only she don't and it's not all that far to the guy I had to see, so I just walked it."

The address was near St. Vincent's Hospital, less than a ten-minute walk away. It was all very loose, thought Sigrid, looking at the rough timetable. The chances of finding anyone who could confirm Orland's wait by the telephone were remote. They'd check the friend, of course, and the deli—see if he and his pastrami sandwich were remembered and if so, try to put a specific time on the transaction.

Time was their problem. They were talking a leeway of minutes. Less than fifteen minutes after Orland left the auditorium, Emmy Mion was dead.

"Do you have a key to the alley door?" asked Sigrid.

"No way, Jose," he answered fliply.

"You came back this afternoon. Why?"

"No reason." His brown eyes met hers, then darted away. "Nothing else to do. Everybody's usually up after a show and it's fun to sit in, hear them critique it. When I get here, there's a photographer from the *News* just leaving and he says what's happened. Listen, I'm freaking and the cops won't let me in so I walk around to the alley and come in that way."

"I thought you said you didn't have a key."

"I don't. The door's unlocked."

Sigrid looked sharply at Elaine Albee.

"I'll find out," Elaine promised, making a mental note of it.

"Hey, Lieutenant, don't you believe me?" Orland asked cockily.

Sigrid ignored his gibe. "When did you last see Emmy Mion?"

"Yesterday morning. I'm out for orange juice and the *Times* and she's passing by my corner, coming here, so we stop and talk a minute."

"Did she seem concerned about anything? Upset?"

He shook his head. "Nope, she's just like always— revved up about today's performance, happy about the way things are going here. She gives me a copy of the program and I'm telling you: getting killed by one of those bastards is not on it, believe me," he said bitterly.

"Who do you think did it?" asked Sigrid.

"Listen, Lieutenant, if I know that—" He made a helpless, palms-up gesture. "She also tells me she's gonna move out on Eric, move in with Ginger or maybe live alone awhile. 'Feature me as a nun, David?' she says. Believe me, she was never a nun. Moving out though, yeah, that'd frost him."

"Wingate West?"

"Naw, he's too ditsy, but Cliff Delgado? Listen," he said, leaning forward with the ice cloth in his hand, all flippancy gone from his face, "that's a volcano looking to erupt, believe me."

By five-thirty, Sigrid was ready to disband her troops and call it a day. All the major witnesses had been questioned, wheels had been set in motion at headquarters and computer nets cast. Follow-up on the audience could start tomorrow. The whole theater had been thoroughly searched for potential leads, right down to the letters Emmy Mion had sealed and stamped only a few hours earlier. Ulrike Innes had been called back for that chore since she seemed to be the one most conversant with Mion's office routines. Sigrid had hoped they might cast light on the dead girl's frame of mind, but the envelopes held only routine end-of-the-month dance class bills.

With nothing solid to give them a handle on why Emmy Mion had died, Sigrid dismissed her officers. "We'll pick it up in my office tomorrow morning."

With the dramatic onstage murder immediately interrupting local radio broadcasts and an early television news program using it as the leadoff story at five, the theater's telephone rang nonstop. Roman Tramegra had written a new message for the answering machine and Ginger Judson had taped it so that callers now heard that the weekend's performances would continue as scheduled in tribute to the troupe's late colleague, "whose joyous vision brought the 8th-AV-8 Dance Theater into existence."

(Ginger's tremulous voice had broken on the word "joyous" and Cliff Delgado, who was handling the mechanics of the taping, refused to let her do a tape-over. "It'll tug at their heartstrings," he told her cynically.)

In the green room, Eric Kee and David Orland established a wary truce and, to Roman's wonder, everyone seemed to take it as a matter of course that Orland would dance tonight. In fact, the six dancers had begun to discuss the mechanical problems caused by substituting a male dancer for a female.

"Who's dancing Emmy's solo?" asked Helen Delgado in her rich contralto. She had changed into her working clothes, a thigh-length paisley tunic over black stretch pants, and carried a half-bolt of gauzy white cheesecloth. "It'll take me at least an hour to whip up another ghost costume. Rikki? Ginger?"

Roman noticed that both women seemed instinctively opposed to the idea.

"David's the logical choice," said Ulrike.

Eric and Cliff protested, but Rikki overrode them. "It's less complicated. That way, we five can dance the first scene as we've rehearsed it, David improvises the solo, and the only place we'll have to make changes is when he comes in at the middle of the goblin dance."

"Listen, you don't want me to solo, I understand," said David Orland, tensing again. "I can probably fake the first scene."

Eric and Cliff looked at Win, who shrugged. "Up to you, guys."

"Rikki's right," Eric said reluctantly. "We just don't have time to rework both scenes before eight o'clock tonight."

"Okay," said David. He propped his foot on the edge of a chair and began untying his sneaker laces. "I'll need to listen to the tape a couple times and then maybe we can do a quick run-through from where I come in with the goblins?"

"Tape first," Helen Delgado said decisively. "Sergio

can bring it to my room and you can listen while I rig a new ghost costume."

"Certainly," said the composer, who had sat wordlessly behind his thick glasses until commanded by Helen's flashing dark eyes. All bony arms and legs, he scurried out to set up a tape player in her workroom.

The others began to murmur about supper, but Helen paused in the doorway to remind them of the horrible but unavoidable task that had to be performed before the show could go on. "There's an extra scrub bucket under the sink," she told them.

Eric Kee's honey-colored face turned pasty as he realized the meaning of her words. "No," he moaned. "God, no! I couldn't!"

Roman Tramegra's own stomach roiled and he sat very still, hoping no one would suggest that a scenarist might pitch in at this point.

"Men! You're all a disgusting bunch of babies." Scornfully, Ginger Judson jumped down from her cross-legged perch atop a table. Her orange freckles stood out against the sudden pallor of her face but she tried to carry it off with bravado. "Women always get stuck cleaning up the messes you make."

She jerked open the doors beneath the sink and one of them slammed into Cliff's shin.

"Now just a goddamned minute, okay?" he snarled, but Ginger was past caring.

With tears streaming down her face, she banged a yellow plastic bucket into the sink, dumped in a half-bottle of pine-scented liquid cleanser, and turned the faucet on full.

Chapter 10

The little red message light on the answering machine connected to her bedroom phone was blinking when Sigrid got in shortly past six-thirty. She executed the playback sequence, then kicked off her sensible flat-heeled shoes and stepped out of her gray wool slacks as she listened.

The first message was another wrong number from a private elementary school on the Upper East Side, only this time, instead of an acerbic female, the recorded voice was sorrowfully masculine. It regretted to inform her that "your son Jason missed two unexcused days of school last week."

Similar messages had begun appearing on her tape soon after classes started in September and Sigrid had phoned the school three times before giving up. No wonder Jason continued to skip, she thought, unbuttoning the black cotton shirt. As long as the school's machine kept calling her machine, his parents would assume he was safely tucked away on that college prep assembly line. She could hope Jason was using his freedom to visit the zoo or the planetarium or one of the city's many museums, some place that would actually plant a seed; but experience told her he was probably holed up at a laser tag maze.

An electronic beep signaled the start of a second message which tumbled out of her machine in a breathless and utterly familiar rush. "—so unless something comes up, I'll be there all weekend." As usual, her mother had been unable to wait for the beep. "Let's have lunch together Monday at that dim sum place, okay? Twelve sharp."

Despite traces of a lingering southern accent, Anne Harald met life on the run and passing fifty had not slowed her down. If anything, she seemed to have picked up her pace, as if more had to be crowded into every interesting minute before her time ran out. Usually, she rattled on long enough for Sigrid to deduce most of the message by internal clues. Not this time though. Sigrid would have to wait until lunch on Monday to learn Anne's weekend location.

Another electronic beep was followed by a moment of silence, then an unfamiliar voice said, "Oh, never mind," and hung up.

By this time Sigrid had stripped to a lacy bra and

underpants that were surprisingly frivolous when one considered the unflattering and severely tailored street clothes she usually wore, and she stood in front of her open closet wondering what to pull out for the evening. Nauman had said dinner when he called her from California last weekend, but the connection was poor and she wasn't sure what he had in mind.

Or what she wanted him to have in mind.

The next beep made the question academic. "Siga?" Oscar Nauman's voice was a rumbling baritone. "God, I hate talking on these damn machines. Look, a pipe's burst—Connecticut—so I have to go—place could wash away and where the hell plumbers? Worse than doctors on a weekend. Sorry. I'll call."

Deflated, Sigrid sat on the edge of the bed, rewound the tape, and then lay back against the ivory linen coverlet as the short message played again. By now she was used to the way the artist's speech turned to verbal shorthand whenever he was excited or upset and she had no trouble deciphering his diatribe about the impossibility of finding a plumber on a Saturday night.

Nauman's East Side apartment was a bachelor efficiency, little more than a place to sleep and change clothes during the week while he attended to his duties as chairman of the art department at Vanderlyn College. Connecticut was where he had his studio, where he actually painted, and where most of his notebooks and sketchbooks were stored, not to mention a cache of early works for which three museums were dickering. Early in their acquaintance Sigrid had visited Nauman's Connecticut house to help one of his former students, and she was willing to concede that a broken water pipe on those premises probably constituted a true emergency.

On the other hand, this was the second weekend in a row that Nauman had canceled their evening plans.

Sigrid rolled to the middle of the bed and sat with her legs akimbo, an elbow on each thigh and her chin supported by cupped hands. It was her favorite position for serious thinking.

Was Nauman avoiding an evening alone with her?

They had met back in April during a homicide inves-

tigation in the Vanderlyn art department. He was chairman of the department, a world-famous artist, nearing
sixty; she was a no-nonsense police officer, absorbed by
her work and disinclined toward any emotional entanglements, much less with someone almost twenty-five years
older than she.

For reasons which she still hadn't fathomed, he had
marched into her life and tried to change her dress, her
palate, her resistance to intimacy. Nothing she did or said
could drive him away, and as spring turned to summer and
summer cooled into autumn, she continued to treat him
much as an oyster treats an unwelcome and highly irritating grain of sand which has intruded beneath its reclusive
shell and refuses to be dislodged: without realizing what
was happening, she gradually accustomed herself to the
unfamiliar and complex emotions which he aroused in her,
emotions her heretofore orderly psyche had never
experienced.

It wasn't until a young naval officer provoked him to a
jealous outburst that she finally recognized how important
Nauman's opinion of her had become. Until then, Sigrid
had believed the mirrors which told her that her face was
too thin, her nose too long, her mouth too wide; that her
breasts were too small and her body too skinny; that
nothing about her physical appearance fit the mold of
standard beauty and sexuality.

Suddenly reflected in the glare of Nauman's jealousy
and frustration, however, Sigrid had abruptly realized that
there might be other standards. For the first time in her
life she began to feel desirable, a woman who could be
cherished for very individual reasons by an exceptional
man.

Curious, and still more than a little awkward, she had
lowered her defenses and waited to see what would happen next.

Nothing.

Whether by coincidence or design, their schedules
had immediately quit meshing. If she wasn't working
overtime, he was jetting off into the sunset to jury a show
or to some exhibit or other of his pictures. In the last ten
days, there had been only one hasty lunch together in an

overcrowded restaurant—hardly the time or place to make him aware she was ready to take the next step even if she'd known what the next step was.

With the old insecurities beginning to nibble at the edges of her fragile new self-esteem, Sigrid slid off the end of her bed and hesitated before the mirrored closet door. Her body seemed all awkward angularity now and her left arm still carried the ugly red wound where a would-be rapist had slashed her earlier in the month. Not a very appealing sight, Sigrid told herself, and at that moment she even repented the giddy impulse which had cut off her hair. Instead of the sensible braided bun that had kept her dark tresses away from her face and out of her eyes for so many years, it was now a mass of layered waves that flopped across her forehead in frivolous disarray.

Sigrid frowned at her reflection and decided that her long neck and short hair made her look exactly like one of those weird African cranes with their ridiculous feathered topknots that were always showing up on Channel 13's nature programs.

How long, she wondered, would it take for her hair to grow out to braidable length again?

Gloomily, she reached inside the closet for a warm robe and barely noticed that it was a lovely black wool, banded in cords of red and gold, which Anne had brought her from Peru. Without Nauman around to make her self-conscious about it, clothes were merely something to warm her body or cover her nakedness and she did not linger before the mirror long enough to see how the black robe made her gray eyes lucent or how its graceful lines softened the imagined angularities of her thin figure.

Instead, she wandered out to the green-and-white tiled kitchen she shared with Roman and peered into the huge, well-stocked refrigerator. When she lived alone, she had always known exactly what she'd find in her small refrigerator: a head of wilted lettuce, a piece of cheese, milk, juice, a stick of butter, and perhaps the remains from a carton of salad or something she'd hurriedly picked up at a corner delicatessen the night before.

With Roman such an exuberant culinary adventurer, the possibilities were now perplexingly endless: assorted

cheeses, three kinds of salad greens, leeks, chives, arti-
choke hearts, bottles of homemade dressing, mustards,
pickles, and a dozen covered pots and bowls filled with
leftovers which, in Sigrid's opinion, ranged from the merely exotic to the totally inedible.

She closed the refrigerator, pulled down one of the
green-enamel saucepans hanging over the stove, and dumped
a can of tomato soup into it. Had Roman been there, he
would have insisted upon garnishing the soup with a sprig
of dill or basil and a dollop of heavy cream and he would
have brought out tins of imported crackers. Sigrid added
half a can of water from the tap and rooted around in the
cupboard till she found some plain saltines. In her present
mood, she felt an obscure need to regain some of her
former asceticism, to recreate a time when her choices
were fewer and much less complicated, when it was her
work that gave her puzzles to solve, not her personal life.

She poured the hot soup into a bowl and tuned
Roman's small portable television to a news program just
as a video camera tracked the removal of Emmy Mion's
shrouded body from the theater. Dispassionately, Sigrid
watched herself deliver a brief statement that was shortened
even further by a beer commercial. After eating, she
carried *The New York Times* and a glass of rosé into the
living room and nestled upon the white linen couch as she
opened the paper to the crossword puzzle.

The apartment, a ground floor appendage to an indus-
trial building on the Lower West Side, belonged to the
sister of Roman Tramegra's godmother and when it became available back in August, Sigrid and Roman had
agreed that they would respect each other's privacy and
overlap only in the kitchen and the tiny walled garden
(Roman's *giardino*) in front. Accordingly, the living room
basically reflected her own tastes: neutral-toned couch and
chairs and uncluttered surfaces. But even though Roman
had his own small sitting room in what had once been the
maid's quarters, he could not resist adding a few colorful
touches out here: an oriental rug in soft red tones, a
couple of needlepoint cushions for the white couch, lush
floor pots of ferns, and hanging baskets of bright pink
geraniums for the courtyard window behind the couch.

She drew the line, however, when Roman tried to sneak in a three-foot-tall replica of a seated Balinese temple goddess. (It wasn't the goddess's bare breasts nor even its six arms that jarred her so much as its garish red-and-gold robes.)

Sipping her wine, she settled into the puzzle. The daily ones were seldom difficult enough to occupy her for very long, but she relished clever word play and today's crossword contained several outrageous puns. It was finished much too quickly, though, leaving Sigrid with a restlessness which thoroughly annoyed her. Why should this one empty evening be so much more difficult to fill than all the empty evenings before Nauman charged into her life?

When Roman let himself in at ten-thirty, he was surprised to find Sigrid at the dining room table with an open briefcase and papers spread before her.

"Working?" he boomed. "I thought you and Oscar—?"

"He was called out of town," said Sigrid, "so I thought I'd catch up on a few things."

From the kitchen came a low clunk, then silence as the washer switched itself off. Roman followed her out to watch while she transferred the load to the dryer. "And you waxed the floor! My dear Sigrid, you needn't have done that."

"I didn't feel like watching a program on African water birds," she said wryly.

Roman hung his corduroy jacket on the back of one of the bar stools, smoothed a strand of thin brown hair across the top of his head, and began measuring coffee into a brass Italian espresso pot. "Had I known you were free, I'd have invited you to see our ghoulish little fantasy."

Sigrid straightened up with her hands full of wet lingerie. "Those people actually danced tonight?"

"And danced *marvelously*! It was standing-room-only and critics were there. Someone said the *Times*, too, but that's undoubtedly wishful thinking." He filled the pot with water and set it over a medium flame on the huge chrome-and-black-iron range.

Sigrid started the dryer. "What did they do about Emmy Mion's solo?"

"If I do say so myself, it was *inspired*!" Roman beamed. "Neither of the women wished to do it and I knew the men weren't too keen on giving the spotlight to David Orland—after all, he is *not* a member of the troupe, you see, and the 8th-AV-8 would hardly benefit if critics took him to be its star soloist—" He paused to explain the difficulties in substituting Orland for one of the men in the first and last scenes.

"So who did you use?" Sigrid asked.

"*No one!*" exclaimed Roman. "I wrote a few lines for Eric and at the end of the first scene, there was a blackout while he told the audience that the next dance belonged to Emmy and that they must imagine her small ghostly figure dancing for them one final time. Then the music started, Nate Richmond narrowed a pure white spotlight till the beam wasn't much wider than my fist, and that little spot of light *danced*. It was sheer *magic*. My dear, there wasn't a dry eye in the house."

Water boiled up in the espresso pot and a rich aroma of dark-roasted coffee filled the kitchen. Roman poured them each a tiny cup and as they sipped the hot liquid, he said, "You didn't tell anyone today that we are friends, did you?"

"No, why?"

"No reason," he replied with suspicious airiness.

"Roman?" she said sternly.

"My dear, I shall be the *soul* of discretion. No one will suspect a *thing*," he pleaded. "*Do* say I can play Watson to your Holmes just this once. Think how useful I can be in your investigation if no one knows our connection."

He looked like a large anxious Saint Bernard who had sniffed a juicy T-bone steak just beyond his reach.

"You'll have absolutely no official status," Sigrid warned him, "and the minute you do something foolish—"

"I shall be more inscrutable than Charlie Chan," he promised happily. "More invisible than the Shadow."

Chapter 11

When Sigrid arrived at headquarters Sunday morning for the day's briefing, she found her office crowded. Bernie Peters was trying to rev himself up with a second cup of black coffee. His bloodshot eyes and deep yawns betrayed another colicky night with his new son. Mick Cluett sat off to one side, immersed in the sports section of the Sunday paper, while Matt Eberstadt absentmindedly fumbled in the box on Sigrid's desk for another jelly doughnut as he read through the reports the patrol units had submitted.

"I thought you were on a diet," teased Elaine Albee, moving the doughnuts out of his reach and offering them to Sigrid as the lieutenant took her place behind the desk.

"I didn't have any breakfast," Eberstadt alibied.

Sigrid glanced at the depleted choices and selected a squashed doughnut filled with raspberry jam. "What about fingerprints, Lowry?"

"No luck, Lieutenant," Jim Lowry replied, confirming what they had feared. The iron scaffolding from which Emmy Mion had been flung was covered with overlapping fingerprints of all six dancers. "I even found a clear set of Orland's prints on the lower rungs. But up near the top, where they say that jack-o'-lantern was standing when he threw her, nothing but smudges."

To add to their lack of leads, Bernie Peters reported a less than fruitful interview with the composer, Sergio Avril. "The guy's blinder'n a bat, Lieutenant. Claims he can barely see across the stage even when it's all lit up, so he's got no idea who the jack-o'-lantern was."

Sigrid set her coffee mug down fatalistically. "I suppose he can't say if Kee or Delgado were in their places across from him?"

Peters shook his head and Eberstadt chimed in, "That's

the skinny little guy with the thick glasses, right? If it tells you anything about the condition of his eyes, I saw him mistake one of those stuffed goblins for a person."

They all agreed that those life-size puppets were not going to make life any easier.

"What about the alley door?" Sigrid asked Elaine.

"David Orland was right. It was unlocked when I examined it. I asked our boys in blue if they'd checked it earlier. No one remembered."

"So Orland could have walked out the front and come back in through the alleyway," mused Jim Lowry.

Mick Cluett lowered the sports section to listen phlegmatically as the others batted possible theories back and forth, but if he had theories of his own, he didn't offer them.

For the next few minutes, the others tried the glass slipper on every foot without really knowing what would make a perfect fit: there was Eric Kee's possessive jealousy, Cliff Delgado's lust, David Orland's spurned love, and Wingate West's what?

"Laziness?" suggested Elaine. "Maybe they were going to can him for Orland."

"No," said Eberstadt, folding the empty doughnut box into a neat square and carefully depositing it in Sigrid's wastebasket. He hoisted his belt to tuck in his bulging shirt. "West may act goofy offstage but everybody says the guy can dance."

Eventually they became aware that Sigrid wasn't with them and Bernie Peters said, "What do you think, Lieutenant?"

"I think we're going at this wrong," Sigrid said bluntly. "Stop focusing on who for the moment and think why."

Albee had been dabbing at a drop of jelly which had fallen on the skirt of her dark blue sweater dress and she lifted her blonde head. "Motive?"

Jim handed her another napkin. "Or who profits?"

Eberstadt nodded sagely. "And what changes now that she's dead."

"That, too," Sigrid agreed. "But even more, why was Emmy Mion killed yesterday afternoon on a spotlit stage in front of a hundred people? Those four men were her friends. Any one of them could have maneuvered her into a dark alley, someplace deserted and without any witnesses."

"Hey, that's right!" said Lowry, his rugged face animated as the alternatives sank in. "Why didn't he kill her Friday? Or wait till after the second show last night?"

"He could have poisoned her champagne or brained her with the empty bottle when no one was looking," nodded Peters.

"Instead," Albee concluded triumphantly, "he killed her in the most public place possible. On stage, front and center."

"They're all performers," said Lowry, "but that's carrying performance a bit far."

Whenever the lieutenant sat so quietly watchful with her thin fingers laced on the desktop before her, something about her erect carriage stirred subconscious memories in all her officers of certain intimidating teachers they'd each had in grade school. Even though the severe, old-maidish bun had recently been replaced by a much shorter and softer hair style, no one equated it to a softening of her manner; and when her cool eyes silently moved from one speaker to the next, even a latent chauvinist like Bernie Peters suddenly started feeling as if he ought to raise his hand and wait to be called on before speaking.

"Maybe he couldn't wait till after the show?" he offered diffidently.

The lieutenant gave a half-nod of approval. "Why not?"

Peters shrugged, but Albee glimpsed the direction Lieutenant Harald was moving toward. "That phone call!" she exclaimed. "Maybe Emmy Mion learned something dangerous and she let it slip just before the show started and he had to kill her before she told the others. Or us," she added, thoughtfully running her fingers through her blonde curls. "Several people mentioned how rigid she was about some things—especially anything illegal."

"Yeah," said Peters. "And who was with her when she got the call? Eric Kee! Maybe that fight they had wasn't all about the Judson kid."

"Kee told us she was expecting a call," Sigrid agreed, "but he denies knowing she actually received it."

"Of course he'd deny it," Peters said scornfully.

It was something else to bat around.

In the end, Sigrid told Cluett, Eberstadt, and Peters to keep it in mind as they interviewed the remaining witnesses. It was also something that Lowry and Albee might dig at when they'd finished at Emmy Mion's apartment this morning.

"Do you think someone will be at the theater?" asked Jim.

"They performed last night and they plan to dance this afternoon," Sigrid said.

Before they could react to that news, a clerk rapped at the door. "Lieutenant Harald? There's a Dr. Ferrell to see you."

The psychiatrist. "Ask her to wait five minutes," Sigrid said.

As she finished her instructions to the others, the psychiatrist's presence reminded her of something. "Albee. What was the name of that child that was killed last winter?"

"Child?" Elaine Albee looked at her blankly. "Oh, yes. Helen Delgado mentioned her. A little girl from one of the dancing classes." She began to thumb through her notebook.

Once again Sigrid missed Tillie's solid unimaginative presence. He might lack flair and panache, but he would have promptly supplied the information she wanted. Unfortunately, Tillie was still in the hospital, lucky to be alive, and in his absence she would have to make do with assistants who were possibly brighter but much less meticulous. She repressed a sigh. It was going to be a long three months.

"Sorry, Lieutenant, I guess I didn't write down her name," Elaine said, bracing for a reprimand.

Fortunately Sigrid had found what she wanted among her own notes, as well as the picture she'd kept of the murdered child. "Amanda Gillespie. Disappeared on her way home from a dance class at the theater last February and later found in a snowbank."

Her gray eyes fell on Cluett, who had returned to an article about the New York Jets. "Cluett, get me the records on that case, please."

He looked up with a broad vacant face. "Ma'am?"

"You *are* with us, aren't you, Cluett? Amanda Gillespie. I want to see the file on that homicide."

"Yes, ma'am." Cluett stowed his newspaper under the chair, heaved himself to his feet, and went off to do as asked.

As the others set out on their own tasks, Sigrid told them to send in Dr. Ferrell.

Chapter 12

Sigrid had formed no mental image of the psychiatrist who had first pronounced Emmy Mion dead, so she hardly expected an elderly bespectacled Viennese in a heavy tweed suit to walk into her office. On the other hand, she wasn't quite prepared either for a tangle of blonde tresses, clear blue eyes, and a perfect size eight in a cashmere suit and high-heeled Italian boots.

So much poise and beauty made Sigrid immediately aware of her own shortcomings—her nondescript gray jacket and navy slacks, that absurd haircut. *She* had a silk scarf similar to the one Dr. Ferrell had looped around her neck for a vivid splash of color, thought Sigrid. Anne had brought her one home from her last mad dash to Paris. It was probably just what today's white shirt could use, so why hadn't she worn it? And she'd recently started experimenting with makeup, but the habit wasn't automatic yet and in the morning's rush, she'd completely forgotten about it.

"I'm glad you came, Doctor," she said stiffly, offering the other woman a chair. "I understand you've been connected with the dance theater since last winter."

Dr. Ferrell remained standing with a quizzical smile

on her lovely lips. "You really don't remember me, do you, Sigrid?"

Sigrid looked at her more closely. "No, I'm sorry. Have we met before?"

"St. Margaret's!" Christa Ferrell laughed musically, drawing a chair up beside Sigrid's desk. "I was a grubby little lower former when you were one of the lofty upperclassmen. You haven't changed a bit, though. I knew you immediately!"

"Oh?" Sigrid promptly heard the inanity in her own voice.

"Don't worry. I know you're too busy to launch into old home week, but I was so surprised to see you up there on the stage yesterday in charge of a homicide, even though I *did* wonder—"

Whatever she wondered was left unsaid as Christa Ferrell draped her black wool coat over a nearby chair. "If St. Margaret's only knew!" Her gloves and purse joined the coat. "I never see your name in the alumnae news."

"I'm afraid I don't keep up with it," Sigrid muttered. She sat down at her desk and pulled her notepad into position, unconsciously trying to restore some semblance of formality between them. "So. Helen Delgado told us you're a psychiatrist. That you worked with the children when one of their classmates was murdered last winter?"

"God, yes! Wasn't that horrible? You weren't there then, were you?"

"No, another officer handled that one."

At that moment, Mick Cluett halted in the doorway carrying the Gillespie file. After sending him off to interview his share of names from last night's audience, Sigrid scanned the high spots of the investigation into little Amanda Gillespie's death.

"They said she was a sweet-tempered child, very affectionate and obedient. Followed all the rules," said Christa Ferrell, who remembered the whole episode and seemed willing to help. "And you know the first rule city parents teach their kids."

Sigrid nodded. "Never talk to strangers."

"The other children said she wouldn't have, either. That she was too timid to say boo to a cockroach. My nephew, Calder, had just turned five when it happened and even though he didn't know little Mandy very well, there was enough gruesome talk to give the children nightmares and implant unreasonable fears. My brother and his wife were worried that he'd be permanently scarred without help and since my specialty's in pediatrics, of course, I agreed to treat Calder."

She crossed her legs and smoothed her skirt over a shapely knee. "A few days later, Emmy Mion and a committee of parents asked if I'd conduct a couple of group sessions to help the other children manage their grief and their fears, so I did."

Children were a dark continent for Sigrid. "Was it hard?" she asked curiously.

"Not really." Christa Ferrell smiled. "Grief therapy for young children is mainly a matter of just guiding the discussion until they talk their way through their anxieties and anguish. It helped that Mandy hadn't been battered or sexually molested. It would have helped even more if they'd found her killer, of course. Children handle things better when everything balances out."

It was said almost as an afterthought, but Sigrid felt rather as if she ought to apologize for a departmental lapse in efficiency. "Will you repeat the procedure now that Mion's been killed?"

"If the parents and staff wish me to, certainly I will." Her blonde hair swept the shoulder of her blue suit as she tilted her head to consider. "I wonder if the dance classes will continue, though? The Gillespie child's death had nothing to do with the theater, but *this* time—My sister-in-law's already saying she won't let Calder go back till this is cleared up, and that's a fairly typical parental reaction."

Sigrid laid aside the Gillespie folder to read in greater detail later. "I don't suppose you recognized the jack-o'-lantern dancer?"

"No, I'm really not very familiar with any of them. I did sit in on one of Calder's classes last month. Two of the men—the Chinese-looking dancer and the one with a blonde punk haircut—conducted that particular session but it certainly wasn't enough for me to recognize them in costume yesterday."

"After the lights came back on, do you remember who was where?"

"I wish I could say, but I was concerned for Calder, of course, and there was so much confusion around the stage area, although I must say your policeman handled things very competently."

Again Sigrid was made to feel responsible for the whole department, as if she should thank Christa Ferrell for her commendation. Instead, she limited her thanks to the psychiatrist for her help yesterday and for coming in that morning.

Dr. Ferrell, however, did not reach for her coat. Instead, she smiled at her onetime schoolmate and asked, "Do you believe in coincidence, Sigrid?"

"You mean this child's dance instructor now being murdered, too?"

"No, no." She waved that aside with a graceful flick of her fingers. "I mean the coincidence of our meeting again like this after so many years. Especially since—" She tucked a strand of hair behind her ear and leaned forward confidingly. "This is the second homicide in which we've overlapped. I *thought* your name was familiar when I saw it this summer, but it didn't really connect until yesterday."

"This summer?"

"When Darlene Makaroff was killed. In July. I should have come to you before now because I can really use your professional assessment. You *will* help, won't you?"

"I'm sorry, Dr.—uh, Christa." Sigrid was completely bewildered. "I don't have the faintest idea what you're talking about."

"Darlene Makaroff. She and her two young daughters were Social Services clients—that's where I work, you see—and her lover killed her. Smashed her head in with a hammer. Your name was on one of the reports."

"Really?" Sigrid tried to recall that particular homicide. Back in July?

A chill November wind now harried lower Manhattan and she had trouble separating the Makaroff murder from a half-dozen others. She reached for her phone and had a clerk bring her the file; but even after skimming through the thick folder, memory's bells were only faintly chiming.

Her initials were on the first reports but Detective Bernie Peters had actually completed the investigation. It read like such a routine domestic killing. No mystery, nothing bizarre, just another of those unpremeditated eruptions of violence, like a sudden summer thundercloud that roils up out of nowhere to strike the earth with electrical, destructive intensity and then is gone with only some wrecked umbrellas and leaf-strewn streets to mark the short-lived fury.

Not that Sigrid equated a human death with an inverted umbrella. It would not occur to her to think of her job in fanciful metaphors, but she did occasionally worry about going stale and times like this made her wonder if objectivity were being replaced by indifference.

She skimmed the papers again, trying to visualize the reality behind the official language. A disturbance at a run-down apartment building tenanted by welfare recipients near Thompkins Square. (*Broken plaster and filthy marble tile*, she thought. *Passageways lit by bare forty-watt bulbs, the stench of urine and vomit in the stair-wells.*) Dead at the scene from apparent blows with a hammer was one Darlene Makaroff, female Caucasian, age twenty-four. (*A dress? Jeans? Or, on such a hot night, perhaps she'd been that nude?*) Alleged assailant, one Ray Thorpe, male Caucasian, age twenty, seen fleeing from the Kingston's twelfth floor and identified as the victim's lover.

According to subsequent additions to the forms in his case jacket, Thorpe had narrowly eluded capture in Newark back in September and had recently been spotted in Queens. A watch was being kept on his sister's house there and an arrest was expected any time now.

Just in time for a Thanksgiving arraignment, thought Sigrid, and considering his prior arrest record, Ray Thorpe would have cause for thanks if he didn't get the book thrown at him.

Making a mental note to ask Detective Peters to keep her posted on the case, Sigrid closed the file, aligned it neatly with others in her Out-basket, and looked up to meet Christa Ferrell's clear blue eyes.

"Sorry, Christa. I just don't have a clear recollection of that night."

To be perfectly truthful, her recollection of Dr. Christa Ferrell wasn't all that clear either, although she had no intention of admitting it. She vaguely recalled that they might have roomed on the same hall one year at school, but Ferrell was at least three years younger and Sigrid knew that children always pay more attention to those above them than those below.

She tried to imagine the tousled blonde hair a shade lighter and perhaps longer, to imagine her schoolmate's stylish cashmere suit and wool coat replaced with one of St. Margaret's ugly brown-and-green plaid uniforms; but memory was just as recalcitrant there as with poor Darlene Makaroff. Christa Ferrell's poise and air of bright confidence must have been her birthright, a birthright shared with most of the school's student body, so that was no help either. Few of the girls had been as shy and gawky or as achingly self-conscious as young Sigrid Harald.

Away from headquarters, some of that childhood awkwardness remained; here in her own office, though, she possessed a cool competence.

"I'm sorry," she said again. "If you knew how many domestic homicides we see in—"

"There were two little girls," Christa Ferrell persisted. "They saw their mother murdered. They *must* have been there when you arrived."

"Not necessarily. One of the neighbors might have taken them to a different apartment. Is it really so important?"

Ferrell's graceful shrug conceded the dead end. "It might have been helpful for me to have an objective account of that night."

"Perhaps a social worker?" Sigrid suggested. "Someone from your place?"

"Martha Holt," she acknowledged.

"Too bureaucratic?"

"Oh Lord, no! If anything, just the op. She never forgets that Social Services is supposed to ease problems, not make new ones. All she cared about that evening was getting the kids out of that dreadful place and bedded down somewhere civilized for the night. She told me everything she saw, but I thought you could add something from the police viewpoint, things she might not have picked up on."

"I wish I could help," said Sigrid, still puzzled by Christa's connection with this nondescript case. As a police officer, she knew better than to judge by appearances but "I'd have thought you'd be in private practice," she probed delicately.

Delicacy was unnecessary. Christa Ferrell appeared to find it perfectly natural that everyone would be as interested in the twists and turns of her career as she was herself.

"I'm still trying to decide what I want to be when I grow up," she confided with a smile that was clearly mock-rueful. "My M.D. was in pediatrics, but first-year residency convinced me that my true interest wasn't in the physical illnesses of children. It's their mental problems that absolutely fascinate me." Enthusiasm animated her flawless features and glowed in the depths of her eyes. "Eventually, I'll open a private practice of my own, of course, but right now I'm doing psychiatric evaluations for the city and getting more solid experience than I'd ever dreamed possible. The things these welfare kids have been exposed to! You can't imagine!"

She broke off with an appealing laugh. "Listen to me telling *you*! And you a policewoman!"

She somehow managed to make Sigrid's career choice sound slightly eccentric.

"Well, I can't give you more details of that night," Sigrid said stiffly, "but maybe someone from the beat—"

Again she consulted the sheaf of papers in the case jacket. "The patrolman who got there first was Officer J. T. Hickler. Personnel can give you his address."

She wrote the name on a memo slip and handed it to Christa, who glanced at it and then tucked it in her jacket pocket with so little interest that Sigrid's earlier feeling returned that something more lay behind the psychiatrist's visit than helping with Emmy Mion's murder or recreating the scene of a patient's trauma.

"I guess I'm taking this case too much to heart, Sigrid, but we see so much hopelessness and this one looks like it'll have a happy ending."

"Oh?" Curiosity about where the hook would come made Sigrid more patient than usual.

"Both the kids are cute as Mickey Mouse buttons and there's a couple that wants to adopt them just as soon as Corrie—that's the younger one that I'm working with. She's blocked out that whole evening but I'm beginning to get glimmers of light. Nothing big yet, but little glimmers of light at the 'way far end of the tunnel. So it's really going to be a marvelous success story for the agency."

She paused and looked at Sigrid expectantly.

"That's good," Sigrid murmured inanely. She felt she was being nudged toward some goal, but what?

Christa Ferrell's winsome smile did not falter. "There are so many gloomy *failures* in the services the city provides, so when I heard your mother was doing an in-depth story about the different agencies for *New York Today*, and there was your name on the investigation of Darlene Makaroff's murder, the coincidence was too much to overlook."

So that was it, thought Sigrid, leaning back in her chair and tenting her fingers before her.

Anne Harald's career as a freelance photojournalist had taken her all over the world, where she recorded award-winning images of the human side of war, famine, calamity, and mass upheavals. She had been out of the country on various assignments for most of the year, but was back now with the avowed intention of staying right in New York at least through Christmas.

Sigrid thought she remembered talk about a projected series in which Anne would use actual case histories to illustrate selected entitling laws. "Someone else will write up all the statistics," Anne had said. "All I have to do is prowl around and take the right pictures."

Pictures that would be seen by a wide audience, thought Sigrid. The series would carry a load of built-in grimness, so yes, a segment that illustrated how two little girls were successfully helped would offer welcome relief, especially if they were photogenic ("cute as Mickey Mouse buttons"). With an equally photogenic psychiatrist?

"It would be so good for the agency, too," said Ferrell, with a guileless tilt of her blonde head.

And suddenly Sigrid had a vivid memory of flaxen hair swinging away from a small, childishly pretty face in just the same gesture. She couldn't remember what it was that little Chrissie Ferrell was trying to persuade their hall to do "for the good of St. Margaret's," but she did remember that it was something that would put the younger girl squarely in the school's spotlight.

"You'd have to speak to her about that yourself," said Sigrid.

"I've *tried*. No one seems to know her phone number."

Sigrid had heard similar complaints about Anne Harald ever since she could remember. "Mother moves a lot," she said dryly and leaned forward to flip through the roto-file on her desk for her mother's newest telephone number. "She's out of town for the weekend, but you might catch her later tonight."

Using a slim gold pen, Dr. Ferrell made a careful note in a small leather-bound notebook, then gathered up her purse and coat.

"It's been absolutely marvelous seeing you again, Sigrid. You'll let me know if the Thorpe man's arrested, won't you? And we really must have lunch sometime and talk about good old St. Margaret's."

Sigrid managed to keep a perfectly straight face. "Oh absolutely," she murmured.

Chapter 13

Ever since their first meeting back in April, when they'd mistaken one another for burglars, Roman Tramegra had badgered Sigrid for insider information about various homicide cases. Now that he was legitimately in the middle of such a case, he found the reality more daunting than he'd expected.

A lifelong enthusiast for spontaneous undertakings, Roman had loved the dance company's Hey-let's-stage-a-show-in-the-barn vigor. From Emmy Mion's optimistic can-do management to Nate Richmond's make-do wizardry, the whole troupe enchanted him—even when badgered from both sides by the Delgados' simmering sexualities or made the butt of Ginger Judson's occasionally vicious mimicry. His imagination was unleashed by their youthful energy and dynamic tension, and nothing he could write for them was too outrageous. The more outrageous, the better, in fact. When they included him in their careless rough-and tumble, Roman felt that he was accepted, part of the whole and, best of all, this particular whole was, however humbly, *show business*—splashy, glittering, larger than life.

Murder stripped away the glitter.

Emmy Mion's death had shaken him. That such a lively little sprite should have ended so brutally impaled upon those iron spikes was dreadful past remembering; nevertheless, the real horror, only now sinking in this Sunday morning, was his gruesome realization that her killer wasn't some formless unknown monster but a familiar face, someone he'd shared his tea with, had laughed with, had applauded in delight upon seeing one of his visual bon mots interpreted so precisely.

Yet no shock could completely blunt Roman's insatiable curiosity, his magpie need to know. Had he not, he asked himself, practically *begged* dear Sigrid for this opportunity to test his sleuthing powers? Could he now go home and face her cool-eyed gaze and tell her he had no stomach for murder after all?

Never! He rallied himself and tried to keep his face immobile as he glanced around the green room with what he hoped was artless casualness. Two of its occupants were immersed in the Sunday *Times*. A short account of Emmy's death in the front section dwelled on the bizarre Halloween aspects of the case and quoted a "Lieutenant Sigmund Harald" as expecting an early arrest.

A one-paragraph, mostly favorable review of last night's performance was buried in a back section; and although its overall tone was one of condescension, Roman particularly savored the paragraph's opening lines: "Eerie percussives and an inventive scenario framed a young improv group's offering last night."

An inventive scenarist should be able to spot an amateur killer, he told himself.

Wingate West had stopped by one of the Korean greengrocers in the neighborhood and bought a bag of fruit, which he'd dumped into a large wooden bowl on the table. Cliff Delgado was tearing the peel from a tangerine in small leathery flakes—for once silent on the parallels to stripping a woman—and the pungent oils from the peel drifted across the table and made Roman's nose itch. He scratched it absently and watched Ginger Judson as she tossed grapes one by one into the air and caught them in her mouth without missing any. Young West had cut a hole in the top of his orange and alternately squeezed and sucked the juice as he read the paper.

No mark of Cain upon any brow, Roman thought gloomily. Of course, neither Eric Kee nor David Orland had yet arrived.

Even as that thought formed in his mind, Orland appeared in an aromatic cloud of mothballs, another *Times* under his arm and a pleased expression on his bruised face. "Good news! Friend of mine works at the *Voice*. Says Bledsoe gives us a rave and the paper's going to use most of his copy."

Frederick Bledsoe was another freelance dance critic who'd been in last night's audience. Unfortunately, the *Voice* wouldn't be out in time to do today's performance of *Ghosties and Ghouls* much good. "Next weekend," was the sudden unspoken hope, and even Roman felt himself perking up at the vision of a healthy box office.

They would need it. Several parents had telephoned that morning to cancel their offspring's dancing classes. Rikki Innes and Helen Delgado were even now down in the corner office, taking calls, soothing anxious mothers, trying to keep the company afloat.

Some parents were less anxious than others though, or at least less vigilant, as Roman discovered when he wandered out to the hall carrying a large tray for protective coloration. He planned to begin sleuthing in the women's dressing room since the women were otherwise occupied. Instead, he found the three Pennewelf children lined up like stair steps by the water cooler.

"We weren't doing nothing!" said Adam, the eight-year-old, his instinctive reaction to Roman's disapproving frown.

"Billy wants to see Nate," said Mary, his younger sister.

As usual, Billy the youngest, said nothing. Five-year-old Billy was something of a legend in his own time. Except for Nate, no one else in the troupe had ever heard him speak. Silent and well-mannered inside the theater, he communicated in whispers only to seven-year-old Mary, who relayed everything with "Billy says" or "Billy wants." According to their grandfather, who owned the hardware store next door, Billy had a will of iron and a temper to match. It was Billy who hung around underfoot, completely fascinated, when the troupe had taken over the empty theater. It was Billy who wanted to learn how to dance. And it was Billy who bullied his older siblings into coming along as interpreters once classes began.

"Billy says Nate has pictures for us," said Mary.

"Then by all means let us seek out Nate," Roman said, herding the children before him down the dim hall to the next door, which had a huge light bulb painted upon it.

Roman knocked loudly, then pushed it open. "Company for you, Richmond."

Part workshop, part sorcerer's laboratory, the large boxy room was more cluttered than any child's playroom. Along the left wall, Nate Richmond had built a narrow darkroom from wooden two-by-fours covered in heavy black canvas, which in turn was covered with dozens of photographs of the troupe and most of the children who'd attended classes there. Inside his makeshift cave, he'd tapped into the water pipes which served the bathroom on the other side of the wall. His plumbing probably wouldn't pass a city inspector—some of the joints looked as if they were sealed with chewing gum rather than solder, and holes in the wall had been patched with wide electrical duct tape—but everything seemed to work properly and nothing leaked.

Double-tiered workbenches lined the other three walls. The one nearest the darkroom was devoted to photograph-

ic equipment and supplies, the other two were jumbled
with cannibalized spotlights, Fresnels, electrical flex,
switches, gels, and a hundred other arcane bits and pieces
which meant nothing to Roman's untechnical eyes.

The only cleared space in the whole room was at the
very center and, although Roman had thought that she
was safely occupied in the office, Rikki Innes was seated
on a cushion there at a low round table with her long legs
tucked beneath her, her pale hair loose around that oval
face. Her welcoming smile for Roman turned to dismay
when she saw the three children behind him.

Nearby sat Nate Richmond, who'd been minutely
examining a proof sheet with the aid of a very large
magnifying glass. He held it up to his face and regarded
the children solemnly through one wildly magnified green
eye. "Hello, Pennewelfs. I was just looking at you. Come
and see."

The three raced across the cluttered room. Billy
confidently climbed into the slender man's lap while Mary
and Adam Pennewelf leaned upon each shoulder.

Roman followed and looked over their bent heads at
the proof sheets spread upon the table. The man was truly
an artist with his camera, he thought. Especially with
pictures of children. It was almost as if Nate became a
child himself, playing behind a toy camera, for they were
seldom self-conscious with him and he captured their
level-eyed gravity and their delicious gurgles of laughter
with equal truthfulness.

As Roman picked his way back to the door, past scraps
of spotlights and electrical odds and ends, he heard Mary
say, "Billy wants you to tell him about the alligator again."

"Alligator?" Beneath the thick curly brown hair, Nate
Richmond's puckish face wore a puzzled look. "Did I ever
mention any alligator?"

"He poked his snout up your bathtub," said Adam.
"You told us."

"And tried to bite your toes," Mary testified, her little
face close to his.

"Oh, *that* alligator." Nate nodded solemnly. Rikki
Innes looked resigned as Nate settled Billy more comfort-

ably on one knee and made a place for Mary on the other. "Well, you see, what happened with that alligator is—"

Unnoticed by all except Rikki, Roman closed the door.

The green room was near the center of the wide backstage hall. Nate's workroom was to the immediate left, then the bathroom, then the corner business office. Just beyond its door rose the wooden staircase. Roman heard the telephone ring and Helen Delgado's answering murmur floated through the open doorway.

On the theory that stealth is more conspicuous than brazenness, he passed with a cheery wave to the designer, but her glossy black head was turned away and he mounted the stairs without being seen.

Both railings at each side of the theater were used as catchalls for anything people didn't want to be bothered with taking upstairs immediately and Roman gathered up a sweatshirt and a red kimono that Emmy had used as a dressing gown. Beneath was a pair of purple leg warmers he remembered hearing Ginger inquiring about. And here was his own dishtowel which he'd brought from home because he disliked paper towels.

He draped the clothes on one shoulder, his towel on the other, and continued up.

Inside the big square dressing room at the top of the stairs, a lumpy daybed and two ancient overstuffed chairs were clumped together on the right wall around a scarred coffee table. Snapping on the lights, Roman was startled by the unexpected sight of someone asleep on the daybed.

"Oh, I say! I'm most frightfully sorry," he began, feeling himself a miserable snoop caught in the act. He started to back out of the room, then abruptly realized the figure was one of those life-size puppets. Unnerving how guilt could make the prone figure look human, he thought, stepping forward to pull it into an upright sitting position. Its ghastly mask grinned at the two jack-o'-lantern heads which were piled on the adjoining chair as if engaged in macabre pleasantries over the dirty cups and glasses standing on the coffee table.

Jutting out from the wall opposite the door were four long pipe clothing racks which held an assortment of costumes and regular clothes on wire hangers.

Mirrored panels lined the entire near left wall. They were topped by strip lighting that blazed into brightness when Roman flipped a second wall switch. Beneath was a single counter which must have originally been planned for six people since there were six shallow drawers beneath the counter. Now it seemed to be divided by three chairs spaced haphazardly along its length.

Roman had been coming to the theater for two and a half months, but he'd never had occasion to enter the women's dressing room when it was occupied and he wasn't at all sure which of the three spaces belonged to Emmy Mion. Each seemed to hold a similar clutter of makeup, cold cream, greasepaint, brushes, combs, and assorted boxes and jars.

He set his tray on the end of the counter next to a pair of electrician's pliers, brought over the dirty glassware from the coffee table, then opened the end drawer.

It held a crumpled wad of rubberized athletic bandages, several half-used tubes of liniment, a second pair of pliers from Nate's workbench, a tack hammer from Helen's, and, not too unexpectedly, a wire balloon whisk from the kitchen area. The dancers were always walking away from the utensil drawer with it because its shape made it an instant microphone, holy water sprinkler, or phallus, depending on whether they were improvising rock star, priest, or buffoon.

They took tools just as carelessly, thought Roman, fishing them out of the drawer to return to their proper places downstairs. Only this morning Helen had complained about a missing paint mask and accused Cliff of using it in another of his bawdy skits.

Remembering how Emmy always "borrowed" Nate's pliers to finish off the last few pistachio nuts which were too difficult to crack with her sharp little teeth, he added the tools to his tray, then opened the second drawer. It was even more crammed than the first. Along with an elastic underbelt and a couple of products connected to what he privately thought of as "feminine hygiene," he saw lingerie, two mismatched woolly leg warmers, and a bright turquoise scarf which resembled one he'd seen tied around Ginger Judson's red hair, although they borrowed each other's clothes as casually as they borrowed tools. Nate was grumbling about a jacket and Ginger had recently turned the theater upside down looking for a crocheted shawl till Rikki remembered that she'd worn it home from a party.

As he started to lift the clothing, the doorknob turned. Immediately, he pushed the drawer shut and was innocently removing a saucer crowned with dried apple peelings from the far end of the counter when Ulrike Innes opened the door for two police detectives whom Roman recognized from yesterday. He smiled blandly, tray in hand. "Any more dirty dishes here, dear Rikki? Cups are getting low in the cupboard."

Elaine Albee groped through her mental directory. "Mr. Tramesa, is it?"

"Tramegra," he said in a deep mellifluous bass, wondering if Sigrid had told her colleagues about him. "Roman Tramegra."

"The scene writer, right?" asked Jim Lowry.

"Quite right," he beamed, pleased.

They regarded the large soft man suspiciously. He was dressed all in black today: black slacks, black ankle boots, and a black mohair turtleneck topped with a heavy gold chain which ended in an eagle's head carved of black wood. Was this, Elaine Albee wondered, Tramegra's version of mourning? He hardly looked the type to play housemaid. In fact—

Albee frowned. She suddenly felt that she ought to know this man. For some reason, his name was elusively familiar. Light brown hair brushed over a high dome, hooded brown eyes, and a slightly English accent—surely she'd remember if she'd ever before met this cross between Robert Morley and David Ogden Stiers?

Her thoughts were interrupted as Lowry hefted the tack hammer. "You weren't planning a little breaking and entering, were you, Mr. Tramegra?"

"Hardly," Roman chuckled. "No, as long as I was

rounding up glassware, I decided I might as well return the tools to their rightful places, too."

"Did Emmy Mion use any of these things?" asked Albee, poking through the objects on his tray.

"I can't say. The glasses and cups were on the coffee table, the saucer down there, the tools here—" He gave a vague wave of his hand, not wishing to admit he'd actually opened a drawer. "Rikki?"

The girl stood on her right foot with her left leg held doubled up behind her as she looked around absently. "Some of the glasses. She was as bad as Ginger and me about taking them back to the common room. And maybe the pliers? She used them for nutcrackers. Emmy—she loved pistachios."

She lowered her leg and turned away from them but her sad pale face was reflected in the long mirror and she felt their eyes watching her. She swallowed hard. "You wanted to see her dressing area." Rikki walked over to the middle chair and, in an oddly tender gesture, touched the back of it with the tips of her fingers. "This is where she sat."

Elaine Albee followed and opened the drawers immediately in front of that chair. Jim Lowry saw Roman's frank curiosity and said, "You can go on and take those things, if you want, Mr. Tramegra. Miss Innes will help us here."

"Very good," Roman said and, feeling like a butler in a Noel Coward play, he picked up his tray and exited stage left.

Once out in the hall, however, instead of returning the way he came, he went on down toward the spiral staircase, past a small rehearsal room and two storage rooms to the men's dressing room at the end.

Its layout was almost identical to the women's if not quite as neat. The troupe wore oversized sweatshirts of bright Crayola colors in many of their improvisational routines, and several were piled haphazardly by the clothing racks. Two jack-o'-lantern heads had been carelessly thrown on top; the third had rolled under a table. Fortunately for his cover story, Roman found almost as many stray cups and glasses on the men's long dressing counter. It, too, held a similar array of makeup and grooming aids, but

here Roman had a clearer idea of who sat where: Cliff
Delgado nearest the door, then Eric Kee and Win West.

A jock strap hung from one of the lights over Delgado's
space and a plastic container on the floor beside West's
chair must have held a health salad earlier in the week.
Now it looked like a science fair experiment in exotic
molds. Roman tipped it gingerly into a nearby wastebasket. A weighted tape dispenser which properly belonged
in the office was at Eric Kee's place and Roman added it to
his crowded tray.

Keeping his ears open for sounds out in the hall, he
quickly searched the six shallow drawers beneath the
counter, paying particular attention to those belonging to
Kee and Delgado. If there was something out of the
ordinary about any of them, he couldn't spot it and,
hearing angry voices at the foot of the iron staircase, he
hastily gathered up his tray and went down to join them.

Still smarting from the humiliation of the last two
hours, Eric Kee was half a minute away from slugging
Ginger Judson. His green eyes crackled with anger and
his fists clenched and unclenched. "If you can't do it
right—"

Ginger stood on the first step of the spiral staircase
and her sturdy body was rigid with equal belligerence.
"You're the one who screwed up last night. Don't blame
me if you can't—"

"Just get it right today or get out of my way." His
blue-black hair stood up in angry tufts.

Ginger's face flamed redder than her hair. "And just
who the hell died and left you king?" she shouted.

As the actual sense of her angry words sank in, the
girl moaned and fled up the stairs, almost bowling Roman
over as she pushed past him. The glasses on his tray tilted
precariously and he watched in dismay as one tumbled
over the edge, hit the iron railing, and smashed to the
floor below in a hundred glittering shards.

Chapter 14

Roman hurried down the circular iron steps, his deep voice resonant with basso apologies and warnings. "Do be careful. Shoes, everyone! A broom."

"You stupid dolt!" Eric Kee's black eyebrows contorted in an angry V; his lips thinned into a snarl of rage. "You *know* we dance barefoot. You want to cut our feet to ribbons?"

Offended, Roman halted on the bottom step and drew himself up to his full six feet. "I assure you I do *not* break glasses for personal gratification."

Kee's quarrel with Ginger Judson, followed by the sound of shattering glass, had drawn the others from the green room.

"C'mon, Eric, chill out, man," advised Win West, laying a friendly hand on Kee's arm.

The honey-skinned dancer jerked away and stomped past Cliff Delgado and David Orland, who stood watching silently. As he passed, Cliff said, "Nerves going, pal?" and gave one of his ill-timed laughs.

Eric Kee kept walking. He knew he was being stupid, lashing out at Ginger like that, snarling at Tramegra. But after what he'd been through this morning, what did they expect?

He paused at Nate Richmond's door, heard children's laughter inside, and kept going. As much as he usually enjoyed watching Nate interact with the kids, he was in no mood for a trip to Never-Never Land just then.

Helen Delgado looked up as he entered the office but her smile faded as she saw the expression on his face. "Oh Christ! What's happened now?"

"Nothing." He flung himself into the nearest chair.

Helen gave an earthy snort and waited. Today's en-

semble included turquoise stretch pants and a high-necked
tunic, a jungle print splashed with vivid greens, blues,
purples, and reds. Iridescent rose shadowed her eyes, a
plummy red glossed her lips, her shiny dark hair was piled
on top of her head, and a small enameled parrot sat inside
one hooped earring, while a monkey dangled from the
other one. It brushed the line of her chin as she tilted her
head toward him. "I hate to tell you this, doll, but an
inscrutable Chinaman you ain't."

She didn't get the smile she had hoped for. Eric
pushed up from the chair and began to pace the room.
When he'd completed his second circuit without speaking,
Helen shrugged and turned back to the papers on her
desk. Her seeming indifference loosened his tongue.

"Ginger doesn't give a damn about the way she
dances anymore and Tramegra's down there breaking glasses
on the stairs and I don't know, Helen. Maybe we ought to
pack it all in."

"Because Ginger missed a few steps and Roman's
dropped a glass? Don't you think you're overreacting a
bit?"

Eric continued to pace the room like an edgy tiger.
Helen's designer's eye noted how his black hair and gold-
en skin resembled a tiger's tawny-and-black fur. His slightly
splayed walk even mimicked a caged predator's bitter
frustration.

"Okay, doll, want to tell Mama what's really bugging
you?"

He paused at Emmy's drafting table. Her notes and
diagrams were still spread there just as she'd left them
yesterday morning. He picked up one of her ballpoint
pens. "The police came."

"I know. They were already in here asking if I remembered anything more about the telephone call and
when I'd actually talked to Emmy last."

"Not here," he said impatiently. "At the apartment."

"Ah," said Helen, suddenly understanding.

"They poked through everything. Everything there
was, which wasn't much. You know Emmy. She kept most
of her things here." The sweep of his arm encompassed
her dance books, sketchpads, and scrapbooks, as well as

various knickknacks and souvenirs cluttering the bookcases and pinned to the walls.

"So?"

"So they saw the empty drawers and hangers. And her suitcases. She was moving out, Helen."

"Yes."

"You *knew*?" He dropped the ballpoint pen and strode across the bare wooden floor to look into her brightly painted eyes. "She told you?"

"She didn't have to."

"Emmy wasn't gay." It was a plea as much as a statement.

Helen shrugged her heavy shoulders and the jungle print rippled across her full body. "What difference does it make now?"

"She loved me!" he insisted. "And damn it all, Helen, we were *good* together. What kind of sex would she get with Ginger? Emmy in bed with *her*? Jesus Christ!"

"Don't knock it if you haven't tried it, doll."

As Kee flung himself back into his angry pacing, Helen added, almost to herself, "Maybe it wasn't sex she wanted from Ginger so much as peace."

"*Peace?*"

"Or tolerance."

"I *loved* her," he said solemnly.

"So you loved her, big deal. Peter, Peter, Pumpkin-Eater."

"What's that supposed to mean?"

"That I've been working much too long in children's theater, probably," she said with a wry quirk of her full red lips. "The sex might have been good but Emmy just didn't want to live in your pumpkin shell, Eric."

He wheeled away from the desk and her dark eyes followed him consideringly. "It's too bad you and Rikki never got it on. I bet she'd love a pumpkin shell."

Upstairs, Rikki Innes watched unhappily as the two police detectives went through Emmy Mion's things. They had finished with the dressing counter and moved over to the pipe racks.

"These don't look like costumes," said Elaine Albee, flipping past a plaid jacket and heavy winter coat.

Rikki nodded. "Emmy keeps—I mean, *kept* most of her extra clothes here."

"Even though there was plenty of closet space at Eric Kee's place?" prodded Albee.

Rikki remained silent, wondering how much they knew about what Emmy had planned to do; and Jim Lowry said, "Did you know they were splitting up?"

"I guessed it," she answered reluctantly. "Only they weren't splitting up like you mean. Eric loved her and I think—no, I *know* Emmy still cared for him. She just didn't want to live with him anymore."

"Why was that, Miss Innes?"

He had a nice face, thought Rikki. Not handsome, but open and friendly. She wondered if he was sleeping with the blonde yet. The way he watched her, almost but not quite touching, hinted at an awareness beyond the professional. The way Nate was when—

"Miss Innes?"

"Sorry. I was thinking of something else." Her long hands turned palms-up in a helpless gesture. "Sometimes, maybe even *most* times, one person in a relationship loves more than the other one and there's no way to figure out why. I don't know why Emmy felt she had to move out. You'll have to ask Eric, won't you?"

"Look," said Detective Albee, "I know it seems disloyal to answer questions about other members of the troupe, but your friend was killed, Miss Innes. By one of those men."

"They're my friends, too," Rikki said quietly. "If I knew for sure—"

"Just make a guess," urged Jim Lowry.

"No." There was a mulish set now to her pointed chin. "A guess would be like saying one of them's more likely than the others and then you'd concentrate on him and it'd be awful if he wasn't the one, so you'll—"

Glass broke and furious yells erupted from the end of the corridor. Elaine Albee stuck her head out the door just as Ginger Judson rushed down the hall, her face convulsed with tears. She saw the police officer and her steps faltered, then she hurtled into the bathroom next door.

Before the door could slam behind her, Ginger had fled to the farthest cubicle, hooked its door, then sat down upon the closed toilet seat and simply howled with a mixture of grief and pure rage.

How dared he? How *dared* he treat her like that! She should have stood her ground. Should have spit in his smug face. His smug *male* face. Tears flooded down her freckled cheeks and sobs racked her body.

It isn't fair, she thought. Nobody thought twice anymore about men being bisexual. All the way back to the Greeks even. But *women*— Even Emmy. After they'd *planned*! Then in the dressing room yesterday, in front of Rikki. To say she'd changed her mind, that she wanted to live alone for a while. No love in her eyes when she said it. Only *pity*.

Remembered pain and humiliation spurted through her heaving breast; then she thought of Emmy's small sweet body impaled on those spikes and fresh weeping for what might have been bent her own sturdy frame double again.

As she groped for the roll of tissue to blow her nose, she saw slippered feet appear on the other side of the swinging door only inches from her feet. "Ginger? Are you all right?"

She hadn't heard Rikki enter the room and she was startled by the nearness of her voice. "Go away," she sobbed.

The cubicle door rattled and the noise echoed off the tiled wall. "Come on, Ginger. Let me in. You can't stay holed up there forever. It's only two hours till curtain time."

"I'm not dancing today. I'll never dance here again. Not as long as Eric's here."

"Eric's a pig," Rikki soothed. "Don't let him rattle you. You're better than that."

The hook fell and Rikki pushed the door open to see Ginger huddled on the toilet seat, her face and eyes swollen with tears, her red hair badly in need of a brush. Rikki put her arms around her and drew her from the cubicle.

When Ginger saw Elaine Albee standing before the row of white porcelain sinks, she instinctively tried to retreat, but Rikki held her firmly. "What did Eric do now?"

"He said I was the one who screwed up with the dummies in the crossovers last night and I *didn't*, Rikki. You saw it. He rushed the music. It was more his fault than mine." She blew her nose. "He mixes me up and then blames me."

Indignation seemed to be getting the upper hand on sorrow again, Elaine Albee noted, and temper could spill into indiscretion. She made her face sympathetic. "Is that what he did with your pumpkin head yesterday?"

"And left me with one that wobbled like it had the shakes!"

"Ginger, the heads were all identical," said Rikki.

"No, they weren't. I'd wired one to fit my head better and left it on the dressing counter and Eric took it because he was too lazy to go look for his. Don't you remember how I had to run downstairs and find his at the last minute yesterday? And then how I almost couldn't find it last night when—"

"Wait," said Elaine Albee. "Let me get this straight: Eric Kee wore your jack-o'-lantern head in the first scene yesterday?"

With her copper-colored hair streaming across her shoulders, Ginger Judson nodded vigorously. Behind her, Rikki Innes shook her head but Ginger had her back to the mirrors over the sinks and didn't see.

"So you wore his, right?"

"Yes, but—"

"Wait a minute, please," said Elaine. "Now after the first scene, you took off the head you were wearing and put it where?"

"Under my chair in the wings," the redhead answered promptly. Tears forgotten now, she automatically flexed her legs, beginning some simple warm-up movements.

"But it wasn't there last night. Someone had kicked it under the stairs."

Elaine turned to Rikki. "Miss Innes, you said Eric Kee went up the steps ahead of you yesterday and that he was still wearing his pumpkin head?"

"That's right. They really are all the same," she added, with an indulgent smile for the younger dancer. "Ginger may have tightened the wire inside one of them, but from the outside they still look identical."

"And Wingate West was wearing his as he reached the men's dressing room?"

"Yes."

"But Cliff Delgado took his off immediately and went down the hall toward his wife's workshop—isn't that what you told us, Miss Judson?"

Ginger looked at Albee warily. "Y-es."

"Was he carrying his head or had he parked it somewhere?"

Frowning, the dancer made two deep knee bends as she tried to recall. "I don't think he had anything in his hands, but he was walking away with his back to me." She did another knee bend with her feet pointed in opposite directions, using the edge of a sink to steady herself. "I think he had his right hand down by his side and it was empty, but the other hand was in front of him so I guess he could have been carrying it."

"What about your head, Miss Innes?"

"I took it off as soon as we exited. They're so hot." Unconsciously, her hand mimed wiping perspiration from her fair brow.

"Did you take it upstairs with you?"

"No," said Rikki, shaking her head. "I usually leave it beside my goblin dummy there in the wings."

"Was it still there when you returned?"

"Why certainly." Her face clouded. "I think so." She looked confused. "I don't remember. On the other hand," she added helpfully, "I don't remember it *not* being there, if you know what I mean."

"But you couldn't swear to it," Albee persisted.

"I couldn't either," said Ginger, who'd listened closely even while continuing her stretching exercises. "When I went to look for mine later, remember? It was under the stairs. Somebody *could* have sneaked it out."

"While you were sitting there?" Rikki was dubious.

"I was concentrating on Emmy," the redhead insisted.

Elaine was disappointed. If David Orland had come in through the alley door yesterday, he would have found not one but two jack-o'-lantern heads ready for the taking. For a moment there, she'd thought that at least one of the four men could be definitely eliminated by lack of a disguise. Since it was not to be, she fell back on a previously unanswered point.

"We're beginning to think that something must have happened late yesterday morning, near enough to curtain time to make the killer decide Emmy Mion had to be done away with immediately. You two were with her almost till the last minute. Did she say anything while you were dressing that might give us a lead? About that phone call perhaps? Or something about the men?"

"No," said Ginger. Her voice sounded unnaturally loud in that tiled room.

Rikki hesitated, then shook her head as Ginger took a deep breath and seemed to notice her mottled face and wild hair in the mirror for the first time. "Omigod!" she shrieked. "Look at me! I'll never be ready in time."

She turned the cold water on full force and splashed her face energetically.

Over her bent back, Rikki Innes flashed Albee a rueful smile. "I guess the show goes on."

With Elaine closeted in the bathroom with Innes and Judson for who knew how long, Jim Lowry decided to go back downstairs and sound out Nate Richmond again. Noticing that Kee and the Delgado woman were in heavy conversation as he passed the open office door, he continued on to Richmond's room.

There he found the slightly built lighting designer occupied by two small boys and a girl. The three children looked up at him accusingly, as if he'd horned in on a private party.

*   *   *

"Maybe it's Eric's way of saying he wants to dissolve the company," said David Orland.

He stood with his left leg straight, his right leg extended at a ninety-degree angle to the tabletop, and his face touched his right knee while his hands grasped his right foot. "Otherwise, why get Ginger p.o.'d this near curtain time?"

"Because he's a card-carrying jerk, okay?" said Cliff Delgado, watching Orland's back muscle stretch and contract beneath his thin leotard each time he bent from the waist.

Wingate West took one of the dirty glasses from the tray Roman had left atop the refrigerator, rinsed it out, and poured himself a glass of orange juice from the refrigerator. "He's still jealous," he said lazily. "Weird to be jealous of another woman."

"A waste, too," grunted David as he switched legs.

Cliff Delgado made a coarse remark. "What was she like in the sack?" he asked avidly, looking from Orland to West.

"*There*!" Roman Tramegra bustled through the bright green door, in one hand a broom and in the other a dustpan, which he emptied into the garbage pail near the sink. Glass crashed against the metal sides and clattered to the bottom.

"I defy you to find a *speck* of glass on that floor," he announced cheerfully as he hung the dustpan on a nail beside the sink and added another piece of equipment to his tray of misplaced articles atop the refrigerator. "And I found Helen's paint mask as well."

"All you need is a frilly white cap and apron," sneered Cliff and banged out of the room.

David Orland was glad to see him go. The guy's weird, he thought. The way his eyes glitter and the way he laughs at the wrong time, two beats ahead or behind everybody else or sometimes when nothing's funny. Always trying to find out what everybody else's sex life's like. Especially with Emmy. *Tough tooties, guy. West won't tell you and you're never going to know from me how sweet Emmy was in bed.*

He had a sudden memory of her lying naked there on his mattress on the floor of his room, her funny little face suffused with laughter as he bent over her and caressed her small breasts. The memory was so vivid that he viciously bit the inside of his lip, needing a different, physical pain to block out the pain of knowing that Emmy, sweet Emmy was gone again. This time forever.

Win felt totally mellow, totally focused on the circle of orange within his glass. The Cliffs of the world kept spinning off the walls, wasting so much psychic energy on sex. As if sex were the only thing that mattered. All that humping and bumping and thumping and rumping for one quick spurt and then the afterglow. Glow came a lot easier than that. As long as he had his little packets tucked away beneath the oranges and mangoes in the vegetable crisper... he didn't abuse it. Emmy'd been wrong there. And when you thought about AIDS and herpes and all the rest, his glow was a lot healthier than the way she'd switched partners every ten minutes.

The liquid circle of orange grew larger and larger as he stared into its depths, remembering an orange sun going down at the end of summer and Emmy's salty body lying beside him on the beach towel, mellow with sunshine and the champagne she'd brought in an ice bag. "You and Nate," she'd said softly. "You're both such effing innocents. Sometimes I wish the three of us could just go away and dance on the moon."

"Nate doesn't dance," he'd reminded her, loving the way her pointed little ears poked through the edges of her hair.

"So he can work the moon and you and I will dance." She'd shaped her body to his in recumbent ballet. "No Rikki, no Eric to hold us down. We'll fly, float away."

"Hey, West, you okay?" asked Jim Lowry.

The swollen orange sun melted into orange juice again. Win swallowed it down, then turned his mild brown eyes upon the police officer. "I'm okay," he said. "You okay?"

David Orland laughed sourly. "Welcome to Doctor Goodthink's therapy group."

* * *

"It was hard to get any of them to concentrate long enough to answer our questions," Jim Lowry complained as he and Elaine summed up their findings for Sigrid back at headquarters. "Helen Delgado and Nate Richmond both claim they didn't see that Mion was abnormally upset about anything. Delgado said she didn't even see Mion after lunch; and Richmond said she ran in for some pictures he'd done of her Monday-afternoon class and seemed okay then. Once they started getting ready for this afternoon's performance, we decided to call it a day."

"That was a good try on eliminating Orland, though," Sigrid told Elaine.

That young woman absently pushed a pencil through her tousled curls and said, "Jim and I were thinking he might be out of it altogether anyhow."

"Oh?"

"On the one hand"—she held out her small square hand and ticked the fingers off with her thumb one by one as she made her points—"Orland doesn't have an apparent motive to kill. Unless we can prove he had a key, he couldn't count on finding the alley door open. Innes and Judson say they usually left their pumpkin heads by their wing positions but not always so he couldn't be sure they'd be there yesterday; and finally, if we think Emmy Mion was killed because of something that happened shortly before show time, then Orland *is* out because he can prove he was uptown the whole time."

"No one saw him at the theater until the kid on the door let him in," said Jim, "and someone was with Mion the whole time." The borders of his notepad were doodled over with ringed fingers remarkably like Elaine's.

"What about during the first scene?" Sigrid asked. "Wasn't she alone then?"

Well, yes, they admitted. But that was only a few minutes. Not enough time to goad someone to kill her, and even if she had, why hadn't he struck her down then? Why complicate things by waiting till she was onstage?

Why indeed? Sigrid thought gloomily. She returned to Albee's impression that Ginger Judson was holding back something that happened in the dressing room moments before the curtain.

"No idea what that could have been?"

"No, but if Judson was lying about it, Innes backed her up. And don't forget that Mion came out on the landing when the show was ready to begin and told them to break a leg. That doesn't sound like she was upset, does it?"

They tossed it back and forth with Peters and Eberstadt, who had returned from fruitless gleaning among an audience unable to name the murderous jack-o'-lantern.

"One thing though," said Jim Lowry as the conference was breaking up. "That scenarist—Roman Tramegra. I know he's not our killer. Not with that shape. But Lainey and I caught him in the women's dressing room today. He *said* he was rounding up dishes missing from the green room; I think he was snooping."

"Ah," said Sigrid, abruptly at a loss for words. "I—um—He's a friend of mine. We don't have to worry about him."

"All the same," said Elaine later that evening, when she and Jim were seated over drinks, "remember that Gill woman who turned up during the Maintenon bombing? She asked the lieutenant if somebody named Oscar was mad because she'd moved in with Roman. How many guys named Roman do you think Lieutenant Harald knows?"

"She's living with Tramegra?" Grinning broadly, he signaled for another drink. "Talk about your odd couples!"

Chapter 15

Personal notes of Dr. Christa Ferrell, re: Corrie Makaroff *[Sunday, 1 November—It occurs to me that in addition to clinical notes, I should be keeping a journal of "color" background for the paper I plan to submit next summer to the regional conference of psychotherapists. Touches of human interest will make a livelier presentation.*

Sigrid Harald's name was on one of those police reports & then when she turned up again yesterday at that dreadful death, the coincidence was too good not to take advantage of—a real stroke of luck. Ever since her mother came & talked at one of St. Margaret's career days, I've always made it a point to read the credit lines at the edge of photos in magazines & news journals & her byline's there several times a year. If I can get Anne Harald interested in this case—well, they do say a picture's worth a thousand words.

Measurable difference between S.H. & her mother. Repressed resentment there? S.H. was standoffish & quiet at school, a classic loner, while A.H. seemed friendly, open, easy to talk to. Pretty, too, as I recall. S.H. must take after her father?

S. such a neatnik at St. M's—never got called down for messy room. Everything picked up or hung up. Probably why she went in for police work. Fetish for order? Don't remember any signs of wanting power. She never went out for any offices.

Mustn't get sidetracked with S.H.'s hang-ups tho. This journal's about the Makaroff children. I'll begin with Martha's broad motherly face which looked troubled when she entered my office at the mental health center in mid-August & asked if she could bother me a minute.]

Martha Holt is one of Social Services' best field workers, a concerned human cog in a bureaucracy so hamstrung by red tape, budget cuts and overwork that it sometimes forgets it's supposed to ease problems, not make new ones.

[NB—For the past year I've been doing psychiatric evaluations for NYC, getting in some solid experience before opening a private practice of my own, & I've already seen more hard-core misery than I'd ever imagined possible back in the suburban hospital where I interned & certainly more than I'd been led to expect during those classes at my comfortably affluent med. school.]

The problems caused by grinding poverty are so discouraging that I know I won't last here much longer, but Martha's been at it twenty-three years. Often frustrated and occasionally depressed, she somehow goes on doing her bit to make the world a better place for her clients.

My specialty is pediatric psychotherapy, which is why she brought her anxieties about the Makaroff children to me that morning rather than to one of the generalists on the staff. I've untangled some emotional knots before they tied up a child's psyche and I think I've helped avert a few psychoses, but it's not as simple as working with Calder and his little friends at that dance theater where every child comes from a loving, middle-class home. Working at Social Services is like handing out bandaids when tourniquets and pressure bandages are needed. For every child we save, there are three dozen more locked into a life of poverty, illiteracy, joblessness, and hopelessness. Burnout's an occupational hazard here, yet Martha can't seem to stop caring.

She laid the case folders on my desk: one for Darlene Makaroff and each of her daughters—Tanya, not quite ten, and Corrie, just past four.

The folders gave the usual facts and Martha's running comments filled in around the edges. Darlene Makaroff had been one of six children, mother on welfare, father's whereabouts unknown. Pregnant with Tanya at fourteen, two abortions, then a second full-term pregnancy; fathers of both daughters unknown. The usual Social Services applications, AFDC granted. Job-training programs abruptly ended. Several drunk-and-disorderly convictions, the daughters temporarily removed to foster care three or four times. General neglect, but no evidence of physical abuse.

"She wasn't a mean person," Martha sighed. "Just weak and undirected."

I turned to the last page in the folder and saw why Martha used the past tense. Two weeks before, Darlene's latest boyfriend had smashed her head in during a drunken brawl.

"According to the police reports, he was using a

hammer and screwdriver to loosen a stuck window. Darlene started yelling at him, and the whole situation spun out of control."

She was DOA at the hospital.

The man, Ray Thorpe, had a history of juvenile violence, Martha said, and is still at large.

[NB—Hard not to compare Darlene Makaroff with Dr. Christa Ferrell. I'm older than she was, but I've lived in clean shining places with nutritious meals, pretty clothes, a family who love & encourage me. I can reasonably expect marriage or an equally rewarding relationship, perhaps children eventually, certainly a full professional career. My life's still opening up while Darlene Makaroff's is closed forever.]

And what of Darlene's daughters? Will they follow their mother's pattern?

"They have a chance now," Martha said earnestly. "Let's help them make it, Christa."

The girls were there during the brawl, she told me, and had actually seen their mother killed. In fact, it was nine-year-old Tanya who had dialed 911 and screamed for help.

As soon as she was notified, Martha had gone to that dreadful welfare building and brought the two children to her own apartment for the night. Tanya had sobbed herself into quivering exhaustion but little Corrie had gone numb.

"Tanya's going to be okay, I think," said Martha. "It's Corrie that has us worried. She's like a sleepwalker. She moves and eats and sleeps, but she doesn't play and she doesn't speak unless you ask her a direct question."

"Two weeks isn't an excessively long grieving period," I said.

"Is she really grieving though?" asked Martha. "She doesn't cry or reach out for comfort. Mrs. Berkowitz says it's like she's blocked everything out."

"Mrs. Berkowitz?"

"The girls' foster mother. Lovely woman. She took them earlier this year when Darlene got six months' real time for her last d-and-d. The children were crazy about her, especially Tanya. In fact, when Darlene got out of jail and demanded them back, they cried all the way home. Mrs. Berkowitz wanted to adopt them, but Darlene wouldn't hear of it."

My antennae went straight up on that. If Corrie had resented her mother for taking them away from Mrs. Berkowitz, she might be carrying a crippling burden of guilt. Childish logic could lead her to believe she was somehow responsible for Darlene's death.

"What was the relationship before Mrs. Berkowitz entered the picture?"

"Well, you know how children are," Martha sighed. "Whatever *is* seems normal when they're that young. Darlene was their mother and I doubt if it ever occurred to Tanya or Corrie not to love her. Certainly Darlene was always talking about how much her babies meant to her."

"Especially if she were drunk?" I suggested cynically.

"She could get sloppy and sentimental," Martha admitted.

"And when she was sober?"

"I told you, Christa: Darlene never actively abused the girls. She might forget to feed them or make Tanya go to school or wash the sheets every time Corrie wet the bed, but that wasn't because she didn't love them."

A poor sort of maternity, I thought, but I knew it could have been worse.

Much worse.

I've seen the battered ones. The cigarette burns. The bruised little faces and bloody buttocks.

"I gather that life with Mrs. Berkowitz was considerably different?"

"We're very lucky to have the Berkowitzes in our foster program," Martha said fervently. "He's a plumber and she's a born homemaker. They can't have children and there are so few Caucasian infants available for adoption these days. They were naturals for us."

"Do they still want to adopt the Makaroff girls?"

Martha nodded. "Funny how it happens. They've had other children longer, but something blossomed with these two last winter. Corrie quit sucking her thumb and wetting the bed and Tanya started getting A's on her schoolwork. Darlene's mother certainly doesn't want them; so if we can get Corrie straightened out, the paperwork ought to sail through the courts."

"I suppose it's possible that Mrs. Berkowitz had so displaced Darlene as a mother figure that the child feels guilty about her death," I said cautiously.

Martha beamed. "I *knew* you'd help."

[NB—probably should describe my office in full detail when I write this up, especially since I've given so much thought to it & am rather pleased with the results. Except for the city-issued file cabinet, all the furnishings are mine. No clinical formality for me. (& certainly nothing as sterile as Sigrid Harald's office. Barely any touch of color there.) Instead, I've created a cheerful family room: bright carpets, chintz chairs & couch, &, under the window, open shelves with dolls, stuffed animals, other toys.]

Two days after my conversation with Martha Holt, Mrs. Berkowitz sat on the couch across from me with a little girl on each side.

Sheila Berkowitz is thin and pleasant-faced. Late thirties, strawberry blonde hair, no makeup. She wore white sandals and a blue cotton sundress. No jewelry except for a wedding band, a modest diamond engagement ring, and clip-on earrings of blue plastic. She displayed unconscious signs of nervousness about being in a psychiatrist's office, but was trying not to communicate that nervousness to the children.

School was still closed for the summer, but she proudly confided that Tanya had been conditionally promoted to the fourth grade.

Considering how much time the child has lost from school because of her mother's negligence, I decided Tanya must be a good student and I said so.

"I still have to catch up with arithmetic this summer and pass a test when school starts," Tanya said shyly.

She is a wiry child. Pale skin, a freckled nose, changeable blue-green eyes, and light brown hair tied in a ponytail with a blue ribbon that matched her blue plaid shorts. After an initial shyness, her natural friendliness came through and soon she was chattering about school and eyeing my toys.

Four-year-old Corrie still has some baby fat in her cheeks and legs but she is of similar build and coloring as her sister. Her twin ponytails were secured with perky red bows and she wore a little red playsuit and white sandals. She did not squeeze against Mrs. Berkowitz's side as Tanya had when they first met me, but neither did she shrink away. She simply sat where put and gazed at me without curiosity or fear.

Since Tanya responded so well, I asked if she would mind talking with me a few minutes while Mrs. Berkowitz and Corrie waited outside.

"N-no," she said, but timidity came back as she watched her sister and foster mother exit.

It didn't take me long, though, to put Tanya at ease again. At nine, she is still young enough to be beguiled by what I call my baby doll games. Very young children will actually use the dolls as surrogates to act out their rage and hostility; the older ones will let their guard down because the toys give them something to do with their eyes and hands.

"This is my oldest baby doll," I told Tanya, pulling a rather shabby Bitsy Betsy from the back shelf. "What was your first doll's name?"

By the end of our second session, I had a reasonably clear picture of what life with Darlene Makaroff had been like for her daughters. Whenever children chatter about toys and games and the people who give or withhold presents and love and nurture, they cannot help but reveal their own emotional ambivalences.

I soon knew that going to the Berkowitzes that first time when Darlene was in jail had been a great revelation for Tanya. It wasn't just that the apartment was bigger, brighter, and cleaner, although it was; nor that the food tasted better and the beds slept warmer, although they did; nor even that she and Corrie had new toys and never-before-worn jackets for the first time, although they had.

No, it was the intangible security of a known routine that seems to have captured Tanya's imagination. For the first time in her young life, breakfast, lunch, and bedtime came at the same hours every day. School was no longer a sometime thing. There was structure and order. A far cry from the hand-to-mouth life her true mother provided.

Tanya evidently tried to carry her newfound orderliness home, but "Mommy said I was getting too prissy and anyhow, lots of times she didn't feel good enough."

"Too drunk," I thought to myself. We continued to talk and play and, bit by bit in that second session, we edged closer to Darlene Makaroff's death.

"I'll bet Corrie was pretty scared when that man started hurting your mom," I said.

"I was, too," she whispered and her small hands twisted the dress she had taken off a Raggedy Ann doll into a knot. "Ray hit her and hit her and then he ran away and Mommy was all bloody and I called the police and then Mrs. Holt took us to her house and then Aunt Sheila came and got us and said we were going to be her and Uncle Lyle's little girls from now on."

"Do you like that?"

"Aunt Sheila lets me run the vacuum cleaner," the child answered obliquely. "And she's going to show me how to crochet."

"What about Corrie?"

Tanya looked at me warily. "She likes Aunt Sheila and Uncle Lyle, too."

I backed off and, in a few minutes, Tanya volunteered, "Maybe she's afraid Ray's going to come back."

"Are you afraid?"

"No!" she answered scornfully. "Uncle Lyle would knock him down with his big pipe wrench."

As we put the toys back on the shelf, I found myself in agreement with Martha's lay assessment: Tanya will be all right. She might regret her mother's violent death, but she has a deep-seated, almost primal, need for the routine and order Darlene had never provided. She is also pragmatic enough to know that one minus one equals zero, and this pragmatism has allowed her to embrace without guilt the satisfying regimen that the Berkowitzes offered once her mother was gone.

Tanya did seem worried about Corrie, but if I could solve that problem, I felt she could integrate the whole experience into her subconscious with no lasting ill effects.

"Good luck with your arithmetic," I smiled as I returned her to Mrs. Berkowitz, who waited outside.

Corrie did not resist when I took her hand and led her across the vestibule to my office, but I could not get her to respond that first day.

She wouldn't choose anything from my shelves and if I gave her a doll or toy animal, she merely held it, scarcely looking at it, until I took it away and gave her another. I tried pictures, balloons, we even sat on the floor and rolled a yellow ball back and forth; but it took me five sessions before she would smile or speak beyond the simplest yes/no to my questions.

We scheduled three sessions a week.

While Tanya and Mrs. Berkowitz sat in the waiting room and plowed methodically—and contentedly—through a third-grade math workbook, Corrie and I tried to push through the gray cotton wool that seemed to muffle all her emotional nerve endings.

At least *I* tried. Corrie gave no outward signs, but experience (and all the textbooks) said that *something* had to be happening underneath. It was only a matter of time.

By Labor Day, Tanya could rattle off the multiplication tables up to eight times ten, and Corrie trusted me enough to take a teddy bear off the shelf of her own volition, an authentic bit of progress.

By mid-October, Mrs. Berkowitz reported that Tanya had been moved into the top section of her fourth-grade class and Corrie finally told me the names of the family of dolls she had constructed.

"This is the mommy," she said, setting a wasp-waisted Barbie doll on the hassock.

(Martha H. had described Darlene Makaroff as a pretty woman with light brown hair.)

"This is the big sister," said Corrie, but I had already guessed that Tanya was symbolized by the large brown-haired doll with a miniature schoolbag on its shoulder.

"And this is the little sister."

Instead of a doll, "little sister" was the small teddy bear Corrie had first touched back in August, a honey-brown creature with black button eyes and a red satin bow around its neck.

"Big sister" and "little sister" were soon joined by the "aunt," a rag doll whose embroidered features do somewhat distantly suggest Sheila Berkowitz's.

Corrie is a good mimic and when the various dolls "spoke" to each other, I could soon tell without looking which person was being acted out:

"Who wants an ice-cream cone?" Aunt Rag Doll would ask.

"Me!" cried the schoolgirl doll.

"Me, too," piped the little bear voice.

"Then let's pick up our toys and come out to the kitchen," said Aunt Rag Doll.

[NB—I've been encouraged from the beginning by "little sister's" willingness to follow the "aunt's" instructions. This indicates to me that, whatever the problem, Sheila B. herself does not set up negative vibrations in Corrie's subconscious & this bodes well for the future.]

Once Corrie became comfortable with me, I began some gentle probing. "What does the mommy say?" I asked.

"Nothing," answered the child. "She doesn't feel good."

I didn't push and a few minutes later, I heard "little sister" say, "I'm thirsty, Mommy."

"That's *my* ginger ale! Leave it alone," said the angry high-pitched voice that signified Darlene.

"Mommy, I have to go to school," said the schoolgirl doll. "I have to say my timeses to the teacher."

"No, you don't. I'm sick this morning. Fix you and Corrie some cereal and then you can watch cartoons, okay?"

The mommy/Barbie doll dominated the next few sessions and I was saddened to hear the maudlin endearments when the doll was drunk and the casual neglect when it was sober. There's been a constant stream of "don't bother me," or "you kids keep it down, I've got a headache." Several times I heard, "Over my dead body. She's not your real aunt" or "I don't care if she *did* say you could come visit. You're *my* honeybunches, not hers."

Last week I asked Martha H. if Darlene used the phrase "over my dead body" very often or if it were one of Corrie's embellishments and she gave a tired smile. "Darlene said it all the time. Ironic, isn't it?"

"It could be significant," I told her. "If Corrie wanted to live with the Berkowitzes, she might have taken Darlene literally."

"Wishing for Darlene's dead body?"

"Not consciously," I speculated. "But when it happened, she got her wish, so now she may feel she caused Darlene's death."

[I'm thrilled with how perfectly my baby doll games are working. Everything's meshing like a textbook case. Do hope I can interest Anne Harald in this case. It would be a pity not to show the public one of Social Services' happy endings. Taxpayers do get so tired of hearing what's wrong with the city. I know I do.]

Chapter 16

November was beginning messily and meteorological reports were already making pessimistic noises about early snow flurries, possibly by the end of the week.

From Sigrid's office, Chinatown was only a brisk walk away through narrow rain-lashed streets. Despite its distance from Wall Street and the difficulty of finding a cab in the near-freezing rain, her mother's favorite dim sum restaurant was jammed with its usual noon-hour crush of gray suits from the financial district. Even so, Oriental faces outnumbered Occidental and testified to the authentic excellence of the restaurant's reasonably priced food.

As tall as most of the men crowding past her, Sigrid paused in the entry to shake water from her beige rain hat and to scan the steamy interior, where the smell of damp wool blended with the comforting aroma of fresh noodles, hot sesame oil, and a dozen different Chinese herbs and vegetables. Eventually, she saw her mother waving from a far corner.

Anne Harald had arrived early enough to secure two places at the end of a long table and she had already snagged three dishes from the loaded trays carried from the kitchen in endless relays by deft Chinese waitresses.

"Shrimp toast, fried wontons, and steamed noodles," Anne greeted her happily, gesturing at the dishes with her chopsticks. "I know you like spring rolls, but they haven't come by yet."

Sigrid unbuttoned her raincoat, draped it on the back of her chair, and straightened the cuffs of her white shirt. "You also know I like a fork."

"Now don't be provincial, honey. You're never going to get any good if you don't keep practicing."

Sighing, Sigrid obediently picked up her chopsticks and tried to make her long slender fingers imitate her mother's efficient movements. Anchoring the bottom stick was no problem, but to manipulate the upper one into picking up anything smaller than a whole shrimp was a clumsy effort at best. It didn't help that a Chinese tot seated diagonally across from her at their table was effortlessly maneuvering delicate wisps of noodles to his mouth in a dazzling display of chopstick virtuousity. Between mouthfuls, his black eyes seemed to appraise her own performance.

Sigrid resolutely ignored him, managed a bite of crispy shrimp toast, and bent her dark head toward Anne, the better to hear her mother's words above the noontime din.

Only in the color of their hair and eyes did the two resemble each other. As much as she loved her mother, Sigrid had always felt gawky standing next to her. By the age of thirteen she was well on her way to her full five-foot ten-inch height, a good six inches taller than Anne; and she tried not to mind when her mother's well-meaning southern relatives repeatedly assured her that breeding meant more than beauty, that all the Lattimores possessed charm and Sigrid would too if she would only relax and let it flow.

Sigrid considered herself an early realist. At thirteen, her wide gray eyes had observed what value the world placed on physical beauty and while she didn't think her features were particularly repulsive, she knew she couldn't compare with any of her female cousins south *or* north. Her neck was too long, her mouth was too wide, her forehead too high, and her skinny frame, all arms and legs, refused to curve in any of the proper places. Buying clothes became such an ordeal that Sigrid was left with a lifelong hatred of department store mirrors.

Nor did her hair please her any better. It may have been the same color as Anne's but it had always been straight and so silky-fine that, until her recent and absolutely irrational fit of madness, she had pulled it straight back from her face in an easy-to-manage knot at the nape of her neck, a sharp contrast to Anne Harald, who wore hers in an explosion of short curls which had only begun to show traces of silver in the last year or two.

Now in her early fifties, Anne's slender body was still shapely beneath her burgundy sweater, and the waist of her gray corduroy skirt was only two inches larger than the skirt she'd worn when she eloped with Leif Harald. A light film of makeup smoothed away all trace of wrinkles except for the fine laugh lines around her hazel-gray eyes, and thirty-odd years in the North hadn't erased all the drawl from her voice either.

"—and everybody's been real sweet about talking to me," she said, completing her description of the city officials she'd spoken to that morning about the *New York Today* series she planned to do on how the city handled its social problems.

"Well, they'd be fools to give the runaround to a photojournalist of your standing, wouldn't they?" Sigrid asked reasonably; then said, "Yes, please," as a passing waitress offered a dish of pearl balls.

"And here I thought it was all because of my southern charm," Anne smiled.

She was probably only half-joking, thought Sigrid. "There's nothing wrong with being good at what you do, Mother."

"I know. It's just that—"

"'A business lady shouldn't be all business?'" she asked, rudely mimicking one of Grandmother Lattimore's favorite dicta.

"Mama didn't expect any of her daughters to have to earn a living," said Anne, in defense of her own mother's prefeminist teachings. "And speaking of your grandmother, what are you getting her for Christmas?"

"Oh Lord! We've just passed Halloween. I haven't even *begun* to think of Christmas. What does she need, do you think? What would she like?"

"I *know* what she'd like." Anne's lips twitched with a mischievous smile. "Let me tell her you're having an affair."

"Mother!"

"Well, you know how she worries about your love life. Next to news of a marriage proposal, it would be the best present you could give her."

"Except that it wouldn't be true," Sigrid said stiffly.

"But I thought sure that you and Oscar—I mean, you cut your hair, started wearing makeup—"

Anne Lattimore Harald had been caught with a foot in two worlds. Needled on the one hand by a traditionalist mother who felt that no woman could be fulfilled without first acquiring husband and children, and concerned on the other hand that her analytically minded daughter was insufficiently connected to the passions of the heart, Anne had found herself with mixed emotions when Oscar Nauman suddenly appeared in Sigrid's life.

It had never occurred to her that Sigrid's first real love affair might be with a man even older than she herself. Nauman's reputation as one of America's leading artists helped, of course, but what actually made her keep any reservations to herself was the humanizing effect he'd had on Sigrid. In the last two months, she'd felt closer to her daughter than at any time since childhood, and sensing Sigrid's new vulnerability, she now leaned forward solicitously. "You haven't quarreled with him, have you, honey?"

"No quarrel. It's just that—oh, I don't know. The art department at Vanderlyn's in the middle of reaccreditation, and if he's not flying up to Toronto for an exhibit of his work, then he's off to California to judge something or other or pipes are leaking in Connecticut. It's not important. I don't have time now anyhow. I've got my own hands full with Tillie gone."

"How's he doing?" asked Anne, momentarily diverted.

She had not approved when Sigrid decided to follow in Leif Harald's footsteps and seldom inquired about Sigrid's work, but she knew about Detective Tildon's close call when a bomb exploded beside him in October.

"He hopes to be home by Thanksgiving, but they don't expect him back to work before the first of the year."

Sigrid absently rubbed her left arm, souvenir of her own most recent brush with death, and her voice was unemotional, but Anne knew her daughter. "You miss him, don't you?"

"He's a good partner." Sigrid turned uncomfortably from Anne's penetrating gaze. "Here come the pork-stuffed peppers. You want some?"

"We'll split a portion," Anne said equably, and to Sigrid's relief, she let the conversation move on to family gossip and the weekend she'd just spent out in Port Jefferson with her niece by marriage, Sigrid's cousin Hilda. "She wanted me to take some new pictures for their Christmas card. The baby's getting awfully cute. They think he'll be walking by Christmas."

They spoke of Thanksgiving plans, a movie they'd both seen, and eventually their talk wound around to Anne's *New York Today* series. "You'll never guess who called me about it last night: one of your old friends from St. Margaret's."

"I know. She came by my office yesterday. But Christa Ferrell wasn't exactly a friend, Mother. We roomed on the same hall one semester, that's all."

"Oh? From the way she talked, I thought you two were closer than that. She sounded real sweet."

Sigrid murmured noncommittally and with her chopsticks poked at the savory pepper before her. A knife and fork would make the meal so much easier, she thought longingly. Across the table, that small Chinese boy was smugly polishing off another dim sum dish with flamboyant dexterity.

There was nothing quite so annoying as a smart-alecky child who knew he possessed a skill you lacked.

"Are you going to use Christa Ferrell in your article?" she asked as she pondered the mechanics needed to separate a bite-sized morsel from her whole stuffed pepper.

"I might. She made a good point about how easy it is to find adoptive parents for infants but not for older children. And these two—their age, the psychological trauma of seeing their mother murdered—it should make dramatic copy. She's going to let me sit in on the last couple of sessions with the younger one."

"Won't that interfere with her treatment?"

"Nope," said Anne, expertly quartering her fried pepper. "She says there's a one-way window between her office and a cubicle next door so that I can watch without the child knowing I'm there. She uses something called baby doll therapy. Ever seen it?"

Sigrid shook her head. "I've heard about it, though. Lawyers use a similar procedure when molested children have to testify in court. It's easier for the children to describe what's happened to them if they can point to a doll's body and talk about it instead of their own."

"It sounds fascinating," said Anne. "And very visual."

Sigrid refilled their teacups and left the lid of the pot tipped back. An attentive waitress immediately hurried over with a fresh pot.

"Serendipitous that you investigated the mother's death," said Anne.

"Actually, I didn't." Again, Sigrid explained how she'd merely put the machinery in motion.

"Then you haven't seen the children?"

"No, but don't worry. If Christa Ferrell says they're photogenic, I'm sure they will be."

"Is she?"

"Very," Sigrid said dryly.

Anne gave her an appraising look, a look Sigrid had

learned to dread over a lifetime of failures to live up to her mother's image. "I thought you promised me last year that you were going to give that suit to the Salvation Army."

"I like this suit," Sigrid said, feeling thirteen again as she hunched into the shapeless black wool jacket. "It has proper pockets, it's warm—"

"It looks like something you've slept in," Anne interjected.

"—and it's loose enough to hide my gun."

Anne held up her hands in surrender. "It's just that Macy's is having a wonderful sale and I saw a blue tweed jacket that would do terrific things for your eyes. It would go with everything and—"

"Not now, Mother, okay? I've really got to get moving." She signaled for their bill. "We have a temporary replacement for Tillie and—"

"Someone unmarried?" Anne asked sweetly.

Sigrid laughed in spite of herself. "Hardly. Cluett's an old-timer from one of the Brooklyn precincts, finishing out his forty years. I gather there's a wife and grandchildren even."

"Cluett?" Anne had suddenly gone very still. "Not *Mickey* Cluett?"

"Mick, yes. Do you know him?"

"Not for a million years," Anne said slowly. She fumbled in her shoulder bag for a filigreed gold compact and renewed her lipstick. "He and your father rode patrol together a few months when Leif first joined the force."

By then, their waitress had totaled up the number of empty dishes between them and Sigrid reached for the bill.

"No, I'll get the check if you'll get a new suit," said Anne, but for once Sigrid recognized her mother's tactics.

"You always change the subject when Dad comes up," she said. "I've just realized that. Why, Mother?"

"Don't be a goop, Siga. We often talk about him." Anne slipped on a gray wool car coat and wound a burgundy scarf loosely over her hair. "Don't forget your hat. Did I have gloves?"

Sigrid remained seated. "Never about him and the force."

"Really, Sigrid! Even if that were true, which it isn't,

this is hardly the time or the place to begin. People are waiting for our chairs." Anne made an unconvincing show of looking at her watch. "I've got to run, too. I just remembered that there's a sublet opening up near Columbus Circle and I was supposed to let them know by this afternoon if I wanted it."

This time Sigrid was distracted. "You aren't going to move *again*, are you? I thought you liked the Chelsea area."

When other women were bored with a place, they usually junked their old furniture or called in the decorators. Anne Harald notoriously kept her old furniture and instead changed her apartments as frequently as the seasons. Sigrid abhorred chaos and upheaval and remembered with horror a childhood period when Anne moved them into five different apartments within the space of fourteen months. No wonder St. Margaret's had come to feel so safe and so blessedly fixed in time and space.

She snatched up her raincoat and hat and hurried after her mother, who had already threaded her way through the crowd to the cash register at the front. By the time Sigrid caught up with her, she had paid and was about to step outside.

The rain had slackened into a chill drizzle, but after their hour in the overheated restaurant, the wind felt icy and made their goodbyes brief. Sigrid leaned down and Anne stood on tiptoe to kiss her cheek.

"I'll call you soon," she promised. Sigrid caught a familiar whiff of jasmine cologne and then Anne had disappeared into Chinatown's narrow clamor.

As she turned in the opposite direction and headed back to work, however, Sigrid found herself remembering all the times her mother had indeed managed not to talk about Leif Harald. At least not about his police career. Family events, yes. Anecdotes that kept his memory vivid for a daughter who could barely remember him, yes. But of the work which must have occupied half his waking hours, almost never. And despite being a professional photographer, she had taken only one or two pictures of him in uniform.

Taken, Sigrid now wondered, or kept?

Was it because Leif Harald had been killed in the line of duty? Something about his death?

Last month, for the first time, Sigrid had finally learned that her boss, Captain McKinnon, had been partnered with her father, and had actually been there when he was killed. In the time she had worked for him, Sigrid knew that she'd spoken McKinnon's name several times in conversation with Anne; yet, until she witnessed an accidental meeting between Anne and the captain, she'd had no suspicion that the two had once known each other.

Anne had immediately taken off for an assignment in South America, refusing to discuss it; and when Sigrid confronted McKinnon, his only response had been a terse admission that Anne blamed him for Leif's death.

"Is she right?" Sigrid had asked bluntly.

"Read the records for yourself," McKinnon had told her.

She had. There was nothing among those yellowing papers to change the way she'd always imagined her father's death or to conflict with the bare facts Anne had told her when she was old enough to understand: acting on a tip, Detectives Harald and McKinnon had tried to arrest a suspected felon thought to be hiding in a seedy hotel just off Times Square.

The felon was not considered dangerous and had never before been known to carry a weapon. Reading between the lines, Sigrid sensed that her father had gone in overly confident, with only minimum precaution.

His confidence had cost him his life.

McKinnon had been backup and he'd returned the felon's fire, killing him instantly. No mystery there.

Yet Anne shied away from Sigrid's probing questions. Why?

Chapter 17

On the way up to her office after lunch, Sigrid signed for a packet from the medical examiner's office and when she reached her desk, she read through the technical language that officially confirmed what Christa Ferrell had ascertained informally on Saturday: Emmy Mion had died from massive trauma to and hemorrhage of the left carotid artery.

The force with which the dancer had been thrown upon the spiked fence had contributed other serious injuries—the report detailed broken ribs, ruptured spleen, collapsed lung, internal bleeding. Those she might have survived, but not that sharp iron point through the side of her neck.

No surprises there, but then Sigrid reached the description of what the dead woman had worn, all of which would have been sent to the department's property clerk: a tattered white cheesecloth dress, a sleeveless white Lycra leotard, white cotton underpants, a taffeta hair ribbon, a pair of gold stud earrings, a gold pinkie ring with the initial E on it.

Officer Paula Guidry's photographs of the crime scene had come in that morning and Sigrid leafed through the prints until she found a close-up of Emmy Mion's head and shoulders. Using the brass-bound magnifying glass that doubled as an occasional paperweight, Sigrid examined the photograph in minute detail.

Odd, she thought.

Guidry was a thorough photographer and she had taken the same shot from three different angles, yet Sigrid still couldn't see it.

She flipped through the rotary card file beside her telephone for the number to Dr. Cohen's direct line. Through her open door, as she waited for the assistant medical examiner to answer his phone, she saw Elaine Albee, Jim Lowry, and Bernie Peters returning from lunch and signaled for them to join her.

"Cohen here," said a flat nasal voice in her ear.

"Lieutenant Harald," she answered, tapping the part of the report she wanted the others to read. "About that report you did on Emmy Mion—"

"Yeah?"

"Among her personal effects, you list a taffeta hair ribbon."

"Yeah?"

"I've examined the photographs and I don't see any ribbon. Where was she wearing it?"

"She wasn't. It was in First National."

"*What?*"

"Between her boobs. That's what my grandma used to say. You want to hear more about my grandma or can I get back to this alleged vehicular homicide you interrupted?"

Elaine Albee volunteered to go request the ribbon from property and while they waited, Sigrid remembered to ask Bernie Peters about the Darlene Makaroff-Ray Thorpe case. The freshness of his memory for the details surprised Sigrid, but then, of course, he'd actually worked it, she thought, and having two little girls of his own must have personalized the tragedy for him.

"Cute kids," he concluded. "I'm glad they won't have to testify."

"They won't? How do you know?"

"They picked Thorpe up in Queens last weekend; the arraignment was Tuesday. He bargained a manslaughter-one."

"Tuesday?" Sigrid's voice went cold. "I read the case file yesterday. There's nothing in it about Thorpe's arrest *or* arraignment."

"Still on my desk," Peters said sheepishly. "I guess I'm a little behind in my paperwork."

"At least a week," Sigrid agreed, her eyes icy with disapproval. "Have it on my desk, complete and up-to-date, before you leave today."

Jim Lowry shifted uncomfortably in his own seat and looked relieved when the tension in the small office was broken by Matt Eberstadt, who stuck his frizzy gray head in the door and waved a square white pastry box. "Dessert, anybody?"

Peters, grateful for the opportunity to distract attention from Lieutenant Harald's censure, said, "I thought you promised Frances you'd stick to fruit for dessert." Frances Eberstadt had enlisted in the losing battle with her husband's waistline.

"This *is* fruit," grinned Eberstadt. "Apple-raisin turnovers."

The ribbon with which Elaine Albee returned was a plaid taffeta, predominantly red and blue, an inch wide and eighteen inches long, and so crumpled and creased that it'd lost most of its original crispness except for an inch or two in the middle that was now stiff with dried blood.

Sigrid frowned. "Emmy Mion had very short hair, didn't she?"

"A pixie cut," Albee agreed. "Much too short for a ponytail. And this ribbon's not long enough to tie around her head. So why was she carrying it?"

Jim Lowry looked up from the sinuous ribbons he had doodled across his notepad. "Probably found it on the floor and just picked it up absent-mindedly—"

"—and put it in Boston Security for safekeeping," said Eberstadt, unconsciously echoing Cohen.

"*Where?*" laughed Elaine.

Eberstadt chuckled. There was a small fleck of apple on his upper lip. "My Aunt Madge had a chest like a chifforobe. If she didn't have a purse with her, that's where she'd carry a letter or handkerchief or folding money. And since she was from Massachusetts—"

Lowry grinned at Elaine and started to add something bawdy then suddenly remembered whose office they were in. The lieutenant was not known for a sense of humor.

Sigrid barely heard their banter. She wove the ribbon ends through her ringless fingers and tried to remember. A small face and plaid ribbons in twin ponytails . . . of course, there were thousands of children and miles of ribbon in this city, but still . . .

The Gillespie folder was still on her desk from yesterday and, yes, little nine-year-old Amanda Gillespie had been strangled with one of her own hair ribbons. Said hair ribbon was described as red-and-blue plaid taffeta, one inch wide, eighteen inches long, and currently being held by property as evidence for when and if a suspect in the child's murder was brought to trial.

That only one ribbon was being held would seem to indicate only one ribbon had been found on the child's body.

"Cluett—" Sigrid looked around and noticed for the first time that Detective Mick Cluett had not returned from lunch.

"Um, Lieutenant." Jim Lowry pointed to a memo which Sigrid had overlooked in her In-basket. "He said he thought he was coming down with the flu or something."

"He looked pasty and his forehead felt a little hot," Albee added as Sigrid read Cluett's note that he was going to see his doctor and probably wouldn't be back to work that day.

She returned it to her basket without comment. "Eberstadt, see if Hentz is around and ask him to join us, please."

"Did that ribbon belong to the Gillespie child?" asked Elaine alertly, as Eberstadt moved past her.

"The description matches," Sigrid replied noncommittally, handing her the pertinent form.

"Oh, Lordy!" Jim was reading over Elaine's shoulder. "If Mion found that ribbon in a place that implicated one of those guys in the kid's death, now *that's* some motive!"

"And it would have to be after she'd gotten dressed or else why stick the ribbon there?" Elaine's face mirrored her excitement. She riffled through her notes, trying to document the dancer's every movement after dressing.

Bernie Peters had been smarting over his reprimand, but now he, too, reached for the description of Amanda Gillespie's ribbon.

Matt Eberstadt returned with Detective Hentz, a trim and dapper officer whose dark hair had begun to show a little gray at the temples.

"You wanted to see me, Lieutenant?" As always, Sam Hentz managed to attach a slight sneer to her title. He didn't like women working homicide and having to maintain a pretense of civility with a younger woman who outranked him clearly galled even more.

His hostility made Sigrid uncomfortable but Hentz was a better-than-average officer. As long as he did his work competently and as long as he didn't openly challenge her authority, she was forced to maintain her own facade of indifference and put up with it. Nevertheless, both of them knew quite well what would happen if Hentz ever goofed and the lieutenant found out about it.

"The Amanda Gillespie case," Sigrid told him, motioning him to a chair.

"I'll stand, thanks," said Hentz, his voice as cool as hers. He did take the file she pushed toward him, however, and scanned it, refreshing his memory. "Okay. What do you want to know?"

"The child seems to have worn her hair in two ponytails most of the time. Two elastic bands and two hair ribbons, yet only one ribbon's listed in the M.E.'s report—the one that strangled her."

"So?"

"Was there a second ribbon?"

Hentz shot the cuffs of his navy-and-white pinstripe shirt, leaned against the door frame, and folded his arms across the front of his crisply tailored charcoal suit, still holding the file. "She was wearing two the last time anyone noticed her as the class broke up, but the only one we found last February was around her neck. We figured the killer kept a souvenir." He nodded toward the one in her hand. "Where'd you find it?"

"Is it the mate?"

"Looks like it. Where'd you find it?" he repeated sharply.

"On the body of Emmy Mion. She was killed Saturday at—"

"At that dance theater over on Eighth Avenue. Yeah, I heard."

"The same dance theater where the Gillespie child had been the afternoon she was killed," Sigrid continued mildly.

She laid the colorful red-and-blue ribbon on her desk and leaned back in her chair. "How thoroughly did you look at that theater last February?"

Hentz met her level gaze with an appraising look of his own. "As thoroughly as we felt the place deserved. If you mean did we search it, no, we didn't. We questioned the dancers, talked to the kids with a psychiatrist present—"

"Dr. Ferrell?"

"Classy blonde. I forget her name. Anyhow, there was nothing immediate to link the theater with the kid's death. She was found four blocks from the place, practically on her own doorstep. Her killer could have been anybody— from the building, from her school, a nut from anywhere in the neighborhood. You know the odds."

"But you did question the parents about the dance troupe?" asked Elaine Albee.

Hentz started to ignore her, but something about the way the lieutenant sat so quietly, watching, made him swallow his irritation. "We did the whole drill, Albee. Not one of those kids had ever complained about being touched or molested in any way by one of those dancers, and parents are damn well on the lookout for things like that these days."

Sigrid glanced around the momentarily silent group. "Any other questions? That'll be all then, Hentz."

But Hentz did not move. "That dancer—you think she found out who strangled Amanda Gillespie?"

"It's the best motive we've come up with yet."

"I hope you're right." Hentz's face was grim. "She was such a tiny little thing and he threw her in a snowbank and just left her there like she was a piece of garbage." His voice took on remembered anger. "Don't leave this one in the open file, Lieutenant. Nail the bastard!"

Chapter 18

With the preliminaries of this case out of the way, Sigrid let Eberstadt and Peters return to work on other ongoing investigations. Those two were concurrently responsible for a rape-homicide, a domestic stabbing, and, from last Friday morning, what looked like a botched murder-suicide pact between an elderly husband and his cancer-stricken wife. Unfortunately the husband's aim was so bad, he'd missed his own heart and was expected to live, which meant he was going to come out of his coma facing an automatic charge of manslaughter-second.

Albee and Lowry went off to compare the taffeta hair ribbon found on Emmy Mion's body with the one still at property. If it matched as perfectly as they expected, they planned to visit the Gillespie child's parents.

Piled on Sigrid's desk was more than enough paper to occupy the rest of her afternoon and that would have been the sensible thing to attack. Or she might have waited until Captain McKinnon returned from a conference and gone in to brief him on the status of the cases under her direction. Instead, as soon as her office cleared, she slipped on her raincoat and hat, left word with the front desk where she'd be and, with a vague sense of playing hooky, headed for the 8th-AV-8 Dance Theater.

Exiting with her fellow subway riders, Sigrid came up a flight of grubby wet metal steps beside a store whose windows reflected the schizophrenia of the season: cardboard monsters and remaindered Halloween candy, drastically reduced, were wedged in with Thanksgiving turkey candies, foil-wrapped chocolate Chanukah *gelt*, and Christmas tree ornaments. The cold rain fell heavily now, making the late afternoon even grayer; and a partially clogged grate at the corner had formed a pool of dirty water at the crossing so that pedestrians were having to take wide detours around and through vehicular traffic to avoid it.

Sigrid turned up the collar of her raincoat, tugged her hat down firmly and sprinted for the theater, which lay two blocks north.

Inside the narrow lobby, she felt an immediate wave of warm air. Someone must have decided that the budget could afford heat. From deeper within the theater came the sound of drumbeats and childish voices.

A young woman holding a clipboard stepped around the partition that separated the lobby from the auditorium and looked Sigrid up and down. "Are you a parent?" she asked suspiciously.

"No," Sigrid replied. "Police."

"May I see some identification?"

Sigrid complied and the woman neatly copied her name and the time onto the sheet of paper on her clipboard. "We're probably locking the barn door too late," she said grimly, "but better late than never. Do you know who killed Emmy yet?"

"We're still investigating, Mrs.—?"

"Weinberg. Liz Weinberg. I have a son and daughter in today's class."

Sigrid vaguely remembered seeing the Weinberg name on a supplementary list of parents not yet interviewed. "You weren't here when it happened Saturday?"

"No, thank God! We had a bar mitzvah up in Syracuse this weekend. Didn't get back till last night and the phone ringing off the hook till all hours while we worked out a schedule. From now on the alley door stays locked and everybody has to sign in whenever the kids are here."

Evidently it had not occurred to the young mother that they might be locking the fox in with the chickens, thought Sigrid, passing into the darkened auditorium.

Up on the brilliantly lit stage, nine children were making enough noise for nineteen. Barefooted, dressed in lollipop-colored tights and leotards, they shrieked with laughter as they tried to adjust their rhythmical march whenever Ginger Judson varied the beat of her bongo drums. They appeared to range in age from five to eight.

The iron fence was nowhere in sight this afternoon. The scaffold tree had been unbolted from its spot at stage right and pushed over into the wings. The cardboard tombstones were also gone and the painted backdrop had been hoisted overhead to uncover the mirrored wall behind.

Sigrid occasionally had trouble differentiating between boys and girls when they were that young, but after watching a few minutes from one of the side pews and seeing them reflected from all angles, she rather thought there were five girls and four boys until she heard Cliff Delgado's voice above the laughter and drum beats: "Okay now, boys march like elephants and girls gallop like ponies"; whereupon five small bodies hunched over with their arms swinging together in front of their heads like elephant trunks.

Although she concentrated on the way Delgado and Judson were conducting the children's dance class, Sigrid was suddenly overwhelmed by such an intense conviction that Nauman was somewhere near that she turned to the pew behind, fully expecting him to be there. Instead, she saw a rather homely young man with a smear of yellow ocher beneath his left ear and a bulky wool sweater that exuded a familiar aroma of turpentine and paint thinner, odors that instantly conjured up a vivid memory of Nauman whenever she smelled them now. Another artist, no doubt.

He gave Sigrid a friendly smile and slipped along his pew till he was close enough to murmur, "Mine's the one with the yellow-and-purple leotard. Which one's yours?"

"I don't have one," Sigrid replied, noting for the first time three unfamiliar women seated six rows down on the opposite side of the theater, two as young as Liz Weinberg, the third several years older. More mothers and a grandmother?

She watched the child in yellow and purple, the tallest of the four girls, as she galloped with the others in and out of the slower-moving line of "elephants."

"Do you always come with your daughter?" she asked.

He shook his head. "We're only three blocks away, but after what happened here Saturday . . . Caitlin—my wife—she thought we ought to take Shannon out of class, but she loves it so much. Just look at her!"

The ponies and elephants tumbled into a noisy heap at Delgado's feet, and if that little girl's blissful face were any barometer, she did indeed love the class.

"Besides," said her father, "I don't figure the kids are in any danger and since they've got that psychiatrist coming back to talk with them today, Shannon ought to be here for it."

"Did she know the child who was killed last February?" asked Sigrid.

He looked at her suspiciously. "You connected with the theater?"

"I'm a police officer," she answered and introduced herself.

"Howard O'Brian," he said. "Yeah, Shannon knew her. Not well, though. They overlapped in this class for a month, then last January the Gillespie girl moved up to the Wednesday-afternoon class for the nine-to-twelve age group. A month later and she was dead." He rested his arms on the back of Sigrid's pew; his eyes followed his daughter's movements onstage. "It's a bitch when something like that happens," he said softly. "You get paranoid with your kids, don't want to let them out of your sight. I walked Shannon everywhere till Memorial Day, till her friends teased her so much she made me stop, and here I am doing it again."

Sigrid nodded toward the other parents. "You don't seem to be alone."

O'Brian frowned. "There's usually fifteen to twenty kids in this session. About a third of the parents have pulled theirs out and maybe they're the smart ones. I don't know. Emmy Mion wasn't much taller than Shannon or Amanda." He leaned closer to Sigrid and the evocative smell of turpentine grew even stronger. "Tell me the truth, Lieutenant: Is some nut running around with a thing against small girl dancers?"

"We certainly hope not, Mr. O'Brian."

"Weird that some guy could sneak in from the alley and waltz right onstage to kill her."

"Is that what they're saying?"

"That's what someone told my wife. That it was some psycho loony Emmy used to dance with out in California who followed her here. We made them promise to keep that alley door locked from now on and somebody's going to sit out in the lobby whenever classes are on to sign people in and out."

Sigrid sat half-turned in the pew so that she could both look at O'Brian and see the stage. "Did your daughter talk much about Emmy Mion?"

"Not more than eighteen or twenty times a day," he answered wryly. "Did you know Emmy could do a somersault in midair, walk on her hands, hey! swing from the rafters, too, for all I know?"

Sigrid smiled. "Nothing negative, then?"

Howard O'Brian's face became serious again. "You

mean any hanky-panky going on, like those day-care centers where the kids were molested?"

"It happens."

"Not here," he said emphatically. "That's the first thing the kids were asked after the little Gillespie girl was killed and we wouldn't have let Shannon stay on if there'd been the slightest hint of any funny teacher stuff. There's always been a good feel about this place. These people really seem to like working with kids. It's not just a job for them—hey, they're only kids themselves. Look at them."

Up on the stage, Eric Kee and Ulrike Innes had joined in with the children for some monkey-see, monkey-do pantomime as Cliff Delgado called out, "Happy! It's your birthday!"

Ginger's bongos gave way to the lighthearted slap and jingle of her tambourine.

"You got balloons for your party! They're so big they almost swoo-oop you off the ground."

As Cliff's voice swooped, Eric and Rikki each swung a child into the air and pretended to bobble him across the stage while the other children mimicked being tugged upward. The musty maroon velvet curtains had been pulled all the way back and Nate Richmond's reflection could be seen standing before his lightboard at stage left. A pixie smile lit his ageless face as he bounced colored lights over the children like confetti.

"Ooops! Billy just popped his balloon!" Cliff called. "Oh, he's sad. So sad, and you're sad for him."

The children drooped around a small boy, Ginger switched back to the drums and beat them in a somber dirge, and the confetti-colored lights merged into a pale blue.

As the class wound down, a slender figure emerged from one of the side doors that led backstage and paused to speak to the three women, who immediately stood up and moved to the rear pews. The figure continued over to Sigrid and Howard O'Brian.

"Hi! I'm Dr. Ferrell and—Sigrid! I didn't realize you were here."

Christa Ferrell beamed at her old schoolmate happily. She wore an expensive-looking green sweater that had whimsical giraffes knitted into its design; and with the sleeves pushed up and her cornsilk hair piled loosely atop her head, she looked as fresh and young as one of the children. Her smile included Sigrid's companion. "Are you a daddy?"

Looking dazzled, Howard O'Brian stuck out his hand. "Shannon's my daddy, yes. I mean, yes, I'm Shannon O'Brian's father."

The psychiatrist shook his hand and explained, "I'm asking all the parents to move as far from the stage as possible so that the children won't be inhibited by your presence when I meet with them in a few minutes."

"Oh sure," said O'Brian and scooped up his scarf and jacket. "Nice talking to you, Lieutenant, and I sure hope you people catch the guy soon."

Christa Ferrell looked at Sigrid dubiously. "You didn't want to sit in on this first session, did you? Strangers are sometimes tricky until I've established trust."

"I'll poke around backstage," Sigrid said. "But when you're through, I'd like to hear how it went."

"Fine." Christa Ferrell moved toward the stage as Helen Delgado rounded the mirrored wall at the rear with a tray that held a pitcher and some paper cups. Today the designer had sleeked her hair back into a smooth braided chignon, and enormous yellow plastic sunflowers bloomed in her ears.

"Now then," she said warmly, "who's ready for juice?"

With six members of the 8th-AV-8 out front among the children, backstage seemed deserted. Beyond the circular iron staircase, the door to the prop room was open so Sigrid stepped inside and looked around. Painted flats were piled against one wall and shelves held a limited inventory of props that reflected the troupe's meager budget: cheap umbrellas, plastic canes, a collection of hats that might have come from thrift stores. Hanging from the ceiling was a net filled with multicolored plastic beach balls, and directly beneath, looking like leftovers from an F.A.O. Schwarz fire sale, were a life-size stuffed lion, tiger, and ostrich in mangy velour.

A table in the far corner of the large room held numerous cans of spray paint; brushes, rollers, and a couple of small face masks hung from nails over the table. Judging by the thick mat of newspapers on the floor and the overlapping layers of colors splattered on both corner walls, Sigrid decided this must be where Helen Delgado painted her flats.

Propped against the fourth wall was the spiked iron fence. Its removal from the stage, unlike that of the scaffold tree, appeared to be permanent.

"We didn't think the children ought to have to keep looking at it," said Helen Delgado from the open doorway.

"Probably wise of you," Sigrid murmured and, as she accompanied the designer down the hall, asked, "Have you learned anything more about the telephone call Miss Mion expected Saturday?"

"Me? Nope. But the phone's been on automatic most of the time since Saturday and who knows whether anyone's listened to the message tape yet?" She balanced the tray with the plastic juice pitcher on one hand and opened the door to the green room with the other. "Eric and Rikki and I've been splitting the clerical work—even Sergio's taken a whirl—but none of us seem to have Emmy's flair for it. I guess she took more of the load than we realized."

Hearing his name as they entered, Sergio Avril looked up like a startled rabbit from the conversation he and Roman Tramegra were engaged in while seated upon that rump-sprung green couch.

"The lieutenant wants to know if that telephone call Emmy expected Saturday ever came," Helen explained, handing the tray to Roman, who carried it over to the sink and began to rinse out the pitcher.

"Oh, dear," said the composer. He turned pink, stood up, and nervously cleared his throat. He was so shy and self-effacing in a threadbare suit too large for his thin frame that Sigrid had carried an impression of smallness. In truth, he was taller than she and even skinnier, with a questing, forward thrust of his head as if continually trying to get his myopic eyes closer to the object in view than his body could decently permit itself.

He cleared his throat again. "Rikki didn't tell you?"

"Tell me what?" asked Helen, her hands resting on her generous hips.

"She was showing me how to work the message tape this morning—you *know* I'm no good with things like that," he bleated.

"Let me guess, doll." She shook her glossy black head in mock disbelief. "You erased the tape."

His face even pinker, the composer nodded. "Not all of it. At least I don't *think* all of it, but—"

"Don't you compose on an electronic synthesizer?" Sigrid asked curiously. "That seems much more complex than a message machine."

"It *is*," Avril sighed, turning his nearsighted gaze toward her voice. "Half the time, what I do is instinctive. Before I met Nate, I could never rely upon duplicating something a second time. He's helped me enormously with programming my compositions. And I know how to work my own tape player, of course, but a telephone's totally different. I *thought* I understood Rikki's instructions but—"

"Okay, okay!" Helen said, holding up an impatient hand. "No need to blither on about it. If it's urgent, people'll probably call back. Don't sweat it, doll."

Relieved, Avril sank back upon the dilapidated couch, removed his glasses, and began polishing them with a less-than-immaculate handkerchief.

"I know you've been asked several times already, Mr. Avril," said Sigrid, "but are you sure you formed no impression of who might have joined Miss Mion onstage Saturday?"

Across the room, Roman pursed his lips at her and shook his head. Sigrid shot a glance at Helen Delgado, but the designer was intent on Avril's answer and didn't see.

Avril stuffed the handkerchief back in his pocket and looped the gold frames around his ears, although as far as Sigrid could tell, the lenses were as smudged as before. "I wish I could say, Lieutenant, but everything's a blur at that distance."

"No wonder," Helen snorted. Deftly, she removed his thick glasses and carried them over to the sink, where she dipped them into the pan of hot soapy water Roman had been using. "I've told you a hundred times that a handkerchief picks up grit in your pocket and scratches the lenses. And a *dirty* handkerchief—how can you be such an idiot?"

"You're right, of course," he said meekly, but Sigrid thought she detected a sly smile that came and went so quickly that she couldn't be sure.

On the other hand, she knew there were men—women, too, for that matter—who pretended to be more incompetent than they actually were. Perhaps this was Avril's way of making himself noticed?

"It's too bad about your eyesight," she said mildly. "You were directly across from Delgado and Kee. It would certainly help if you could alibi even one of them."

"The fence and the tree were between us," he reminded her as his now-shining spectacles were returned to him. "Thank you, Helen. You're very kind."

Helen smiled at him indulgently, a smile that turned to annoyance when her attention focused on the tools atop the refrigerator which Roman had forgotten until that moment.

"I tore the prop room apart looking for that mask yesterday morning," she said. "Where the hell was it?"

"Under the spiral stairs," said Roman. "Cliff must have left it on the steps and it fell off." Archly, he held the rigid cupped plastic shape over his nose and mouth. The filter lining was missing but his words still sounded muffled as he spoke thorugh the air holes. "Don't worry about the operation, *mein liebchen*. I studied under ze famous Dr. Frankenstein."

"Where's the strap?" asked Helen, unappeased, reclaiming her equipment. "If Cliff's broken it, I'll strangle him."

"No sign of a strap," Roman told her. "Your tack hammer was up in the women's dressing room. Along with Nate's pliers. The tape dispenser was in the men's dressing room. I'll just return it to the office."

"If you don't mind, Mr. Tramegra, I'll come with you," said Sigrid. "There are some questions I wish to ask."

"Certainly, Lieutenant."

*   *   *

Once inside the corner office, Sigrid went straight to the answering device on the telephone while Roman pointedly closed the door with a conspiratorial flourish.

"How long has Avril been connected with the company?" she asked when she'd zipped through the answering tape and found nothing of import in the three remaining messages.

"He came in last spring after they got that *fabulous* grant. I *told* you about that."

"That's right; I remember now. And you said he brought you in because you two had collaborated on some poetry readings last winter at the Y."

As Sigrid had only known Roman since the spring, she hadn't attended those readings of his haiku poems set to electronic music. It was not an experience she regretted missing. Although she was receptive to most poetry—especially poetry with enough formal structure, metrical rhythm, and felicitous attention to language to satisfy her sense of order—haiku had never appealed to her. Nor was she much enamored of electronic music. Nauman had tried to educate her ear as well as her eye, but with small success in bringing her very far into the twentieth century. "Teddy Bears' Picnic," by Peter Klausmeyer, a contemporary American composer, made her laugh each time she heard it, and his "The Cambrian Sea" stirred her emotionally—the rest was simply so much sound and fury with little significance as far as Sigrid was concerned.

She clicked through the tape again, then abandoned it to fix Roman with her piercing gray eyes. "Do you think Avril would deliberately erase the tape to protect someone in the troupe?"

"Surely not!" he protested. "I fear that Sergio is something of a cultural snob. He is not ungrateful for their commission—the money has allowed him to continue work on his *serious* music—but he would not consider that a *children's* dance company had purchased his immortal soul. Or even his loyalty."

"If he's that snobbish, why's he still here so much?"

"They feed him," Roman answered simply. "Ginger washes his shirts, Helen mends the tears in his clothing, Win sends him home with vitamin pills and bags of

oranges, Nate helps him understand the machinery that
David and Eric have procured so that he can work here.
Few electronic composers make even a *subsistence* living
with their music. I've never visited Sergio's rooms, but I
daresay they do *not* offer the physical comfort he has
here."

He paused and looked at the telephone thoughtfully.
"He scorns the level of intellect here, yet these same
creature comforts *clearly* offer an inducement to preserve
the status quo."

"So that if he heard something on the tape which he
thought would wreck the company—?"

"He might indeed erase it deliberately," Roman concluded. "*If*—and it's a large if, my dear—*if* he could figure
out how to *manage* the erasure with Rikki standing right
there watching. He truly is *frightfully* incompetent with
unfamiliar mechanical contrivances."

"I'll speak to Innes," Sigrid said. "In the meantime,
have you learned anything I should know about?"

"Alas, no. Ah, but wait a moment! Something Ginger
said this morning makes me think that Emmy was *not*
going to move in with her as she'd thought."

Sigrid was puzzled. "Mion was going to stay with
Kee?"

"No. Evidently she told Ginger while they were
getting dressed Saturday that she planned to camp out in
one of the storage rooms upstairs until she could find a
place of her own. A *single* place."

An interesting tidbit, thought Sigrid after Roman left
her—"If I stay too long, it will look *suspicious,*" he had
whispered with relish—but she couldn't see that it ad-
vanced their knowledge of why Emmy Mion had been
killed. Except that it was one more piece in the puzzle.

She looked around the large office and once again
wished that Tillie were working this case with her. He
would have seized on so many details about the room: the
pictures of dancers and children, the books on choreography, the slapdash messiness of Emmy Mion's creative area
as opposed to her managerial orderliness. He would have
seen significance in the way her desk had been ransacked
while her drawing table seemed to have been left untouched.

Most of what he noticed on a case was irrelevant. Sigrid knew she usually discarded eighty-five percent of what he diligently brought to her attention, but at least she would have considered each point and would not now be sitting here with the uneasy feeling that she was overlooking something obvious. Well, sighing over Tillie's absence wouldn't help, she scolded herself. She got up and walked around the office, consciously trying to look beneath the surface of each object that met her eyes.

Roman had left the door ajar when he left and some twenty minutes passed before Sigrid heard sounds in the hall. A child appeared in the doorway. "Is Nate here?" it asked.

"Down here, Calder," she heard Nate Richmond call from further along the hall, as she caught sight of Christa Ferrell rounding the corner from the stage.

"Ah, there you are, Sigrid. Don't disappear on me, Calder. I shouldn't be more than a minute."

Christa Ferrell closed the door. "I let the session run longer than I expected," she said, consulting the delicate gold watch on her wrist as she tugged down the sleeves of her green sweater. "We made a good beginning though. The children were quite forthcoming. There's a lovely trust between them and the company."

"You let the dancers stay?"

"Oh, yes. This is a group process, you understand. We're not trying to resolve every conflict in their individual lives; we're merely allowing them to validate and deal with this particular trauma. The dancers can speed up the process by helping to channel the responses, so to speak. Get their emotions about Emmy Mion out in the open more quickly so we can see where we stand."

"And where *do* you stand?"

"Well, there's the expected grief and bewilderment; also the guilt."

"Guilt?"

"Oh heavens, yes! A young child always feels guilty when something goes wrong in his world. He thinks that if he'd been a better child, obeyed all the rules, this wouldn't have happened. It's a perfectly normal response. Counseling and therapy help him understand that bad things can occur independent of his personal behavior." She glanced at her watch again. "Sigrid, I'm sorry, but I really do have to run or I'm going to be late for my session with Corrie Makaroff. And did your mother tell you? I'm *so* pleased she's going to use Corrie and Tanya."

"I'm glad you reminded me," said Sigrid. "I'll send you all the details if you want them, but one of my officers told me today that Ray Thorpe was apprehended last weekend and has already been arraigned. He's pleaded guilty. The Makaroff children won't have to testify."

"That's wonderful! What will he get? Life?"

"More like six to ten years maximum," Sigrid said dryly.

"You're kidding!" Christa's blue eyes were shocked. "A man violently murders a woman and that's all the time he serves?"

Sigrid shrugged. "I'm told six years can feel like a lifetime in some of our prisons."

Chapter 19

They had copied the address from Amanda Gillespie's case file. Situated on West Nineteenth Street a half-block off Eighth Avenue, it proved to be a four-story brick town house with a high stoop, polished brass fittings, and sturdy black iron filigree at the basement and first-floor windows. Jim Lowry pulled open the outer door to a minuscule entryway paved in white marble and Elaine Albee pushed the button marked 2a—*K. Gillespie*.

Static hissed from the speaker beside the buttons and a crisp feminine voice said, "Yes?"

"Detectives Lowry and Albee, Mrs. Gillespie," said Elaine. "NYPD. May we speak to you about your daughter?"

"*Police*? Oh dear God! What's happened to her? Is she hurt?"

Kicking herself for assuming that the dead girl was an

only child, Elaine Albee quickly leaned toward the speaker again. "We're here about Amanda, Mrs. Gillespie."

There was a long pause.

"Mrs. Gillespie?"

"Yes, all right." The crispness had gone out of the woman's voice.

The buzzer sounded to unlock the inner door and the two police officers passed through into a stairwell made light and airy even on this gray day by a large skylight. The stairs were carpeted in deep blue pile and the white wallpaper was sprigged with small flowers of the same rich blue. All the woodwork seemed freshly painted in clean white enamel. A ten-speed bike was propped under the edge of the stairs near the door of the rear apartment and a child's yellow rain hat had been left on the newel post for someone to claim.

As Elaine Albee and Jim Lowry rounded the landing and walked up the second flight, a door opened at the top of the stairs. At first glance, the woman who waited for them looked like a teenager called from her homework assignments: straight brown hair that fell to her waist, jeans, a baggy red sweater with pushed-up sleeves, woolly red socks, no shoes, a yellow pencil tucked behind one ear, another pencil in her hand.

Then they saw the deep lines beside her small tight mouth and more bitterness in those dark brown eyes than an ordinary American teenager could marshal.

"Mrs. Gillespie?" smiled Elaine.

"Yes." There was no answering smile.

Elaine introduced herself and Jim Lowry. "May we come in for a few minutes?"

Mrs. Gillespie hesitated, then stepped back.

Although the apartment felt small, inside it was as bright and cheerful as the stairwell. It overlooked the street and there were baskets of swedish ivy hanging from window hooks; pots of red geraniums bloomed on the sills; baskets of bamboo and palms sat on the floor. A daybed covered in patchwork quilts and piled with small animal-shaped pillows doubled as a couch, and two Boston rockers were pulled up near it around a low round table of scrubbed pine. In front of the windows was a large drawing table and an open, three-shelf metal cart that had been converted into a sort of rolling supply cabinet. It held dozens of bottles of colored inks, drawing pencils, and a coffee can that bristled with crow quill pens.

But what immediately caught and held the eye were the many pen-and-colored-ink drawings which enlivened the plain white walls. Matted in bright red, green, or navy blue, all were framed in narrow white plastic and all were of children—children splashing in puddles on idealized city streets, flying kites in a pristine park, tumbling with puppies, chasing butterflies; children limned in sunlight. Elaine paused before one of a dimpled toddler who had found a speckled ladybug on the daisy she held.

"That looks exactly like a birthday card I sent my two-year-old niece last month," she said.

Mrs. Gillespie perched on the stool behind her drawing table. "It probably was."

The penny dropped. "I'll be darned!" said Elaine. "I didn't connect it before. Gillespie. Are you the Gilly of Clarion Cards' Gillyflower line?"

In spite of herself, Mrs. Gillespie looked gratified by the recognition. "Hardly anyone ever notices the name. Gillyflower is Clarion's smallest line."

"My sister-in-law adores them. There's a Clarion cardshop near my building and she always stocks up when she's in the neighborhood."

Elaine did not like her sister-in-law and she now remembered with guilt how she'd deliberately selected the most sugary-sweet card she could find, knowing that her sister-in-law would consider it just too cute for words. (She'd later made it up to baby Belinda by taking the kid to the park and letting her drip chocolate ice cream all over her new pink sweater.)

Something of a frustrated artist himself, Jim Lowry peered curiously at the surface of the drawing table. "Is that going to be a Christmas card?"

"The first week in November? Goodness, no. We work at least six months ahead. This is for a boy's birthday around the Fourth of July."

She tilted the drawing toward them. Nearly finished, it showed a perfectly adorable little boy dressed in a red shirt, droopy blue jeans, and scuffed white sneakers and holding a sparkler. Off to the right sat a puppy with its equally adorable head cocked at an inquisitive angle as it watched the shower of burning sparks.

"My sister-in-law would love it," Elaine said truthfully.

Jim Lowry knew her well enough to catch the nuances. He cleared his throat formally. "We're sorry to have to bother you like this, Mrs. Gillespie."

"No, it's okay. I understand you have to keep coming back, asking." She added another blade of grass to the tuft growing beside the puppy.

Elaine glanced at Jim. "Perhaps we weren't clear, Mrs. Gillespie. Amanda's case is still open, of course, but we're actually working on Emmy Mion's death."

The woman's long hair had fallen across her face as she drew. She pushed the strand behind her ear and looked up with a startled air. *"Who?"*

"Emmy Mion," said Elaine. "One of the dancers who worked at the 8th-AV-8 Dance Theater. You didn't know she was murdered Saturday?"

"No." Mrs. Gillespie gave a vague, encompassing gesture of her hand. "No television. My last husband took the color console when he left and I haven't bothered to get another."

She sat quite still and listened as the two police officers explained how Emmy Mion had died, then sighed softly and went back to her meticulous pen strokes across the picture. "I guess that's the real reason she didn't call back."

"She called you? When?"

Mrs. Gillespie sat up on the stool and pushed her heavy hair back from her face with both hands, keeping her fingers clasped at the nape of her neck as she spoke. "I don't know when. Kelsy—that's my fourteen-year-old—spent the weekend with her father down in D.C. because this morning was the deadline on a Father's Day card." She grimaced. "Not exactly my favorite holiday so it wasn't coming easily. Anyhow, I turned off the phone around eight Saturday morning and put on the answering machine so I wouldn't be disturbed and then I forgot to check the messages till after dinner. I don't remember which was first, but if it's any help, hers was either just before or just after one from a friend who called up on the spur of the moment around noon to ask if I wanted to meet her for lunch somewhere."

Elaine eyed her telephone. "I don't suppose the message is still there?"

"Sorry." Mrs. Gillespie unclasped her hands, bundled her hair into a loose pile on the top of her head, and deftly secured it with three drawing pencils. "There wasn't much to it. Just that she thought she'd found something of Amanda's and wanted to know when it'd be convenient to bring it around."

"Did she give you any idea of what that something might be?" asked Lowry.

Mrs. Gillespie shook her head and the lines beside her mouth seemed to deepen. "I called the theater late last night and left a message that I really didn't care what they'd found. Whatever it was, I didn't want it back."

Carefully and precisely, she inked in a small brown spot on the puppy's head.

"It was Amanda's missing hair ribbon," Elaine said gently.

Mrs. Gillespie placed another brown spot on the puppy's rump. "Look," she said. "I know you people are only doing your job, but I've got this job to finish as well, and really there's no point in just going over and over and—oh damn!"

As she dipped her pen into the small bottle, her shaking hand upset it and brown ink ran across the drawing. "Damn, damn, *damn!*" she moaned.

While she dabbed at the stain ineffectually, the front door opened and a teenage girl entered. Her brown hair and eyes proclaimed her Mrs. Gillespie's daughter; otherwise, she was a Madonna clone in short skirt, black lace-up granny boots, and excessive makeup. She stared at them curiously as she dumped a load of schoolbooks on a chair and stuck her furled umbrella in a large butter churn beside the door. Then, sensing something strained about their silence, she said, "Everything okay, Mom?"

"It's all right," Mrs. Gillespie answered raggedly. "I just messed up the picture. Another do-over. Kelsy, these are police officers. Detective Albee and Detective Lowry. They're here about Mandy."

"Oh, Christ on a flagpole!" Kelsy Gillespie picked up her books and angrily flounced from the room, flinging back over her shoulder, "Let me know when they've gone, okay?"

They heard a door bang down the hall.

"I guess she's still upset about her sister," said Lowry. "Were they very close?"

She gave a half-negative turn of her head. "Though teenagers don't tell you much. Amanda worshipped her, but she seemed to get on Kelsy's nerves a lot. There was that five years' difference in their ages and then, too, Kelsy didn't like Amanda's father. I thought she was just jealous of him, but kids know, don't they? He turned out not to be very likable in the end."

Karen Gillespie's voice held a detachment which implied that the things of which she spoke no longer had the power to hurt.

She put aside the blotting paper she'd used to dry up the spilled ink and covered the ruined drawing with a sheet of tracing paper. "He paid child support every month on the button, I'll give him that; but I told him if he ever tried to see Amanda, if he ever so much as *spoke* to Kelsy again, I'd swear out a warrant for his arrest."

Elaine Albee suddenly felt tired. No matter how many statistics she read, no matter how often she heard about it, she knew she'd never get used to finding it in nice middle-class homes. "He molested your daughters?"

Mrs. Gillespie did not look up. "One of the side benefits to working at home: You learn about things before they get out of hand." Her pencil moved rapidly across the sheet in seemingly random strokes. "He liked to give the girls their baths. Mandy was two, Kelsy seven. I heard Kelsy cry out and I ran into the bathroom and there he was in the tub with them. He—" The pencil lead snapped and Mrs. Gillespie took a deep breath. "I took the girls to a friend's house that night and I gave him twenty-four hours to pack up anything he wanted and get out of our lives. And before you ask it, I'll tell you that he went back to New Mexico six years ago, and he conducted his regular

Shakespeare seminar for eighteen graduate students the day Amanda was killed. Those other detectives checked."

"Amanda's name wasn't really Gillespie then?" asked Elaine.

"No. I'd been using the Gilly signature on my pictures and Clarion Cards had started buying my designs before I married him, so I kept the name." She stuck the pencil into a battery-operated sharpener on the tabletop and held it there until it was ground down to a stub. "After what happened that night, I told everybody that Amanda was a Gillespie from then on, too. My first husband—Kelsy's father—he didn't mind and it was no one else's business."

"I know you've been asked this before," said Jim, "but please consider it carefully one more time: Isn't it just barely possible that one of those dancers could have tried to molest Amanda?"

Mrs. Gillespie threw the stub into a nearby wastebasket and took up a fresh pencil. "Anything's possible, isn't it?"

There was another tension-filled pause, then she said abruptly, "Look, I'm not a very huggy, touching person. I wasn't brought up like that. My parents loved us, but they weren't physically demonstrative. That's just the way they *were*. We certainly didn't feel slighted or neglected, my brothers and I. Kelsy's a lot like me, but Amanda— It was different with her. She was always nuzzling up to me, leaning against me, kissing me goodbye every time she left the apartment.

"Those dancers— I went to a couple of Amanda's classes. They seemed very"—she twirled the pencil slowly between her fingers as she searched for the right word— "spontaneous. They hugged the kids, patted them, let them sit on their laps or snuggle up when one of the others was giving instruction. Amanda liked that. But we had talked about the difference between healthy touching that makes you feel loved and touching that troubles you."

Her eyes met Lowry's. "If it happened, she would have told me."

"Unless she didn't get the chance," he said.

"Unless she didn't get the chance," she agreed bleakly.

"Mrs. Gillespie," said Elaine, "may I talk to Kelsy a minute?"

"I don't mind. Kelsy might. Her door's the first on the right."

Until then Elaine had been standing with her raincoat over her arm. She handed it to Jim and went down the hall to tap at the closed door.

When there was no answer, she opened it.

Kelsy sat on her bed, granny shoes tumbled on the floor, her stockinged feet drawn up beneath her. "What do you want?" she asked sullenly.

"Just to talk a minute. Okay if I come in?"

The girl shrugged. "Suit yourself."

Elaine stepped over the books, moved aside a pile of clean laundry, and sat down on the end of the other twin bed. She looked around the room. No cutesy kids here. The walls were thick with posters of rock groups. "Van Halen," she said, tilting her blonde head to one of the posters over the bed. "What did you think of their last album?"

"Look, could you just cut the crap and get to the point?"

"Excuse me?"

Kelsy pushed her back against the headboard and stretched out her legs in an impatient gesture. Her eyes smoldered with resentment. "We both know you don't give a damn about what I think of Van Halen. You just want to soften me up so I'll tell you what I know about Mandy."

"All right, Kelsy. What *did* you know about Mandy?"

"Nothing."

"Don't you care about catching the person who hurt your sister?"

"She wasn't *hurt*, Detective Albee," Kelsy said brutally. "She was killed. K-I-L-L-E-D. And anyhow, she wasn't my whole sister. She was my half-sister."

"I see."

"No, you *don't* see. Look, I'm sorry Mandy's dead but you guys won't leave it alone. You keep coming and coming, and every time it makes my mom cry for hours and then she drinks too much and it just screws everything up."

Despite her tough words and her years-too-old make-up, a child's grief trembled behind that shaky facade. She clutched a fat pillow to her chest and Elaine flinched to see that her fingernails had been bitten into the quick.

"I'm sorry," she said softly. "Want me to go?"

"Why'd you come here today anyhow?"

"Someone else has been killed, Kelsy. One of the dancers at the theater where Amanda had classes."

"Yeah, I heard about it at school today. So?"

"Your sister—sorry. Your *half*-sister wore her hair in two ponytails the day she died but only one ribbon was found. The dancer who was killed Saturday had the other ribbon on her person. We're beginning to think she may have been killed because she learned who murdered Amanda."

"Oh."

Silence grew in the small room as Kelsy buried her chin in the pillow and contemplated her toes. Elaine glanced around again. There was nothing in the room to suggest a younger girl might have shared it, yet somehow Elaine knew that she had.

As if reading her thoughts, Kelsy swung herself to the floor and pulled out the bottom drawer of a nearby bureau. It was packed full. The teenager pushed aside stuffed animals, some composition notebooks, and a unicorn music box, and brought out a flat wooden box with a hinged lid that locked with a tiny key which Kelsy kept hidden beneath the lamp atop the bureau. Inside the wooden box were a couple of birthday cards, a report card, a red satin ribbon with "Second Place" imprinted in gold letters, and a thick sheaf of familiar-looking black-and-white photographs. Many were blurred and under- or over-exposed, obvious discards which the child had salvaged and claimed for her own; but just as many were duplicates of pictures that still hung on the theater's office walls.

Kelsy thumbed through to a group photo of the whole troupe. "Which one was killed?" she asked. "Her?"

"Yes," said Elaine. "That's Emmy Mion."

"Mandy liked her a lot. And this one, too. Helen somebody."

"Helen Delgado. What about the men?"

"She had a crush on this guy." Kelsy found a smudged four-by-six picture of Nate Richmond. There were tack holes in each corner as if the photographer's own self-portrait might once have found a place on these walls that were now devoted to rock groups. "He let her help him in the darkroom once in a while. Big deal. She used to moon about him all the time. He looks like a wimp to me. Now *this* guy has sexy eyes, doesn't he?"

"This guy" was Wingate West.

"Did Amanda like him?"

"I guess. And that one, too. Eric? He's part Chinese. That one there, though, she didn't much care for him."

"Him" was Cliff Delgado.

A sudden gust of wind outside rattled the sash and hurled rain against the window.

"Why didn't she like him?"

Kelsy shrugged. "I don't know. There was just something about him. She said he used to weird out. You know, laugh at things that weren't funny sometimes. I think he scared her a little bit." Her voice turned deliberately scornful. "She was such a scaredy-cat about everything anyhow. Afraid of the dark, afraid of ants, afraid of getting yelled at—I mean, just *look* at her!"

The eight-by-ten photograph was a three-quarter figure. Hair that had been back-lighted so that its probable mousey brown appeared to be spun from gold. Twin ponytails tied with plaid ribbons. A shy smile that revealed brand-new front teeth. She was not especially pretty nor particularly photogenic, yet her eyes had looked straight into the camera lens and they had been filled with love.

"Wouldn't you think a scaredy-cat like that would have enough sense to run away?" Kelsy asked angrily.

"You sure would, honey," said Elaine and put her arms around the weeping girl and held her tightly.

Chapter 20

Sigrid sat on the stool behind the drawing table where Emmy Mion used to choreograph simple dances for the children and more complex movements for the troupe. She had unpinned pictures from the wall and now the dancer's small heart-shaped face smiled up at her, circled by photographs of Eric Kee, David Orland, Cliff Delgado, and Wingate West, the four male dancers.

In a second outer circle she had fanned the photographs of Ginger Judson and Ulrike Innes, the two remaining female dancers, and of Helen Delgado, Nate Richmond, and little Amanda Gillespie.

She had stared at these faces until she felt she knew their smiling surfaces intimately. Yet what lay beneath remained *terra incognita,* and it was getting late. She might as well go find Rikki Innes, hear her version of how Sergio Avril had erased the message tape that morning, and then call it a day.

Wearily she switched off the light over the drafting table and the shadowed eyes sprung into relief. Eyes were supposed to be the windows of the soul, Sigrid thought, leaning forward with her elbows on the table and her chin propped in her cupped hands; but these eyes told her nothing.

The only light in the office now was the desk lamp in the opposite corner and Sigrid sat so motionless that she must have blended into the background clutter, because when the children crept into the room, they seemed unaware of her presence.

The situation instantly called up a memory that Sigrid had completely forgotten until that moment.

Seated in a shaded part of her grandmother's herb garden on a late spring day, she had just finished solving a rather complex diagramless crossword puzzle and was enjoying that absurd sense of pleasure which comes from creating an ordered pattern out of random data when a rustle of dry leaves on the other side of the low stone wall caught her attention. Remaining absolutely still, she saw a mother bobwhite lead eight fuzzy chicks over the wall, through a bed of lemon-scented geraniums, and down the graveled path almost to Sigrid's feet.

Sigrid was neither a naturalist nor someone who automatically cooed over small baby animals, but that spring morning she had discovered that there was some-

thing unexpectedly fascinating about watching wild crea-
tures when they don't realize they're being observed, and
she now experienced a similar fascination in watching the
three children cross the room as noiselessly as some
half-feral animals might cross a forest floor.

She didn't move; she'd barely blinked; yet, as if
they'd suddenly caught her scent, the children froze and
three pairs of eyes immediately swung in her direction.

"We weren't doing nothing," said the taller boy.

"No?" Sigrid asked skeptically. She switched the drafts-
man's light back on and the three, two boys and a girl,
edged toward the door.

"Don't go," she said. "I want to talk to you." One of
the women had said that some children had been around
and underfoot Saturday morning. These children?

Once again she missed Tillie's help. She was always
awkward with children but Tillie had three of his own and
could usually achieve an instant rapport. For once, though,
she got lucky. The Pennewelf children had grown accustomed to trusting most of the adults connected with the
theater and they came over to her willingly enough. In
fact, before she could stop him, the younger boy scurried
up her legs and onto her lap as nimbly as a tame squirrel.

"Billy want to see," said the girl, standing on tiptoe
herself to peer over the top of the high drafting table.

Sigrid went completely rigid. Holding a child on her
lap was well outside her normal range of activities.

Billy didn't seem to notice. He held up the picture of
Emmy Mion for his siblings to see.

"Emmy!" they chorused.

He laughed, scooped up the rest of the pictures, and
began to show them one by one as if he were a teacher
conducting a sort of flash-card drill.

"Cliff!" said the other two obediently. "Eric . . . Nate
. . . David . . . Rikki . . . Helen!"

They fell silent before the next picture and Billy
turned it around so he could see. Unconsciously putting
her hands around his waist so he wouldn't slip, Sigrid
looked over his shoulder and saw that it was the picture of
Amanda Gillespie.

"Do you remember her?" she asked them.

The older boy and girl stared back silently until the child on her lap nodded.

"Billy says it's Mandy," whispered the girl.

"She died," said the older boy.

"And Emmy yelled about her," said the girl.

"Now Emmy's dead."

For a moment, Sigrid felt as if she were caught up in a Greek chorus.

"Who did she yell at?" she asked. "And when? Saturday?"

Before they could answer (or not answer if so decreed by the tyrannical little choragus on her lap), the spell was snapped by the sudden appearance of Jim Lowry and Elaine Albee, who both looked soaked to the skin as they noisily entered the office.

Billy slipped through her hands like smoke and the three Pennewelf children vanished from the room.

"Guess what, Lieutenant?" said Lowry, shaking water from his raincoat. "Emmy Mion called Mrs. Gillespie around noon Saturday, told her she thought she'd found something of Amanda's, and asked her to call back."

"And Mrs. Gillespie finally returned her call late last night with a message that she didn't want whatever it was," said Albee. She tossed one of the towels on the radiator to Jim and applied a second one briskly to her own head. The rain had turned her loose curls into tight frizz, but the short walk down Eighth Avenue had restored her equilibrium. "The message is probably still on the tape there."

"No, it isn't," said Sigrid and told them how Sergio Avril had erased it, supposedly by mistake, although she hadn't yet heard Ulrike Innes's account. "Was there a reason it took the Gillespie woman two days to respond?"

"I think she didn't want to have to talk to anybody here," Jim said.

"He's probably right," said Elaine and described their interview with the dead child's mother and half-sister, from the incident of sexual abuse to young Kelsy's festering grief. "She pretends she doesn't care, but she's kept a whole drawerful of Amanda's favorite things."

Sigrid agreed that Amanda's crush on Nate Richmond

was predictable, given the gentleness with which he seemed to treat all children, but she wondered if they ought to make too much of the child's latent fears of Cliff Delgado. "It might have been merely a case of his seeming so much more intense than the others."

She told them of her strange session with the Pennewelf children, and Jim was ready to go round them up again, but Sigrid was hesitant. "If you find them alone, fine. But if there are any troupe members around, let it go for now and just bring me Ulrike Innes."

Sigrid returned the pictures to the wall. She couldn't remember the exact order, but doubted if it mattered. They seemed to have been placed there randomly anyhow. By chance this time, Ginger Judson's wound up beside Emmy Mion's.

"Did you know that Mion had decided not to go through with her plans to move in with Judson?" she asked Elaine.

The younger woman had just discovered the smear of makeup Kelsy Gillespie's tear-washed face had left on her pale gray blouse and was dabbing at it with the damp towel. "I wondered about that," she said, looking up. "She'd recently brought most of her clothes to the dressing room upstairs. Do you suppose that's part of why Judson was so hysterical yesterday?"

"Perhaps. Roman—Mr. Tramegra—" She turned to get another thumbtack and saw that Elaine was staring at her with bald curiosity. "You wanted to say something, Albee?" she asked icily.

"No, Lieutenant." Elaine hastily gave her attention to her soiled blouse.

"As I'm sure I mentioned, Roman Tramegra is a personal friend. It might, however, prove awkward for him here should the company learn of our friendship, so I expect you and Lowry to keep silent about it."

"Certainly, Lieutenant." Meekly, she spread the damp towel on the radiator to dry.

Appeased, Sigrid relented slightly. "His presence here may even help us. He seems to think that Emmy Mion told Judson while they were dressing Saturday that she was going to camp out here in the theater for a while until she could find a place of her own."

Having dragged two chairs over to the radiator, Elaine draped her raincoat on one, Jim's on the other. "Even if Judson mentioned it to one of the men, what would be so urgent about Mion getting a place of her own that he had to get rid of her right then and there?"

"Could it be the fact that she was going to camp here in the theater first?" Sigrid asked thoughtfully. "Is there something going on here that one of them wanted to prevent her from discovering?"

"Well, she got uptight when she thought their synthesizer was stolen property. Maybe it really was," Elaine suggested. "Maybe this was a transfer point for bootleg electronic equipment?" Distracted, she ran her fingers through her damp hair. "But then, how would that fit in with the Gillespie child and the ribbon Mion found?"

"Her timing on leaving Kee and moving in here could still be sheer coincidence," said Sigrid. "We'll have to—"

She broke off as Jim returned with Ulrike Innes.

"Sorry to have taken so long, Lieutenant, but Miss Innes had to help the hardware dealer from next door find his three grandchildren."

"Those Pennewelfs," said Innes, shaking her fair head ruefully. "They're like little mice the way they dart in and out. Especially Billy. At least the other two are in school most of the day. He only goes a half-day. His grandfather's always over here looking for him. Take your eyes off him for a moment and he scurries through any little mouse hole."

She paused and a pleased smile lit her oval face. "Emmy had already sketched out most of the choreography for our Christmas recital. Billy will be perfect for 'Not a creature was stirring, not even a mouse.' We'll let him keep scurrying all over the stage so that the narrator has to read the line twice as if to drum it into the mouse that he's supposed to be still. The children love that sort of silliness."

The dancer suddenly seemed to remember that she hadn't been invited to the office to discuss the Christmas recital. "Sorry. You wanted to ask me something, Lieutenant Harald?"

"Yes, about the telephone message tape. Mr. Avril tells me that you were instructing him on its use when he erased all the messages this morning."

"Yes?" she asked with an air of cautiousness.

"Would you say it was an accident or deliberate, Miss Innes?"

"A complete accident," she answered promptly even though her china-blue eyes shied away from Sigrid's steady gaze. "It was all my fault. I *know* Sergio's bad with machinery, but he insisted on helping me this morning and I'm afraid I wasn't thinking clearly."

To demonstrate how it had happened, Innes leaned across the desk. "He was there at the phone and I was over on this side. I told him to press the right button, meaning the one on his right as he faced the machine, and he thought I meant *my* right. By the time I realized what had happened, half the tape must have been cleaned and if there were any messages on it . . ." Her long hands flew up in a gesture of resignation. "Too late."

"I see," said Sigrid. It could have happened that way. On the other hand, if Sergio Avril had wished, he might have willfully misunderstood her directions. By itself it proved nothing.

"One more thing, Miss Innes. Would you describe for us what happened in the dressing room Saturday shortly before the performance?"

"I'm not sure I know what you mean," said Innes, nervously pleating the folds of the oversized blue sweatshirt she wore over her leotard and tights.

"Didn't you witness a conversation between Emmy Mion and Ginger Judson?"

"Y-yes."

"Is there some reason not to repeat it?" Sigrid asked patiently.

The young woman seemed to consider. "I guess not," she decided. "There wasn't much to it. Emmy merely told Ginger that she'd decided not to take her up on her offer. Emmy wanted to move out of Eric's place and Ginger had offered to share her place. Emmy said yes and then I suppose she changed her mind."

"And how did Miss Judson react to Mion's announcement?"

"Well, she got a little upset and ran out of the room." Innes glanced over at Elaine Albee. "I suppose you told her about Ginger falling apart yesterday?"

Elaine nodded.

"Dancers can be as temperamental as actors at times," said Innes defensively. "It doesn't mean a thing in the long run. Honestly."

"Did she mention it to any of the men, do you think? About Miss Mion's plans to camp here in the theater for a few days?"

"I really don't know. You'll have to ask her, won't you?"

But by the time they were finished with Innes, Ginger Judson had already left and she didn't answer her telephone.

"I suppose we might as well call it a day, too," Sigrid said.

It was almost dark when they stepped outside, and the rain had thinned to a fine mist that kept the sidewalks wet enough to reflect the gaudy neon lights that flashed and glowed up and down the avenue.

"Drop you, Lieutenant?" offered Jim. "The car's only a couple of short blocks up."

"No, thanks," she said, slightly disappointed to find the hardware store next door locked tight, its interior dark. She had hoped to see the Pennewelf children again. "I feel like walking."

"See you tomorrow," they called and turned uptown.

Eighth Avenue was clogged with rush-hour traffic heading north from lower Manhattan. Taxis duked it out with buses at every intersection and there seemed to be more horns and squealing brakes than usual, or was it, Sigrid wondered, because sounds carried better in damp air?

Nauman would know, she thought, and suddenly felt

quite melancholy. She gave herself a mental shaking. It was absolutely stupid to be pining about like the lily maid of Astolat. Oscar Nauman was a famous artist, educator, and obviously busy man and she'd probably misinterpreted his simple acts of friendship for something that would horrify and embarrass both of them.

Chapter 21

Personal notes of Dr. Christa Ferrell, re: Corrie Makaroff [Monday, 2 November—Everything's falling into place beautifully. When I returned to the office this afternoon after a session with Calder's movement class at the 8th-AV-8 Theater, I found Anne Harald here already beginning to interview Martha Holt. She's as attractive as I remembered— a little gray in her hair, a few lines around the eyes. I just hope I still look as good at her age.

M's a little dubious about the value of our department's being included in A.H.'s mag. article; wonders if we won't be perceived as blowing our own horn somehow. (As if horn-blowing's sordid & slightly suspect. M's a dear, but has old-fashioned view of selflessness that lets others walk all over her at times.) Anyhow A.H. & I reminded her that come budget time, higher visibility might get us a bigger slice of the pie.

Took A.H. down to my office, explained why I had so many toys (& made it clear that said toys were out of my own pocket—not supplied by the dept.). Only had time to show her the soundproofed observation room with its one-way window, which is next to my office, before Mrs. Berkowitz arrived w/ Corrie Makaroff.]

Through informal police channels, I learned today that Ray Thorpe, Darlene Makaroff's lover (and killer), was finally captured last week and will plead guilty to the murder, which means that Tanya and Corrie will not have to face him at a jury trial.

[NB—get technical jargon from Sig. H. re arraignments, degrees of manslaughter, etc.]

While Corrie waited outside, I discussed this new development with Mrs. Berkowitz. In view of Tanya's suggestion that her little sister might be afraid that Thorpe would return and hurt her, I thought it might reassure Corrie to know that her mother's killer had been caught and would now be punished. Perhaps this fear has indeed constituted part of her blockage.

Mrs. Berkowitz eagerly deferred to my judgment.

When Corrie entered, I took her upon my lap and kept my account of Thorpe's capture and incarceration to simple concise statements. She listened silently, as if the words were nothing more than a description of the weather.

"Do you want to ask me anything about Ray?" I said gently.

She shook her head and slipped off my lap, so naturally I didn't force her and within only a few minutes, she was completely at ease again.

She set up her family of dolls upon the hassock and began playing with them. Unlike the last few sessions, though, Aunt Rag Doll was neglected for vignettes with Barbie/Darlene.

[Theoretically, I probably should have waited for Corrie to make the connections herself, but with A.H. observing, decided it wouldn't hurt to nudge things along a bit.]

Casually, because I didn't want to undo any of our progress, I brought out a G.I. Joe doll and stood it in the open. Approximately ten inches tall, dressed in jeans and work shirt, G.I. Joe is quite definitely a masculine icon, with dark hair and beard. I rather suspected it might already represent Ray Thorpe because Corrie's eyes always flicked in that direction whenever I mentioned his name.

"He's been bad," I told Corrie, careful not to give the doll a name. "He hurt someone and then he ran away. But the police caught him and now he's in prison where he can't ever hurt anybody again."

Corrie didn't comment. She continued to play with

the other dolls, but at one point she looked at me directly and said, "Never ever?"

"Never ever," I promised, feeling that little thrill every psychiatrist must experience when the breakthrough begins.

Corrie studiously avoided that section of my toy shelves until the very end of the day's session. Just before I opened the door to the waiting room, she looked over at the G.I. Joe manikin and said, "He was *very* bad."

[I think A.H. was impressed w/ the session. She asked intelligent questions afterward. Complimented me on my camera awareness. Says she got a—her words—"charming shot" of Corrie on my lap. Had a dinner engagement w/ Matteo Accongio—a very sexy(!) heart specialist from Rome—but told her I could delay it if she wanted to discuss things further over a drink. She asked for rain check as she's moving later this week & needed to pack or something. Did ask me where I get my clothes. Get the impression she'd like to smarten Sig. up some. Prob. hopeless but mother love's classically blind. Gave her the names of my favorite shops. Suppose she can afford them. Wonder how much photojournalism pays?]

Chapter 22

Below West Fourteenth Street, Eighth Avenue veers west, and as Sigrid reached Abingdon Square, the rain began again with an earnestness that signaled an all-night soaking. The clouds overhead reflected a sullen yellowish brown and hung so low that they completely masked the tops of the Trade Center, the Empire State Building, and any other buildings more than twenty stories high.

Into Sigrid's mind came a stray line of poetry: *"For the rain it raineth every day."*

She sheltered in a doorway on Hudson Street with three other homeward-bound pedestrians and weighed her options. Her apartment was less than twelve blocks away, down near the river and too far west of Seventh Avenue for the subway to be of any help. As for buses, even if Hudson suddenly reversed itself and became one-way southbound, she'd still be three and a half blocks from home when she got off the bus. Not that Hudson Street showed any signs of reversing polarity. Abingdon Square was clogged with traffic and all of it pointed north.

A taxi didn't enter into her considerations. New York City taxis react to water like the Wicked Witch of the West and instantly melt away with the first drops of rain. Only tourists or incurable optimists expect to find an empty cab during a rainy rush hour and Sigrid was neither.

As so often happens, choice had devolved into necessity: she had chosen to walk, so walk she must.

Narrowly avoiding a kamikaze bicycler who whizzed past draped in flapping sheets of fogged plastic, Sigrid crossed Hudson and plunged southward, dodging umbrellas and briefcases, sprinters and sloggers.

"For the rain it raineth every day. . . ." What came next? *"Hey-ho!"*? No, that didn't sound right. She stepped around a street vendor who was doing a brisk business in cheap umbrellas. Umbrellas? Umbrellas triggered something about a *"just and unjust fellow."* A rainy spring day? Yes, and a tall-windowed brownstone house near Prospect Park, Aunt Edda fuming because her sister had gone off with her umbrella the night before, and blue-eyed Cousin Hilda chanting mischievously:

> *"The rain it raineth every day,*
> *Upon the just and unjust fellow,*
> *But more upon the just, because*
> *The unjust hath the just's umbrella."*

Sigrid frowned as she waited for the light at Perry Street. *"For the rain it raineth every day"* felt gloomier than Hilda's teasing verse. More like the refrain in a dirge and as inevitable as the final nails hammered into a coffin.

An icy rivulet ran from the brim of her hat down the

back of her neck and she pulled her collar up to divert the
flow. There were people who actually *liked* walking in the
rain, she reminded herself. A hundred different poems,
novels, and movies celebrated thunderstorms and April
showers with undampened enthusiasm. Idiots wrote songs
about it for other idiots to sing. Her pant legs clung wetly
to her ankles and her shoes squished with every step. She
remembered Gene Kelly splash-dancing along city sidewalks. What was so damned romantic about getting soaked?

"*For the rain it raineth every day,*" she reminded
herself grimly. Especially in November.

As she crossed West Tenth Street, she misjudged the
curb and went down on one knee. Her only injury was a
scrape on her right palm, but a passing car completed her
drenching with a tidal wave of dirty gutter water. Feeling
gloomier than this raw November evening, she trudged
the last few blocks, past locked warehouses and deserted
buildings, sustained by two visions: a steaming tub of
fragrant hot bubbles and her warm dry bed.

Number 42-1/2 was a solid green wooden gate set into a
nondescript high brick wall. Sigrid unlocked the gate and
entered a small courtyard where narrow herb beds had
flourished riotously for Roman Tramegra all summer. Now
that the bee balm and lavender had faded and the dogwood
in the center had dropped its red leaves, everything was
beginning to look brown and tattered. Beneath the tree,
ankle-deep in wet leaves, a three-foot statue of Eros faced
winter's onset with a stoical smile on his marble face.

Pelted with rain which hadn't slackened for a moment,
Sigrid hurried across the garden and let herself into the
vestibule. There she lingered a moment, her wet coat streaming onto the mat as warm air surrounded her at last and the
aromas from Roman's kitchen welcomed her home with
promises of pea soup and buttery, onion-flavored croutons.
She had lived alone for so many years that she'd been
cautious when Roman suggested sharing this particular apartment. Tonight, for the first time, she admitted to herself that
it was comforting to come home to someone.

She hung her hat and coat on the halltree, stepped

out of her ruined shoes, and walked down the short hallway, bracing herself for Roman's clucks and fussing when he saw how chilled and wet she was.

"It smells wonderful in here," she said, then halted in the doorway.

Instead of Roman's soft bulk before the stove, it was Oscar Nauman's lean height.

"Hello," he said and then his penetrating blue eyes swept her bedraggled form. "Are you all right? What the hell's happened to you?"

"I walked home," she said, drawing herself up defensively.

"In the rain? You?" he snorted. "I thought you hated to walk in the rain."

"I do."

"You're drenched." He crossed the green-and-white tiled floor to take a closer look. "And shivering. And why are you barefoot? Oh, God! Is that blood on your hand? You were mugged, weren't you?"

"No, I wasn't mugged," she said, snatching her hand away. "I fell and scraped my hand. That's all. Where's Roman?"

But she spoke to his back, for he was already striding across the living room and down the hall that led to her bath.

"I'll start your tub," he said. "You get out of those wet things before you catch a chill."

From pure habit, Sigrid started to argue, then remembered that a good hot bath was exactly what she'd planned. Anyhow, only an utter fool would try to make a power play out of spending another minute in these soggy clothes.

She closed the door to her bedroom and immediately put her gun in the top drawer next to her bed, but before she could shuck off the black suit and white blouse, she caught a glimpse of herself in the mirror. Appalled, she hastily finger-combed the dark hair back from her face. No wonder Nauman had started at the sight of her. She could be an ad for a horror movie: stringy wet hair, drawn face, no makeup, clothes that looked as if she'd clawed her way out of a muddy grave.

She stared at herself despairingly, suddenly remembering a squib Roman had pointed out to her in *The Village Voice* last month: "Flying in from London for the opening was the ever-so-elegant Lady Francesca Leeds, who graced the arm of the ever-so-attentive Oscar Nauman."

Nauman had asked Sigrid to go with him to that event, but she had to work. Just as well, she'd thought, reading that little tidbit. No gossip columnist would have thought it worth mentioning had Oscar Nauman escorted a less-than-elegant police lieutenant.

He rapped on her bedroom door. "Tub's full."

His footsteps returned toward the kitchen as she finished undressing, took a robe from the closet, and slipped into the deliciously steamy bathroom next door.

When she reappeared twenty-five minutes later, her hair was dry and soft again, she'd creamed her face and touched her lips with color, and she wore the black Peruvian robe and black slippers embroidered in gold threads which Anne had brought back from a Moroccan bazaar.

As an artist, Nauman immediately noticed how the matte black of her robe emphasized the sable highlights in her hair and turned her eyes a luminous silver, but he'd learned that compliments made Sigrid uncomfortable so he said nothing. He had set the dining table while she bathed and now he ladled Roman's thick split pea soup into shallow bowls.

"Where *is* Roman?" she asked, seating herself before a steaming bowl.

He sprinkled a generous handful of croutons over her soup. "I gave him a quarter and sent him off to the movies."

Sigrid did not smile back. "He's not my kid brother."

"I've noticed the lack of family resemblance," he assured her as he uncorked a bottle and poured the sparkling wine into their glasses.

"Champagne? With soup?"

"Why not? A split of champagne should go very well with split peas." He raised his glass. "Actually, there aren't many things champagne doesn't go with."

Sigrid sipped the wine and she couldn't have said why, but Nauman was correct—as he usually was about food and drink—this particular demi-sec went quite nicely with the faintly smoky flavor of the soup.

As they ate, they spoke of the sudden change in weather from autumn to winter, of an art film he'd seen, a new book she'd read, yet every conversational gambit seemed to dead-end into a strained silence broken only by the clink of silverware against china.

Rain beat upon the living room windows. "Poor Roman," she said. "It's such a wretched night. I wonder where he had to go?"

"I told you," said Nauman, refilling her glass.

"You weren't joking? You actually asked him to leave his own house? Why?"

"He didn't seem to mind. Anyhow I lent him my car. He said there was a nightclub act he wanted to catch over on the East Side. More soup?"

She shook her head and her "Why?" hung between them.

"I told him we wanted to be alone for a while tonight." His eyes held hers. "Don't we?"

Confused, she looked away and her slender fingers toyed with the stem of the champagne flute. "How were things in Connecticut? Did you find a plumber?"

"Sigrid—"

She stood up hastily. "I'll make coffee."

"There's still champagne."

She let him fill her glass a third time, then retreated into the living room and stood looking out into the storm-tossed courtyard. She could see Nauman's reflection in the wet dark glass and an anticipatory shiver swept over her as she felt him pause behind her. Only inches away. So close she could smell the familiar blend of turpentine and German cologne that emanated from his tweed jacket.

"*For the rain it raineth every day,*" she murmured nervously.

"What did you say?"

Sigrid repeated the words. "It's been running through my head all evening. Do you know what it's from?"

"Shakespeare?" he hazarded.

Sigrid handed him her glass, and the black robe swirled in graceful folds around her slender ankles as she turned from him and fled down the hall for her *Bartlett's Familiar Quotations*. Nauman was right. It was Shakespeare. She pulled her battered copy from the bookcase on the far side of her bed. "It's *Twelfth Night*," she called, then saw that Nauman had followed her, a wine glass in either hand.

"It's *Twelfth Night*," she said again, suddenly aware of the bed between them. "One of the Clown's songs—

> *"But when I came to man's estate,*
> *With hey, ho, the wind and the rain,*
> *'Gainst knaves and thieves men shut their gate,*
> *For the rain it raineth every day."*

Despite the wine, her voice sounded like a croak in her own ears.

"Things haven't changed much in four hundred years, have they?" Nauman observed.

He handed Sigrid her champagne across the width of the bed and reached for the book. Without seeming to notice where they were, he put his glass on the near table and sat down upon the bed to leaf through the plays. "This song's better," he said and began to read in his warm baritone:

> *"Tell me, where is fancy bred,*
> *Or in the heart or in the head?*
> *How begot, how nourishèd?*
> *Reply, reply."*

He closed the book with a sardonic lift of his eyebrow. "Care to answer that, Lieutenant?"

She stood mutely and he stretched out his hand to her. "Siga?"

"No!" she said and something between anger and bewilderment welled and darkened in her wide gray eyes. "I don't know how to play games, Nauman. I don't understand the rules. I thought— But then you avoid me and now tonight—"

He caught her hand and drew her down on the bed beside him. "Sh-h," he said. "I had to."

Oscar cupped her face between his strong hands and kissed her lips with infinite gentleness. "I wanted you so damned badly, Siga, that I had to make myself stay away. My doctor decided to go to Jamaica for the weekend and his idiot nurse wouldn't give me the test results—"

"Doctor?" She twisted in his arms, stricken with sudden fear for him. "Tests? What's wrong with you?"

"Nothing. That's what I wanted to verify."

"I don't understand."

"Listen, sweet fool. Haven't you been paying attention to what's happening? It's a whole different game these days. I wanted to make sure it was safe for you."

He gave her his clean bill of health as a more conventional lover might present a diamond bracelet. The sleeve of her robe had slipped aside and he ran his finger lightly down the red scar of her knife wound. "They must have done blood tests on you when you were in the hospital, so—"

"*Me?*" She flung his gift back in his face, suddenly angry. "You have the nerve to ask that of me? I'm not the one out tomcatting with every titled Sue, Jane, and Nancy who jets into New York. I'm not sleeping with every oversexed stud who asks nicely. I'm not—"

He put his hand over her mouth. "I'm not either," he said. "Not since April."

That silenced her.

"Not since April. Not ever again until you shut me out of your life," he promised. "And maybe not even then."

She wanted to answer, to argue, to discuss, but she seemed to have no words, only nerve endings which responded to his lightest touch as one hand slid down the side of her neck and the other undid the fastening on her robe and slipped the heavy dark fabric away from her shoulders.

"Nauman—"

But his breathing had become as ragged as hers.

"No more talking," he murmured as their lips met again.

*   *   *

She awoke sometime in the night when a gust of wind rattled the narrow clerestory windows above the bed and rain beat upon the glass.

Lying on his stomach beside her, his face half under the pillow, Nauman slept soundly. The room was too dark to see the laugh lines around his eyes or the deeper lines beside his mouth. Only the edge of his thick white hair.

It was enough. Sigrid was swept with momentary grief. Did all lovers feel this? she wondered. Lie in bed and count how few the years remaining?

Filled with a bittersweet tenderness, she pushed aside the pillow and smoothed his rumpled hair. His eyes opened at her touch. "Can't sleep?"

"The rain woke me."

They lay quietly for a few moments listening to the wind pound and batter the outer wall. It made Sigrid's bedroom feel like a warm safe haven. Nauman put his arms around her and drew her closer.

Their breathing slowed toward sleep again as rain pelted heavily against the glass above them.

"Not exactly a small rain," he said drowsily and though Sigrid was already half-asleep herself, she understood his allusion to that poignant scrap of sixteenth-century poetry and she fell asleep deeply content, with his hand cupped around her breast and those words drifting through her dreams.

> *O Western wind, when wilt thou blow,*
> *That the small rain down can rain?*
> *Christ, that my love were in my arms*
> *And I in my bed again!*

Chapter 23

Tuesday morning dawned gray and cold. The rains had tapered off, Manhattan's cloud cover seemed to be breaking up, and the weather bureau predicted partly sunny skies by noon.

Sigrid was not a morning person and seldom rose early by choice. The closer to dawn, the further under sleep seemed to take her. This morning she was drowsily aware of Oscar beside her but the pleasure of his hands and mouth upon her body were so much a continuation of the night that she was already half-aroused before she fully realized what was happening.

Afterwards she lay sleepily relaxed while Nauman showered and dressed.

Unfortunately, Nauman *was* a morning person and he sat on the edge of the bed, lifted the pillow from her face and said, "Breakfast?"

Sigrid peered past him to the clock on the bedside table. "What time is it?"

"Almost six. I have an eight o'clock appointment with a grad student. Omelet for you, or toast and coffee?"

Sigrid seldom ate breakfast, but she didn't want to send him away sooner than necessary. On the other hand, she suddenly remembered that breakfast would mean coping with Roman, that other early-morning enthusiast. She wasn't quite prepared to watch Roman scramble eggs or butter toast while he acted scrupulously nonchalant about her newly altered relationship with Nauman.

As if he'd read her mind, Nauman picked her robe off the floor by his side of the bed and handed it to her. "There's a coffee shop over on East Twenty-third that makes muffins with blueberries the size of marbles. I could go find my car and meet you out front in what? Ten minutes?"

"Make it fifteen and you've got a deal," she said, relieved. She started to push back the covers, hesitated beneath an abrupt attack of shyness, then made herself follow through on her first impulse.

Oscar watched her jerky stop-and-go hesitation in wry amusement. Someday, he thought, they might laugh about this moment, but he knew that now was not the time. It was enough that she had come this far. Push for too much, too fast and it could all come undone; so before her self-consciousness could drive a new wedge between them,

he dropped a kiss on her tousled hair and cleared out so
that she could dress in privacy.

The coffee shop was attached to a once grander, now
second-class hotel which clung forlornly to the shreds of its
original beauty. The spacious lobby cried out for fresh
paint and new carpets, for the banishment of the urethane
couches which had replaced velvet, for live holly or aromatic pine boughs in its gracefully proportioned marble
urns instead of dusty plastic poinsettias. The stuccoed
columns were chipped, the murals over the desk were
dingy and faded, and the beautiful central chandelier was
missing several crystal drops. Those that remained were
yellow with smoke and city grime.

The coffee shop itself needed a thorough scrubbing,
the blue vinyl of its tinsel-draped booths had been mended
with duct tape, and food arrived on ugly thick crockery;
but the food was freshly prepared on the premises, por-
tions were generous, and the two waitresses were cheerful
and quick.

The older woman was a comfortable peroxide blonde
who wore a sprig of artificial mistletoe on her blue-and-
white cap, spoke familiarly to her regular customers, and
called everyone "duckie."

Serving Sigrid and Oscar was a short chunky waitress
who looked young enough to be a high-school dropout and
who wore her uniform cap at a belligerent says-who? angle
atop orange-and-pink hair. Her eyebrows had been plucked
into thin arches, her half-inch-long fingernails were filed
to sharp points and painted black. On the limp white lapel
of her tight blue nylon uniform, she wore a button that
read "Anarch."

When the young woman set their steaming-hot blueberry muffins down on the table, Sigrid noticed that her
bracelet was a wide black leather band studded with steel
spikes. ("It probably began life as a dog collar for a two
hundred-pound mastiff," said Nauman.)

"Jam?" she chirped. "More butter? You could probably bathe in it and stay thin. I just look at butter and,
honey, it flies straight to my hips."

She bustled away to return in a few minutes with a tray of bacon and fried eggs for six Korean tourists who sat at a nearby table between the two rows of wall booths and who laughed and chattered merrily as they attacked their breakfast.

After her years of struggling with chopsticks, Sigrid was startled to see the flip side of East-West culture clash.

"You're staring," Nauman told her.

"I can't help it," she said and laughter bubbled in her voice.

"Aren't they just the cutest things?" asked their waitress *sotto voce* as she refilled their coffee cups. "It's their first trip to America and I think they're having a blast." She adjusted her spiked leather bracelet. "They don't talk much English though and I don't guess they're used to knives and forks over there."

The Koreans appeared oblivious to the covert glances of the other customers. Nor were they interested in copying the natives for the conventional application of western cutlery. Chattering and smiling, they moved food from plate to mouth with whichever utensil came to hand. One man had cut his fried egg into long narrow strips which he then draped over his knife and conveyed to his mouth. The woman beside him had balanced a crisp strip of bacon on the back of her fork, while an older man directly opposite dexterously buttered a piece of toast with his spoon.

"I'll never feel as stupid with chopsticks again," Sigrid told Oscar.

"Speaking of chopsticks," he said, "there's an exhibit of Chinese calligraphy opening at the Friedinger Museum tonight. Want to go?"

"Not really." She delicately picked up several buttery muffin crumbs with the tip of her moistened finger and ate them one at a time. "I have a court appearance this morning and if it runs into the afternoon, that'll put me behind on everything else. I'll probably be in bed by ten since you woke me so early."

"Early and often," he said solemnly, then gave her a playfully rakish leer.

Feeling unexpectedly frisky, Sigrid leered right back and was amused by his surprised expression.

Despite the Assistant District Attorney's assurances to the contrary, it was midafternoon before Sigrid escaped from the courtroom. As far as she was concerned the case was open-and-shut. The defendant, a successful podiatrist, had severely beaten his much-younger wife several times and threatened to kill her if she left. She had and he did—in front of three impartial eyewitnesses which included his own sister. His lawyer seemed to be shaping a two-pronged defense: one based on the defendant's battered childhood, the other on minute technicalities related to the way Sigrid and her homicide team had handled the initial investigation.

"What can I tell you?" said the A.D.A. during the recess called immediately after Sigrid had icily fended off all the attacks on her team's competency. "He's got to do something to justify billing a hundred-twenty an hour."

"Starting to feel as if you're standing on the wrong side of the courtroom?" Sigrid asked her.

"Nope. Somebody's got to make it unprofitable for macho podiatrists to bash their wives and it might as well be me." The A.D.A. crushed her cigarette in a sand urn, gave Sigrid a half-salute, and headed back inside.

Rather than return to the office, where the paperwork on other, more routine homicides piled up on her desk, Sigrid checked her notebook and remembered that she had planned to question the brother of a floater who had been pulled from the river yesterday with a bullet in his head and the fingers of his right hand chopped off. Early indications were that he had been a numbers runner with sticky fingers. The brother's address was located close to the 8th-AV-8 Theater, so she would have plenty of time to interview him before the Pennewelf children were likely to be home from school.

Although the brother appeared to be a fairly law-abiding citizen, he spoke knowledgeably and bitterly about the dead youth's criminal connections. Even more importantly, he was angry and grieved enough to name names.

The whole interview, including the phone call Sigrid made to send Peters and Eberstadt out to question those names, took less than fifteen minutes and she arrived at the hardware store owned by the Pennewelfs' grandfather only to learn that the children weren't expected for almost an hour. The older man made it quite clear that he'd allow her to talk to them if she felt it necessary, but not without himself present.

"I shall be glad for your help," Sigrid told him truthfully although she would much rather have Tillie. Mick Cluett's interviewing skills were likely to remain unknown to her, since he had called in sick again this morning.

The theater appeared virtually deserted when Sigrid arrived. The front door was unlocked but no vigilant parent appeared to challenge her since there were no dance classes scheduled for that afternoon. Sigrid walked through the shadowy auditorium and found lights on in the office, Nate Richmond's workshop, and Helen Delgado's two workrooms; but no one was there, not even in the green room.

As she mounted the wooden stairs, she heard voices from the women's dressing room. Inside, Nate Richmond and Helen Delgado were standing by the pipe clothing racks with a large cardboard box and appeared to have just begun sorting through the personal effects Emmy Mion had left behind.

"I got a phone call from California about an hour ago," Helen Delgado told Sigrid. "Her family's arranged for her to be buried in California and they asked if we'd go through her things, dispose of her clothes, and just send home the personal stuff."

Today the designer wore her hair in loose swirls over an almost subdued purple shirt that was cinched at her thick waist with an intricately knotted belt of faux pearls and purple satin cords. Mauve mascara shadowed her eyes, but for the first time, her ears were bare.

As she spoke, she removed a heavy black wool coat from a hanger, checked the pockets, discarded a tissue left there since last winter, folded the coat neatly, and handed it to Nate Richmond, who placed it in the cardboard box.

"We thought we'd give her clothes to that shelter for the homeless over on Tenth Avenue," he said. "Emmy was so small, there's no one here can wear many of her things. The leg warmers perhaps. That's about it."

There was a pasty tone to his skin today that aged his elfin face even more than the crinkled lines already there.

He would probably look like this when he was ninety, thought Sigrid, watching as he shook out a thick woolen jacket of red plaid.

"Hey, this is mine," Nate said. "I was wondering where it got to. I haven't seen it since last winter."

"Really?" Helen answered absently. "I think Emmy was wearing it Saturday morning. Remember? She was a little chilly and didn't want to put on the heat. She probably had it hanging here all summer. Or Rikki. You know how they borrow everybody's clothes."

Nate put the jacket on over his blue turtleneck sweater. "At least it doesn't smell of mothballs."

"Yeah, I caught a whiff of David, too," Helen laughed and, seeing Sigrid's puzzled look, explained, "David Orland's mother packs everything in mothballs. You could really tell that summer was over when he walked in Sunday."

She hesitated over a final winter garment, an outsized blue cable-knit cardigan. "Wonder if this is hers or Ginger's?"

Nate shrugged. "I think I've seen Rikki in it, but like you say—the way they borrow each other's clothes . . ."

"I'll leave it for now," Helen decided and moved over to the dressing counter where she began to remove things from the two drawers Emmy Mion had used.

"There was a locket that belonged to her grandmother," said Nate. "And an amethyst bracelet." He looked around helplessly.

"They're probably in her suitcases," Helen suggested. "Eric brought them over this morning."

The two matched pieces of luggage were of sturdy brown leather and looked quite expensive.

"Her aunt gave her these for graduation," Nate said sadly and Sigrid quietly watched him open the cases.

Inside the first were underthings, T-shirts, two pairs of sandals, a pair of red sequined pumps, an extra pair of sneakers, and some toilet articles. Inside the other were jeans, a couple of skirts and dresses, some knit shirts and sweaters, a manila envelope that appeared to be stuffed with letters and miscellaneous scraps of paper, and a small satin bag that held the locket and bracelet Nate had mentioned plus a thin gold chain and a silver ring.

Not very much for a six-month stay with one's lover, thought Sigrid, leafing through the folder but finding nothing that seemed to connect to Mion's death.

"She kept most of her papers downstairs," said Helen. "Bills, bank records, stuff like that. I guess we'll have to go through those, too."

Her plump hands had almost finished efficiently sorting Emmy's things. Out of both drawers, Helen saved only a string of glass beads, a little heart-shaped brass box, a 35-mm camera (no film), a pearl-handled pocket knife, and a small hinged frame that held the pictures of an older man and woman.

"Her aunt and uncle," said Nate. "They raised her."

"We'll pack everything in the suitcases," Helen decided and Nate carefully transferred all the clothes from the cases to the shelter box except for the red sequined pumps.

"Emmy wore these in the last production we did out in L.A.," he said wistfully.

Helen patted his thin arm and her dark eyes were liquid with compassion. "Want to keep them, doll?"

He shook his head, but instead of sending them to the shelter, he left them in the suitcase along with the manila envelope Sigrid had handed back and the trinkets Helen had salvaged.

Downstairs was more complicated.

"Paper always takes more deciding than cloth," sighed Helen. She brushed her black hair away from her face and pulled open the bottom drawer of the file cabinet. Inside

were two brown envelopes of heavy kraft paper, their flaps
secured by attached elastic cords. One envelope held
Emmy's personal correspondence, old playbills, ticket stubs
and the like. The other was stuffed with her canceled
checks, receipts, insurance papers, and tax forms.

Sigrid asked to see them and, seated at the desk, she
was again struck by the duality of the dead woman's
character. The personal papers had been crammed in
helter-skelter; documents in the other envelope had been
inserted in chronological order with dividers to separate
one category from another. Again, nothing leapt to Sigrid's
appraising eyes.

In a looping scrawl, Emmy Mion had written checks
for regularly occurring bills or for small amounts of cash.
Her savings account totaled $863.79, her checking account
$230, and she appeared to owe $122 on her Visa card. No
unusual deposits or withdrawals.

Most of the letters appeared to be from Mion's aunt.
They spoke of the weather, loneliness, and a concern for
Emmy's health and safety so far away.

Sigrid returned them to Nate, who stowed them in
one of the brown leather suitcases.

"What about her books and notebooks?" Helen asked
him.

Nate stood before the bookcase wedged tightly with
Emmy's dance books and seemed to hunch his thin shoulders into the plaid jacket. "I say send home the notebooks
and sell the rest."

"We ought to keep what she's already done for Christmas, though, shouldn't we?" asked Helen, lifting the
pages on the drawing table.

Abruptly she seemed to notice Nate's increasing past-
iness. Stricken, she said, "Hey, listen, doll. Why don't you
let Auntie Helen finish here and you go fix us a nice hot
cup of tea?"

Gratefully, he acquiesced and left the two women
alone.

"I keep forgetting how long a history he had with
Emmy," said Helen, swiftly pulling notebooks and two
bulging scrapbooks from the shelf, then sweeping Emmy's
drawing pens into a neat handful, which she bound with a

rubber band and placed in the suitcase. She unpinned three of the best pictures of Emmy, sandwiched them between the notebooks, and added them to the suitcase.

In less time than Sigrid would have guessed, Helen finished her selection of the things she thought the aunt might like to have. There was only enough to fill one suitcase.

"Emmy always said she traveled light," said Helen, zipping both bags and flipping the latches shut. "Tea, Lieutenant?"

"Later, perhaps," Sigrid said. She leaned against one of the bookcases with one hand in the pocket of her jacket, the other loosely holding her notebook. "Just now I have a few questions."

"I rather thought you might," said Helen with a mock groan. Her purple shirt had bloused up over her belt while she packed Emmy's things and she drew in her stomach and pulled the shirt taut again. "Rubber hose time?"

"Actually it was Mr. Delgado I wanted to see," Sigrid said coolly, "but he doesn't seem to be around."

"He's taken a part-time job at Bloomingdale's. Pre-Christmas sales. Only fifty-two more shopping days, you know." Helen twisted the ends of her corded belt and her eyes were wary. "What did you mean to ask Cliff?"

"Part of the routine in many homicide cases consists of running the names of the people involved through our computers," Sigrid said. "When I got to the office this morning, I found that your husband's name had popped out. Assault and battery against a female dancer four years ago. I believe he drew a fine and a suspended sentence?"

"One isolated act," snapped Helen. "She was an irritating little no-talent who had the hots for Cliff and when he turned her down, she tried to become the *prima ballerina* with him. Unfortunately, she had lead in her shoes and about the fifth time she made him mess up, he slapped her."

"The report said something about stitches over her eye," Sigrid said. "It must have been a rather hard slap."

"That part was an accident. Cliff was wearing one of those tacky junk rings—I think he was supposed to be dancing the part of a prince or something—and it caught her on the bony edge of her brow. Half an inch either way and he wouldn't have marked her. Honest."

Helen dropped the ends of her belt and her voice deepened with intensity. "Cliff has a temper—I don't deny it. But in the six years we've been married that's the only time he's used his hand on someone instead of his mouth."

Unnoticed by either woman, Nate Richmond had reappeared in the doorway. His face was still drawn and gray. "Tea's ready if you people are," he said wearily.

Chapter 24

Despite her refusals, Nate Richmond brought Sigrid a cup of boiling-hot tea anyway. "No lemon," he apologized, as he set it on the desk in front of her, "and our milk's gone sour—no one thought to buy fresh—but I brought you some packets of sugar. Or would you prefer some of Win's wild honey?"

"This is fine, thanks," said Sigrid, "but you really needn't have bothered."

"No bother." He hesitated by her desk, absently fingering the thin gold ring in his ear. His gnome-like face was solicitous. "Unless you're not allowed to?"

"I beg your pardon?"

"Not allowed to eat or drink anything with the suspects' families? Is that still one of the police rules?"

"I don't think anyone would object to a cup of tea," Sigrid said.

"Anyhow, Helen and I will be in the green room if you need anything."

Left alone again, Sigrid absently stirred the sugar into her cup and considered Nate Richmond's words. She hadn't thought of it before, but yes, she supposed the troupe did form the equivalent of a family—the way they ran in and out of one another's rooms, borrowed without asking, defended, scolded, argued, cosseted. Helen Delgado was like the company's mother, nurturing and earthy; Cliff the unruly bad-boy; Eric Kee the responsible older brother; Wingate West the idle dreamer; while Ginger Judson could be the bratty youngest daughter and Ulrike Innes the sensitive older sister who loyally guards the secrets of the younger ones from parental judgment.

But what role for Nate Richmond? The household's ageless brownie? Spirit of the hearth, or bachelor uncle who creeps down to his basement workbench in carpet slippers?

And who was Emmy Mion?

The father, Sigrid decided, sipping the steaming tea. An easygoing tolerant *paterfamilias* so long as everyone acted responsibly, but also a moralist who would have been at home in a pulpit, according to Helen Delgado. The decision-maker and maker of rules, the drawer of lines. This far and no further, my children, or Papa will spank.

Where had Emmy found Amanda Gillespie's missing hair ribbon and what thoughts had gone through her mind at that moment? She must not have been sure it was Amanda's, though, for she had called Amanda's mother to verify its identity.

They said she was distracted that morning. That she had fought or not fought with both Eric and Ginger, depending upon whose version one believed. Yet she had sensed no danger from her "family." She must have recognized her killer the moment he stepped upon the stage for, according to Ginger at least, she had laughed at the jack-o'-lantern's movements (even though, again according to Ginger, he had done nothing funny at that point) and she had trusted him to hold her safely at the soaring climax of their dance.

If Tillie were here, he would probably have drawn up one of his incredibly detailed timetables with every person's movements carefully charted.

So, okay, Sigrid told herself as she spread her notes on the desktop. Let's do a Tillie on Emmy Mion and see where it gets us.

She found a ruled legal pad and wrote at the top *Saturday a.m.—Emmy Mion*, drew a heavy line, and

began directly underneath with Emmy's arrival at the
theater. Right away she ran into problems. Nowhere in her
notes could she find a reference to the exact time Emmy
had arrived that morning. According to Helen Delgado,
she'd slipped on Nate's jacket, so she was probably one of
the first ones to arrive, before the night chill was off the
building.

And why start with Saturday anyhow when there
were earlier incidents that might have meaning?

By the time she'd pulled all the bits and pieces
together, Sigrid's original timetable was scribbled over
with circles, arrows, interlineations, and two or three
versions of the same story. She tore out the sheet and
copied the main points neatly. It took longer to write out
than she'd expected and when she'd finished, the chart
lacked Tillie's prolix precision; but at least it helped her
spot the points that needed further clarification:

Winter—Emmy Mion living w/David Orland.
February—Amanda Gillespie killed.
Spring—EM living w/Eric Kee.
Friday a.m., Oct. 30—David O. runs into EM who says
    she's moving out of Eric K.'s & will move in w/Ginger
    J. or into the theater. Seems happy & unworried.
                Saturday, Oct. 31
 ?—EM arrives at theater w/some of her clothes.
10–11 a.m.—Run-through rehearsal.
11–11:15 ?—EM checks lighting cues w/Nate R., then to
    Helen D.'s workroom where Helen adjusts EM's dress
    & notices EM's preoccupation; puts it down to
    performance.
"sometime around noon"—EM calls Mrs. Gillespie, leaves
    message referring to "something of Amanda's."
"a little before noon"—Ulrike I. calls Nate to lunch, finds
    EM there who declines to join them as she's expecting
    a phone call. Nate says she came for some old pics of
    Mon. dance class. [NB—Amanda G.'s class? And where
    are those pics? Was that why EM's desk ransacked?
    Or had someone sought the ribbon?]
"a little past noon"—Eric K. lunches w/EM in office. Says

EM preoccupied, as if working something out in her mind.

12:45 p.m. +/—*Eric & EM have words. Overheard by Ulrike I. & Ginger J. EM joins them in women's dressing rm.*

12:45–1:45/50?—*EM in dressing rm. w/Ulrike & Ginger. Tells Ginger she will not move in w/her but will live alone. Ginger rushes downstairs—she says to find the jack-o'-lantern head which Eric took; Ulrike thinks because she was hurt & angry over EM's announcement.* [NB—*Ginger says Eric wore her head on Sat. She left the replacement under her chair but it'd been kicked out under the spiral steps sometime during the afternoon after the murder. Deliberately?*]

1:55 p.m.—*EM stands at top of wooden stairs as other 5 dancers prepare to go on. Blows a kiss, wishes them luck. No one admits speaking to her after that.*

1:55 p.m.—*David O. seen entering auditorium.*

2:00 p.m.—*performance begins. Ensemble dances approx. 8 minutes.*

2:02 p.m.—*David O. leaves auditorium. Tried to make phone call from corner. No verification of precise time.*

2:08 p.m.—*Ensemble exits stage left.*

GINGER: *says she saw Eric, Win, & Ulrike go upstairs, Cliff down the hall, she to her place between curtains. Saw only S. Avril. Saw killer enter from Eric's spot.*

ERIC: *says Win to men's dressing rm., he to lavatory, then to office for his hood, then to his place stage right center as Emmy mounted scaffold. Saw Win's life-size puppet, no one else.*

WIN: *says he went to dressing rm., then to his place upstage right as Emmy being lifted. Saw no one else.*

ULRIKE: *says Eric to lavatory, Win to dressing rm., did not see Cliff. To her dressing rm., then downstairs, Win not in place. Crossed between wall & screen to her place upstage left. Saw Ginger sitting as if mesmerized. No one else.*

CLIFF: *got water, went to john, then immediately to his place downstage right. Saw Ginger seated enthralled*

> *directly across, no one else. Angered that killer in-*
> *truded on EM's solo, thinks either Eric or someone*
> *mimicking Eric.*
>
> 2:09 p.m.—*EM begins solo.*
> 2:12?—*Killer enters from Eric's position disguised by jack-*
> *o'-lantern head. According to witnesses, probably*
> *onstage less than 2 mins.*
> 2:14 p.m. +/—*Killer throws EM onto spiked fence. Death*
> *almost instant. Lights doused. Killer exits in dark.*

Constructing a workable timetable wasn't quite as
productive as completing a diagramless crossword puzzle,
Sigrid decided. Disconsolately, she stared at it but no
orderly pattern revealed itself. Nothing to suggest why
that morning of all mornings Emmy Mion should suddenly
stumble across Amanda Gillespie's ribbon. She had arrived at the theater, rehearsed, worked with Nate on the
lighting, let Helen alter her dress, and then called Mrs.
Gillespie. Did that mean she'd found the ribbon in Nate's
workshop? In Helen's?

But she hadn't been sure, so even though she'd called
Mrs. Gillespie, she'd also gone back to Nate's for pictures,
pictures that probably contained a view of Amanda's hair
ribbons.

The Pennewelf children had been in the theater that
morning and must have seen Emmy with Amanda's picture. "Emmy yelled about her," the little girl had said.

Yelled at whom?

Someone she trusted? Someone who told her, "No,
that can't be Mandy's ribbon. You know me, Emmy. You
know I wouldn't hurt a child"?

And because she trusted, or maybe because they
were both due to go onstage so soon and she could not risk
the performance, she had let him allay her doubts enough
to keep silent until she could prove it one way or the other.

But he had known that once she was sure, she would
not keep quiet. That strict sense of right and wrong of
which everyone spoke would have had her dialing 911 the
instant she confirmed it.

No one had seen David Orland in the theater that day

until minutes before the performance began so it seemed unlikely that Emmy could have confronted him with the ribbon.

Eric Kee, Cliff Delgado, Wingate West. It had to be one of those three.

A little girl had died. A little girl who liked to cuddle and touch and be hugged, but whose mother swore she knew the difference between affection and molestation and would have told if she'd been sexually fondled.

Assume she had, thought Sigrid, her pen doodling question marks around Amanda's name. Assume she'd been frightened by the betrayal of trust and had run from the theater, only to be caught just steps from the safety of her apartment building.

Eric Kee. Cliff Delgado. Wingate West.

If the answer lay in her timetable, Sigrid couldn't see it. Maybe she needed Tillie's mountains of extraneous detail after all.

And yet . . .

Something did glimmer there among the entries. A niggling little point or two which clumped around an alternate theory that was totally illogical. And yet . . .

Sigrid lifted the cup to her lips and discovered that her tea was completely cold.

How convenient, she thought. Returning her notes and papers to her briefcase, she picked up the cup and walked down to the green room.

Helen Delgado was alone there and she looked up guiltily from a thick wedge of German chocolate cake as Sigrid opened the door.

"Caught me," she said. "I tell everyone it's glands or genes, but it's really just plain old gluttony. I love to eat. Freud could probably tell you why."

"Do you think he actually knew?"

"Vot do vomen really vant?" Helen said, savoring a bite of frosting.

Sigrid knew quite well what Freud thought women wanted but she didn't intend to enter upon a bawdy conversation with this woman.

Helen Delgado laughed hugely at the expression on Sigrid's face. "Well, of *course* all women want *that*, doll!

But Freud's a jerk if he thought we wanted it permanently attached."

"May I have another cup of tea?" Sigrid said austerely, moving toward the stove.

"Sure, help yourself," said the other woman, amused. "Want some cake, too? There's plenty."

"No, thank you." Sigrid busied herself rinsing out the cup and procuring another tea bag, and as she waited for the kettle to boil, she asked, "I wonder if you could tell me approximately when Emmy Mion got here Saturday morning?"

The designer paused with her loaded fork in midair. "About eight-thirty or nine o'clock, I guess. Nine's when I got here and I don't think she was much before that. She hadn't turned on all the lights." The fork continued its journey to her full lips.

"And the others?"

"Everyone was here by nine-thirty, but I couldn't tell you who came when. Wait a minute! Nate and Rikki didn't get here till almost ten. He had to wait for the hardware store next door to open. He needed some screws or something. Rikki came on in after we'd finished breakfast and I guess the others had been here at least a half-hour by then."

The kettle whistled and Sigrid refilled her cup. "And to the best of your knowledge, Emmy Mion first appeared preoccupied, as you described it, when?"

"Not during breakfast." Helen finished the cake and stood heavily, pulling down her purple shirt before moving to the sink with that unexpected gracefulness to wash her plate. "She was laughing and talking, keyed up like everyone else; but when I saw her after the run-through, she was—I don't know—quiet. Withdrawn. Preoccupied."

"Who likes the children more than they should?" Sigrid asked abruptly.

"*What?*"

"I said—"

"I *heard* what you said, Lieutenant Harald! I just don't know what the hell you mean!"

"Don't you?" Sigrid stood placidly, stirring sugar into her steaming cup, as she waited for the other to reply.

Helen banged the dishes into the sink, then out into

the drain rack before answering. "That's a hell of a thing to accuse a children's theater of. We all like kids or we wouldn't be in this end of show business, would we? That doesn't make us pedophiles."

She slammed down the dish towel. "Do you think we'd stand for something like that?"

"No," Sigrid said calmly. "Not collectively. But if someone among you kept it secret and hidden—"

"No! No! *No!* How long do you think something like that could be hidden? We live in each other's pockets."

They faced each other across the length of the table and Sigrid said, "Emmy Mion found the Gillespie child's missing hair ribbon."

It took a moment for the import of Sigrid's statement to sink in, then Helen Delgado's plump face was drained of all natural color, leaving behind mauve eyelids and lips that were now a ghastly shade of plum against the whiteness of her face.

"Oh, my God," she whispered and held onto the table for support.

Sigrid hurried to slide a chair beneath her. "I'd prefer you didn't mention this to any of the others yet."

"Of course, of course," Helen murmured brokenly.

Sigrid brought her a glass of water and was relieved to see the color begin to creep back into the woman's face.

"So that's why Emmy was killed," she said. "I was so afraid that Cliff—" She clutched at Sigrid's hand. "You know about Cliff's temper, but I swear to you he'd never hurt a child. Or touch one in that way. It takes a sexy woman to turn him on. Always has. Before I got so fat—before he started catting around—which came first?" she asked bitterly. "The tomcat or the pig?"

Sigrid freed her hand. "What about Eric Kee or Wingate West, then?"

"Win is like a child himself when he plays with them. He's so gentle and sweet. And Eric? No, not Eric. Emmy must have been mistaken."

"Emmy's dead," Sigrid reminded her, but Helen Delgado could not be budged from her position.

Suddenly remembering that she had a spy in Canaan,

Sigrid let it go. "There's another point of confusion, Mrs. Delgado. The jack-o'-lantern heads. Ginger Judson insists that Eric Kee wore hers on Saturday, but Ulrike Innes said they were identical."

"Rikki's right. They are. Ginger always goes off half-cocked," said Delgado. She sipped more water and smoothed her glossy black hair. "I heard she was accusing someone of hiding it on her, under the spiral steps. As if anyone would sabotage the production like that. She probably left it by her chair and in all the confusion, it got kicked aside. Like my paint mask."

"Ah, yes, that paint mask," said Sigrid. "Did you ever find the missing strap?"

"Yes, Roman Tramegra turned it up in the john down the hall."

"You thought your husband took it?"

Helen Delgado looked at her warily. "So?"

"No reason. I was just curious as to why he would have. What was he painting?"

Helen managed a shadow of her usually raucous laughter. "Not painting, doll. Clowning. Cliff could turn a crucifix into a phallic symbol if he put his mind to it. My mask is almost the same size and shape as a medieval codpiece. Use your imagination and see where it takes you."

"I see," said Sigrid. She glanced at her watch and saw that it was almost six. The Pennewelf children!

She impressed on Helen Delgado the need to remain silent about Emmy Mion's hypothetical suspicions concerning the Gillespie child and hurried from the theater.

But once again, she found herself peering futilely into a locked and darkened hardware store.

Chapter 25

Personal notes of Dr. Christa Ferrell, re: Corrie Makaroff
[Tuesday, 3 November—Success! Anne Harald called to

say the first pix look good & that she'll probably definitely
use the Makaroff case to illustrate the Social Services part
of her series. I can't push Corrie too hard, but I didn't
think it would hurt to speed things along. Accordingly, I
called Mrs. Berkowitz this morning; told her I thought we
ought to intensify & that I'd fit Corrie in for an extra
session this afternoon.]

When Corrie returned today, Mrs. Berkowitz was very
distressed. "She seems to be backsliding, Dr. Ferrell. She wet
the bed last night. She hasn't done that since school began.
And she wouldn't talk to Tanya last night or this morning."

I reassured Mrs. Berkowitz that such regression often
signals an inner turmoil that might foretell a major breakthrough and she immediately brightened. "Do you really
think so?"

[NB—the adoption's being held up until I give Corrie
a clean bill of mental health & everyone hopes it will come
soon.]

"Tanya says that as soon as the judge gives her to us,
she wants to call Lyle and me Daddy and Mother," Mrs.
B. confided. "Isn't that wonderful?"

She stood there in my waiting room, in her neat wool
skirt and practical flat shoes, with pride and wonder on
her thin face. She already has one daughter of her dreams,
and I am determined that she shall soon have a second
daughter well and whole.

Since I've begun seeing her, Corrie has lost the rest
of her baby fat and has grown an extra inch in height. This
November day, she wore blue plastic boots, bright blue
stretch pants, and a white pullover with a flower appliquéd
on her tummy. Her curly brown hair was held away from
either side of her face with little flower-shaped plastic bar-
rettes but she seemed wan despite a lingering summer tan.

I took a chance today and prepared the scene before
she came. The G.I. Joe and Barbie dolls that represented
Ray and Darlene lay on the low hassock with the "sisters"
on a nearby chair. I had found a miniature toy hammer
and I placed it on the floor by the hassock in plain view.

At four years old, Corrie understood very well that

Darlene's "ginger ale" wasn't a soft drink; and from the baby doll play I've observed these past few months, I know that she and Tanya tried to keep Darlene from drinking too much. They knew alcohol distorted her personality.

So we sat down beside the toys in our usual position and talked about how people sometimes said or did things they really didn't mean.

"Like sometimes you and Tonnie squabble and maybe you even say ugly things to each other but later wish you hadn't."

Corrie looked at the little bear sitting so close to the schoolgirl doll.

"Grown-ups do the same thing," I said. "They may wish afterwards that they hadn't and then it's too late."

Keeping my voice as casual as possible, I said, "I'll bet even Ray and your mommy used to yell things to each other at times."

Corrie scooted away from my side and spent most of the session curled up in the wing chair with those two figures that represented Tanya and herself. She mimicked a few skirmishes between the bear and the schoolgirl, but her blue-green eyes kept darting over to the hassock. When it was time to return the toys to the shelves, she put away the Barbie doll but did not offer to touch either the G.I. Joe or the hammer.

But I can feel it in my bones. Inside that small head, *something's happening!*

[Called Anne H. after Corrie left & told her that tomorrow's session would probably be the climactic one— that I have Corrie poised for the catharsis which must precede reintegration. Should make for wonderful photographs.]

Chapter 26

Hoping to forestall one of Roman's incredible inedibles, Sigrid stopped at a crowded deli on Hudson Street and stood in line to order a roast chicken, macaroni salad, and a quarter-pound of fresh mushrooms while a local easy-listening radio station broadcast premature Christmas carols for the less-than-merry clientele around her. When she got home, however, she found Roman amid pots and pans in a kitchen redolent of sauerkraut, smoked pork, and German sausages.

"A *Berner Platte* stretches so *nicely*," he said, busying himself with the oven. "Two can be served generously or three moderately. And if Oscar's coming—"

His voice trailed off and he seemed unable to meet her eyes.

His self-consciousness fueled Sigrid's.

"He isn't," she said. "There was an opening at the Friedinger and I thought I'd make it an early night."

"—since last night was so busy?" hung unspoken in the green-and-white kitchen.

Sigrid dumped her cartons on the tiled countertop. "Mushrooms," she croaked. "Salad. But *Berner Platte's* a great idea. We can save the chicken for tomorrow."

She unbuttoned her raincoat and went out into the vestibule to hang it beside Roman's.

"Ale?" asked Roman, setting out bottles and two beer steins. "Or do you want something more full-bodied? I mean, something more *stimulating*? I mean—" His face registered horror at his clumsiness.

"Ale's fine," she answered tersely and withdrew to freshen up and, with a little luck, give Roman time to bring his adjectives under control. She hung up her jacket, put her blouse in the laundry hamper, and changed into a dark red turtleneck sweater, which she'd bought because it was comfortably loose and knitted of plain thick wool. That its rich warm color flattered her own coloring was an unsought bonus.

As she came back down the hall, the gate bell rang. Sigrid pressed the intercom button. "Yes?"

"It's me, honey," said Anne Harald's disembodied voice.

Sigrid buzzed the lock release and, peering through the darkness, saw her mother maneuver through the gate with a large flat box.

"I thought you and Roman might be in the mood for pizza," she said gaily as Sigrid opened the door. An aroma of olive oil, garlic, and oregano wafted in with the chill night air.

"A *party!*" Roman exclaimed. "What fun!"

He kissed Anne heartily upon the cheek, relieved her of the pizza, and immediately popped half of it into the microwave to reheat. "We can begin in Napoli and wind up in Bern. Now the *only* decision, *mes petites*, is should we stay with ale or switch to Chianti?"

Ale won unanimously and Sigrid set the table while Anne filled their glasses and Roman brought the first half-pizza to the table in great ceremony. Sigrid drank deeply and was beginning to relax when the gate bell rang again.

"Now who—?" wondered Roman. "Sit, sit, my dear. I'll get it."

He went out to the intercom and they heard his deep "Yes?" An instant later, he stuck his head in the door and hissed, "Sst! It's *Oscar!*" before hurrying back to open the front door.

Anne glanced at Sigrid in amusement. "Why did that sound like 'Fly! All is discovered!'?"

"God knows," Sigrid said, apprehensively taking another swallow of her ale as she heard Nauman's baritone mingle with Roman's bass.

"Guess what Oscar brought?" Roman boomed. "Moussaka and baklava."

"How sweet," murmured Anne.

Nauman added his coat to the collection building in the hall and joined them looking blown and buffeted by the wind. "I couldn't get the top of my car to stay up," he complained. "Hello, Anne."

She smiled up at him and gave him her cheek to kiss.

"I thought you were going to an opening tonight," said Sigrid, willing herself not to redden under her mother's watchful eye.

"Decided against it. Hope you don't mind?"

"Not at all," she said stiffly and rose to set another place for him.

"What opening?" asked Anne and while Oscar explained

about Chinese calligraphy, Roman looked at the table critically. "All we need are some egg rolls or won ton soup and we could be the UN."

"We could eat with chopsticks," Anne suggested with a mischievous glance at Sigrid.

"No, we couldn't," said her daughter.

Which reminded Oscar of the Koreans that morning and he proceeded to make a witty and visual tale of their inventive use of western tableware.

"You went *out* for blueberry muffins?" blurted Roman. "But that was what *I* planned to make for breakfast."

Anne's hand froze in midair and melted mozzarella slid off the piece of pizza she was serving Oscar. Her eyes, so similar to Sigrid's in color if not in size, darted from Sigrid's face to Oscar's and back to Sigrid's again.

"Is that for me?" Oscar asked mildly.

"Hm? Oh. The pizza. Yes," said Anne. "Siga, honey, I'm afraid I've got pizza all over your tablecloth. Isn't this one my mama gave you? If you'll get a damp cloth—" She looked confidingly at Oscar as Sigrid seized the excuse to leave the table. "You know the nicest thing about pure linen is that you *can* bleach it if you have to. Not like polyester. Of course, lemon juice and sunshine—thanks, honey. I'll just sponge the worst of it."

Doing his own bit to smooth over the awkwardness, Roman chose that moment to bring in his succulent *Berner Platte* in its earthenware casserole dish. He set it in the center of the table and removed the heavy lid with a dramatic flourish.

"*Voila!*"

Unfortunately for the effect he wished to create, the cooked sauerkraut had shrunk away from the surface of the dish to reveal two large white potatoes. Nestled between those rounded shapes was a swollen pink knackwurst.

There was a moment of stunned silence, then Anne began to giggle.

"Oh dear!" said Roman, fumbling for something with which to stir the dish as Oscar threw back his head and hooted with laughter.

Sigrid rolled her eyes in resignation. "Maybe we should have put a notice in the *Daily News*."

*   *   *

Roman's dinners were always long and boisterous and
by the time he had divided three pieces of baklava between four dessert plates and was ready to pour coffee, it
was almost ten and conversation was long since back to
normal. Anne and Oscar had fought to a draw the question
of whether photography should be taken seriously as an
art—Oscar for, Anne against, Sigrid and Roman abstaining;
Roman raved about a current book on the best-seller
lists—Sigrid and Oscar had both disliked it intensely but
for radically different reasons which devolved into a
subdebate; and Anne passed around the contact prints of
some of the pictures she'd taken for the *New York Today*
series which was scheduled to begin in January.

"You were right about Christa Ferrell," she told Sigrid.
"She's wonderfully photogenic."

The individual pictures on the proof sheet weren't
much bigger than commemorative postage stamps and
Roman set the coffee tray on the end of the table and
brought out a large magnifying glass in order to see better.
Oscar slipped on his reading glasses.

"This is an old schoolmate?" he asked. "She's quite
lovely."

Telling herself that she was being stupid, that Nauman
certainly didn't mean to be tactless and that he wasn't
necessarily drawing comparisons, Sigrid rose to set the
cups around the table for Roman and to distribute the
baklava.

"Likes herself, doesn't she?" Oscar commented as
Anne described the case.

"You noticed that, too?" asked Anne. "I thought maybe it was just me."

Absurdly, Sigrid's heart lifted and she looked over
their shoulders at the contact prints.

"No one sits on a low chair with her skirt draped like
that unless she knows she has perfect legs," said Nauman.

"And she made sure that she was either full-face or
three-quarter profile during the whole session, even when
she had the little girl on her lap. See there? See how she
never quite lets the child's face block hers?" Anne looked

up at Sigrid. "I don't know about your friend, honey.
There's just something about her that puts me off and I
don't mean only the way she thinks she's going to come
out looking so good in the article."

"Have you changed your mind about using her?"

"No-o-o," Anne drawled thoughtfully. "The pictures
are good, the story's dramatic, and she's promised me
fireworks tomorrow. I don't walk away from a story just
because I don't like one of the people."

"Fireworks?" queried Roman as he began to pour the
coffee.

"The little girl there saw her mother killed by her
lover last summer but she's been blocking it out of her
mind ever since then," Anne explained. "Dr. Ferrell
seems to think that tomorrow may be the day she unblocks."

Sigrid handed the contact prints back to her mother.
The close-ups of little Corrie Makaroff reminded her of
Nate Richmond's photographs and she described them to
Anne. "He does the lights at the dance theater Roman's
connected with, but he's also a very gifted photographer."

Roman nodded enthusiastically. "Sheer *magic*, Anne!
His portraits of the children would break your heart with
their innocence. Everyone there *likes* the children, of
course, but *Nate's* relationship with them is quite special.
He *becomes* a child when he works with them."

"Peter Pan?" asked Nauman as his fork shattered the
multilayered Greek pastry.

"With a dash of Lewis Carroll thrown in for good
measure," Sigrid said, passing the sugar bowl to Anne.

"The Reverend Charles Dodgson." Anne stirred a
heaping spoonful of sugar into her coffee and added cream
as well. "He photographed children, too. No, not what
you're thinking. Did I sound lascivious? I'm sure it was
quite Victorian and proper. The mamas were always present."

"The Victorians were a curious race," said Nauman, a
propos of nothing that Sigrid could see, so she smiled at
him.

"The mamas may not always be present when Nate
snaps their children," Roman said, "but they *love* the
results. One father bought ten different poses of his two
kids. Makes a nice little sideline for the theater."

"What about the other men?" asked Sigrid.

"You mean the dancers?" Roman smoothed several strands of sandy brown hair across the high dome of his head. "What about them?"

For Anne and Nauman's benefit, Sigrid briefly described Emmy Mion's death and the people involved, embellished by Roman's eyewitness account of her last moments. Roman was astounded to hear that Emmy must have suspected one of the troupe of murdering the Gillespie child, and the other two were drawn into theorizing about the case quite unwittingly. Although Nauman had twice seen Sigrid in action, she seldom discussed her work with him; and, like Anne, he would have preferred her in a safer profession.

But both had read accounts of the young dancer's dramatic death and one of Nauman's students at Vanderlyn was a friend of Ginger Judson's, so they were already familiar with the broad outlines and were interested in having it explained to them how one member of a dance troupe could kill another onstage, in front of an audience, and not be recognized.

"I vote for the costume designer and her husband," said Oscar. "Masks? Hoods? Pumpkin heads? She designed the perfect disguise and he carried out the murder."

"Why?" Sigrid demanded.

He shrugged. "I don't do whys, I just do hows."

"Unfortunately, the D.A.'s office insists that I give them whys, too," Sigrid told him.

"I must admit, dear Sigrid," said Roman, "that it's vastly more difficult to question one's friends about homicide than utter strangers."

"The Gillespie child," said Anne, hewing to cause and effect. "Could she perhaps have been killed because she saw something else? A criminal act of one of the troupe? Or perhaps two people making love who weren't supposed to?"

"Lovemaking isn't a criminal act," said Sigrid and a warm wave of awareness promptly washed over her as Nauman's foot nudged hers teasingly under the table.

Fortunately neither Anne nor Roman seemed to notice. Her housemate was still running over the probabilities.

"Rikki's hopelessly insane over Nate, although Nate can *hardly* be described as oversexed," he mused in a low rumble. "Emmy was living with David Orland back then and it was certainly no secret from Eric; Win and Emmy may have *slept* together but sex doesn't seem terribly important to Win either; none of the men would care *whom* Ginger bedded; and Helen *knows* that Cliff's unfaithful and it doesn't bother her any more than it would bother Cliff should Helen turn the tables."

"Actually, it does bother Helen Delgado," Sigrid told him and repeated part of the conversation she'd had with the designer that afternoon.

"All the same," countered Roman, "she's right about the children. I simply do *not* see how anyone in the troupe could have an unhealthy interest in children and it not be soon apparent."

"Perhaps the child was a coincidence after all," Anne suggested. "Maybe it was a simple crime of passion—one of Emmy's scorned lovers."

"I suggest it was Miss Scarlett in the conservatory with the candlestick," said Roman. "More coffee anyone?"

Sigrid covered her cup with her hand but smiled at Roman even as she shook her head. "You're probably right."

Anne hid a yawn behind her hand. "Too deep for me, chickabiddies. And too late. Me for home and bed."

"I'll drop you," Nauman offered and Sigrid didn't know if she was pleased or disappointed.

While Roman went to fetch a book he'd borrowed from Anne a few weeks earlier, Sigrid followed Nauman and her mother out to the hall and handed them their coats.

"'Night, honey," said Anne. She took the book from Roman, reached up to kiss Sigrid's bent head, then tactfully stepped out into the chilly courtyard ahead of Nauman, who did not have a peck on the cheek in mind for her daughter.

"I shall load the dishwasher," Roman announced, not to be outdone in tactfulness.

Sigrid felt her heart do funny little skips as Nauman embraced her.

"Dinner at my place tomorrow night?" he asked.

"Yes, please."

He smiled at her in the darkness and followed Anne's small figure across the courtyard, paused at the gate, and then turned back to Sigrid, who had remained in the open doorway despite the cold night air.

"Forget something?"

Nauman jangled Roman's house keys in his hand. "I don't think I can start my car with these. You must have given me Roman's raincoat."

Now that he mentioned it, Sigrid realized that the raincoat he'd left in was at least two sizes too large.

"Freud says there's no such thing as an accident," Nauman observed when he'd retrieved his own coat and found his car keys.

"Smart man, Freud," Sigrid murmured, not at all displeased to repeat their goodnight kiss.

But later, just as she was almost asleep, she came wide awake with a sudden certainty as to why Emmy Mion had died on Saturday instead of Friday or Sunday.

And Freud was wrong. There *were* such things as accidents.

Chapter 27

Wednesday morning dawned clear and sunny, cool enough for coats but warmer than the day before. Mick Cluett still had a chesty cough but at least he was at the morning briefing in Sigrid's office.

As coffee and doughnuts made the rounds, Sigrid said, "Glad to see you're feeling better, Cluett," then moved briskly through the review of her team's caseload as each member brought the others up to date on current lines of investigations.

She was pleased to hear that the leads she'd given

Peters and Eberstadt yesterday had borne fruit and that a suspect had confessed to killing the floater.

"The D.A.'s office called," said Elaine Albee, brushing powdered sugar from her blue tweed jacket. "That podiatrist's trial went to the jury late yesterday and it took them only twelve minutes to return a guilty verdict."

Sigrid had deliberately saved the Emmy Mion investigation for last; and after other business was out of the way, she used the timetable she'd constructed yesterday to review what they'd learned so far. As for what she now suspected, she waited until after she'd dismissed everyone except Elaine Albee and Mick Cluett.

Cluett cleared her file cabinet and desk of empty paper cups and dumped them in her wastebasket along with the doughnut napkins as Sigrid outlined her speculations, but he gave her all his attention when she described how the killer might have lulled Emmy Mion's suspicions.

"How good are you with children?" Sigrid asked Elaine.

The younger woman shrugged. "Average, I guess."

"The little Pennewelf boy—I think he's named Billy—goes to school a half-day in the afternoons," Sigrid said. "See if you can get him to tell you who Emmy yelled at about Amanda Gillespie and then meet us at the theater." She looked at the time. "Say in two hours?"

As Elaine left, Sigrid gave Cluett Sergio Avril's address and told him to sign out a car. "This early, he'll probably be at home."

In short terse sentences, she told him precisely what he was to ask the composer and what he expected to hear when he joined her at the theater. "But no leading questions," she warned. "If it's what I think, I want it to come in Avril's own words."

Mick Cluett hoisted his beefy frame from the chair beside her desk and then hesitated.

Sigrid looked up from her paperwork. "Question, Cluett?"

The older man started to answer but was seized by a paroxysm of coughing.

He was carrying at least fifty extra pounds, thought Sigrid, and if his flushed face were any indication, his

blood pressure was probably too high. His dark suit fit
well enough, but the buttons of his shirt strained at his
belly, and his collar was too tight. How many years since
he'd seen the inside of a gym, she wondered, or chased
anyone down a dark alley? And why had McKinnon specialled
in a detective of Cluett's age, in his condition, instead of
leaving him to finish out his forty in Manhattan Beach?

"Cluett?" she repeated as his cough subsided.

"I'm okay. I probably should have taken off another
day but I don't have much sick leave left and—" Again he
hesitated.

Sigrid frowned. "You wanted something?"

"It's just that I've been thinking, Lieutenant. Your
name and all."

"Yes?" she said icily.

Mick Cluett shifted uneasily under her cool gaze, but
plunged on. "You wouldn't be any kin to Detective Leif
Harald, would you now?"

"My father."

Mick Cluett cocked his head. "Well, I'll be damned!"
he said, studying her openly. "Leif Harald's kid. I *thought*
there was something familiar about your name." A broad
smile creased his puffy face as he sat back down in the
chair, clearly prepared for a long and comfortable session
of reminiscing.

Sigrid knew it was to be expected. She remembered
her father only in vague and unconnected snatches but
always with laughter; and since childhood, she had watched
Anne turn strangers into instant friends with her ready
smiles and easy southern charm. People who had known
only her parents always assumed that Leif and Anne's
daughter had to have inherited their gregariousness.

"You got Leif's tallness and his eyes," said Cluett,
unconsciously paralleling her thoughts, "but not much of
Anne, did you?" He looked suddenly abashed. "What I
mean is, well, she was a little thing, wasn't she?"

Sigrid knew very well that he was remembering her
mother's beauty rather than her height, but she nodded.

"Hair like yours, though. She still living?"

"We had dinner together last night," Sigrid acknowledged. "Detective Cluett—"

"Aw, call me Mickey," he said expansively. "Everybody else does and hell! I bounced you on my knee a couple of times when you weren't big as a minute."

Sigrid mentally gritted her teeth at his familiarity. It was always difficult to make herself speak of anything personal. Especially here. She had kept her off-duty life rigorously separate from her work. Not for her the easy camaraderie the others seemed to fall into, the surface chitchat of daily intercourse. It was easier to hide her self-consciousness behind a facade of reserve. In the past year she'd learned to trust Tillie enough to begin to lower her guard with him, but she knew that most of the others considered her a cold and sexless automaton. They might not dispute her competence, but she knew that she made them uncomfortable.

Mick Cluett seemed to feel he had her pegged, though, for he was now rattling on freely about the old days. "Why, I broke your dad in when he first signed on the force. They used to put all the rookies with me for their first six months. I was working over in the old Sixteenth Precinct when Leif came aboard and I remember—"

"Detective Cluett," she interrupted crisply with a pointed glance at her watch. "I suggest we continue this another time. You've now somewhat less than two hours to interview Avril before we meet with Albee at the theater."

"Oh, yeah. Right, Lieutenant," he said, getting to his feet heavily. But there was a hurt expression on his broad face as he left.

Yet when she was alone again, Sigrid did not immediately return to work, for, by his loquaciousness, the old detective had stirred a half-memory of her own. She crossed to the file cabinet and pulled out a folder. When Captain McKinnon had suggested she read the records of her father's death, she had photocopied a set of those yellowing reports for her personal files.

Now she leafed through them until she came to a report filed by the driver of one of the patrol units which had replied to McKinnon's call for help.

It was signed by Michael Cluett.

*   *   *

Since the hardware store didn't open till ten, Elaine Albee had planned to seek Billy Pennewelf at home three blocks away; and the store was still dark when Sigrid passed. Inside the 8th-AV-8 Dance Theater, however, she found Eric Kee and Win West in the corner prop room where, under Helen Delgado's supervision, they had begun to construct simple props and backdrops for their Christmas production. Eric was cutting out basic toy shapes from heavy cardboard: a drum, a ball, a teddy bear which would be painted and then stapled to scrap blocks of two-by-fours so that they could stand around the tree.

Win was at work on the tree itself, dreamily pasting strips of newspaper onto a chicken-wire skeleton.

"When it's sprayed green, and draped in some tinsel, it'll look enough like a tree," Helen said confidently.

Sigrid looked around the workroom, noting the slap-dash lack of order in the way the designer kept her supplies and equipment.

She wandered back down the hall to the dimly lit stage. The dusty velour maskers on each side were in place again and the life-size goblin puppets were piled beside the light and sound boards, but the back screen was still rolled up above the mirrored rear wall. Sigrid stood quietly at the center of the stage and tried to place each member of the troupe.

There was where Sergio Avril claimed to have stood, there Ginger Judson claimed to have sat. Cliff Delgado there, separated from Eric Kee by one of the maskers. There from Win West's spot, Rikki Innes claimed to have seen Ginger diagonally opposite before Rikki crossed between the screen and mirror to her own place, again separated from Ginger's by a velour masker.

Closely witnessed only by Ginger, the killer had entered from Eric's place to Sigrid's left, had danced with Emmy for but a short moment or two, lured her to the top of the scaffold over here, then smashed her down onto the fence to spill her life's blood upon the stage floor there, where one spot was scrubbed cleaner than the rest.

"Lieutenant?"

Sigrid turned to see Elaine Albee watching from beyond the proscenium.

"You were right on the money, Lieutenant."

Sigrid swung herself over the edge and motioned Elaine to one of the pews where they could speak without the risk of being overheard.

With commendable brevity, the younger detective reported on her approach to Billy Pennewelf's mother and the mother's no-nonsense request that the child answer her questions. "One thing," Elaine concluded. "Billy said Emmy was angriest—and I'm quoting him directly—'over his holes.' Does that make any sense to you?"

Sigrid nodded. "I think it does." She looked at her watch. Cluett should have been here by now. Well, they'd have to continue without him.

They went backstage through the side door, down past the wooden steps, past the office and the bathroom, switching on lights as they went, to Nate Richmond's workroom. Elaine turned on the lights there and Sigrid immediately went past her into the makeshift cave which served as the light wizard's darkroom.

It was as Sigrid remembered from her cursory examination on Saturday: the pipes and faucets that serviced the darkroom were jury-rigged taps on the bathroom plumbing next door. Most of the cracks on the bathroom side had been legitimately patched with wide electrical duct tape to prevent light from leaking into the darkroom; but as she'd expected even before hearing Billy Pennewelf's testimony, concealed beneath a calendar and the instruction sheet from a box of toner were two small holes, covered by easily movable flaps, on either side of the leaky toilet next door about half-way up the wall.

He would only have had to wait until a child turned its back to the wall and dropped its underpants to take as many surreptitious pictures as he liked, the camera sounds masked by the constantly running water in the tank.

"Amanda Gillespie told her sister that he used to let her help him in the darkroom," Elaine said. "Maybe the flap wasn't closed tightly that day and light leaked in. Or maybe she walked in on him as he was taking pictures."

Even as she spoke, the outer door opened and Nate Richmond entered, followed by Ulrike Innes.

"Ah." He smiled at them. "I thought for a moment I must have left the lights on. Were you looking for. . .?"

His words died away as he stepped into the darkroom and saw the open flaps over his sink.

"Yes, Mr. Richmond," said Sigrid. "We were hoping to see the pictures Emmy Mion found Saturday when she came looking for pictures of Amanda Gillespie's class. I can't believe you would have destroyed them after the trouble you went to to make them. And to steal them back."

"I—I don't know what you mean," he faltered, his face ashen.

Ulrike Innes placed her strong body in front of him protectively. "Aren't you supposed to have a search warrant before you invade someone's privacy?"

Elaine snorted. "Mr. Richmond didn't seem to mind invading the kids' privacy," she said hotly.

Sigrid held up a restraining hand.

"We can, of course, get a warrant if you insist—"

"Don't bother," Richmond said wearily. "I'll show you."

"Nate!" cried Rikki, swinging around to face him. "What are you doing?" The pale oval of her face was terrified for him.

"It doesn't matter, Rikki," he soothed her. "I haven't done anything wrong. Not really. You'll see."

Above the sink was a set of metal shelves which held yellow boxes filled with photographic paper, developing chemicals and the like. Nate stood on a step stool and brought down one of the eight-by-twelve boxes.

Inside were dozens of black-and-white photographs of partially nude children, some printed through gauzy filters, the others in sharp detail.

"And this is how you get your jollies?" asked Elaine, repulsed.

"No!" he said. "See, Rikki? That's why I couldn't talk about it, not even to you. Everyone looks at pictures like this and yells *Voyeur!* But I'm *not!*" He was almost in tears as he pleaded his case to Sigrid. "I'm not, Lieutenant. I love children, but for themselves alone. Their sweetness, their innocence—everything about them. I'd never do anything to mess that up. I don't lust for them. Not like dirty-minded people think. It's only that their bodies are so beautiful, so delicate. Look at the curve of that small bottom, the way her skin almost glows with an inner luminosity. They grow up and out of that beauty so quickly."

He fanned out some of the pictures. "I look at these pictures and I feel like Wordsworth. Remember? 'Not in utter nakedness, but trailing clouds of glory do we come from God.' Heaven really does lie all around young children— so much immortal beauty and so fleeting."

Rikki was sobbing openly now and he put his arm around her. "Don't cry, Rikki."

"Only pictures?" she sobbed. "I didn't know. I thought you had—Oh Nate, I've been so frightened for you. When I heard Emmy storming about a photograph—"

"Somehow I left one of these mixed in with the prints of last winter's dance class," said Nate. "She came in with a plaid ribbon Saturday, said she thought it belonged to Mandy Gillespie. Poor little Mandy."

Sigrid stopped him. "Mr. Richmond, I think it's time to warn you and Miss Innes, before you say anything else, that you do have a right to a lawyer. Albee?"

Stunned, the two listened numbly as Elaine Albee read them their rights under the Miranda ruling.

"Do you understand, Mr. Richmond?" Sigrid repeated when Elaine had finished.

"Yes," said Richmond, "but it's okay, I tell you. I haven't done anything wrong."

"Miss Innes?"

"Y-yes," the pale-haired dancer quavered, "but Nate couldn't have killed Emmy. He was working the lights."

"Killed *Emmy?*" His gnome-like face was shocked. "Of course I couldn't. Look—could we sit down?"

He led them from the darkroom to the low round table in the middle of his workshop and pulled out chairs for everyone. Rikki Innes clung to his side and he patted her consolingly. "Emmy was my friend. We go back forever and in the end I think I did make her understand, though I had to promise I wouldn't take any more of these pictures. You heard her, Rikki."

"Is that what she meant?" Rikki asked, fresh tears sliding down her cheek. "You didn't tell me and then later when she said—"

"When she said what, Miss Innes?" asked Sigrid. "When she said she'd found Amanda Gillespie's missing hair ribbon in the pocket of Mr. Richmond's jacket?"

"What?" said Nate.

"She had moved the rest of her winter clothes to the dressing room upstairs," Sigrid told him. "Either she'd taken your jacket home with her last spring or it'd been hanging up there mixed in with other things. Whichever, something unexpected happened Saturday. The weather changed early Saturday morning and instead of Indian summer, it was suddenly chilly. So Emmy Mion ran upstairs and by sheer accident took the first jacket she came to. Your red-plaid jacket, Mr. Richmond. And when she eventually put her hands in the pocket sometime that morning, she came out with the hair ribbon Amanda's killer had picked up automatically last February."

In a wordless silence broken only by Rikki's hopeless weeping, Nate shook his head as if dazed by the lieutenant's scenario.

Implacably, Sigrid hammered home her accusations. "That's when you knew you'd have to kill Emmy, too."

"But I *didn't*! I *couldn't* have! A hundred people *know* I was upstairs, working the lights from the rear booth."

"You see?" cried Rikki. "You know he couldn't have."

"Yes, but you could have, Miss Innes."

"Emmy's killer was a man," said Nate. "A male dancer."

"No." Sigrid shook her head slowly. "Ginger Judson told us Saturday afternoon that Emmy almost laughed out loud when the jack-o'-lantern first came onstage, even before he'd begun to pantomime Eric Kee's style. Emmy laughed because she had seen Cliff Delgado use his wife's paint mask as a burlesque codpiece and knew that Rikki had stuffed the mask down the front of her tights in order to disguise her sex. Emmy thought it was more fun and games and she died for it.

"When you doused the lights, Miss Innes ran off stage right, then immediately doubled back between the screen and the wall so she'd be in her right place when the lights came back on. As she ran, she removed the mask and pumpkin head and flung them out in the passage where they were kicked under the stairs in all the confusion."

Rikki Innes had folded her arms upon the low table and buried her face. Her pale hair fanned out on the table around her.

"Rikki?" Nate touched her shoulder gently. "Rikki? But you loved Emmy."

She nodded without lifting her head.

"You loved her, Rikki. Why would you kill her?"

She raised her face to him then and that delicate oval was blotched and puffy. "I loved you more, Nate, and she thought you'd killed Mandy."

"But I *didn't*!" he said and exasperation mingled with raw grief in his voice. Then disbelief and horror swept over him. "Oh God, Rikki! Not Mandy, too?"

"I had to, Nate. She saw you with a camera pressed against that hole and figured out what you were taking pictures of. It scared her. And it scared me when she told me. Suddenly, all I could think of was how you always had more time for the children than you had for me."

Her ravaged eyes held his and her voice dropped in shame. "You never make love to me unless I ask. Yet the children . . . forever rubbing against you, your hands caressing them—"

"Not like that!" I never actually let myself—"

"How could I be sure?" she cried, half-angered by his denial of guilt. "You were always here at the theater. If it wasn't for Emmy or Ginger and if it wasn't for me, who else was there? And then Mandy said she was going to tell her mother. I couldn't have that. Whatever you'd done— even if it was *that*—I couldn't let her destroy you. So I said I'd take her to tell her mother and I grabbed up your jacket—and—"

She buried her face again.

It was then that Mick Cluett finally arrived. Sigrid

threw him an interrogative glance and he nodded to confirm that she had reasoned correctly: Sergio Avril had indeed followed Rikki Innes's instructions to the T, which meant he'd been deliberately led to erase Mrs. Gillespie's message.

If Emmy Mion had left the ribbon in her desk drawer as she'd left the picture, Rikki would have destroyed it, too, and there would have been nothing left to link the child's death to Emmy's.

Sigrid rose from her chair feeling drained and soiled. "Book them both," she ordered.

Nate Richmond's head came up at that. "*Me?* I didn't know—"

"You may not be charged for murder," Sigrid said, and her voice had gone as slate-cold as her eyes, "but I will be triple damned if we don't find some way to keep you away from children the rest of your life."

She handed the box of pictures to Elaine.

"But I explained about that!"

"Not to Amanda Gillespie, you didn't," she said and turned away as Mick Cluett unsnapped the handcuffs from his belt.

Chapter 28

Personal notes of Dr. Christa Ferrell, re: Corrie Makaroff *[Wednesday, 4 November—I must not internalize this. I am a professional. Nothing should surprise me. Never again will I let myself forget that, though how any professional could have foreseen—This has been a ghastly day. Anne Harald pretended to be sympathetic, but I can see where Sig. gets her judgmental attitude. How does she know so much about preconceptualization & how dare she apply that tag to me?*

Oh hell—blast—& DAMN!!!

I can see Dr. Hennemann now—short, fat, & dumpy,

with an ugly moustache on her upper lip. "Yah," *she told me a couple of years ago during an evaluation.* "You haf good grades, good skills, good luck, but you rush too quick to diagnosis. Too much preconception on insufficient data."

Well, I don't care. It was a classic case & even if I did preconceptualize a little bit, I should have been right.

Since Sig. H. & I were at St. M's together, A.H. has promised not to use the Makaroff case in her magazine series although she says Sig. will have to be told. (NB— better check with Dad's lawyer about what constitutes slander in case she doesn't keep her word.)

Wish to God I hadn't told Dr. Hennemann I was preparing a paper for next summer's conference. On the other hand, if A.H. keeps quiet about me, perhaps I can still salvage this case. After all, no real damage done. I'll continue to treat Corrie & none of my colleagues need ever know how close I came to screwing up her therapy.

Galls to think how when I called A.H. yesterday to confirm today's photo session, I told her she could expect some really great action pics, that Corrie would probably act out the whole scene. Well, I was certainly right about that, wasn't I? Oh bloody HELL!]

Once again I had set the stage before Corrie arrived: G.I. Joe and Barbie on the hassock, the toy hammer on the floor beside it, the little brown bear and schoolgirl doll on a nearby chair.

Corrie tried to shy away and look at some picture books beside the door, but I led her over to the dolls and again we talked of how grown-ups may say and do dreadful things which they afterwards regret. Especially if they've been drinking.

"It isn't their fault," I reassured her.

Corrie's blue-green eyes looked deeply into mine.

The timing felt so right to me that I said, "Do you remember how your mommy and Ray used to yell at each other?"

Her eyes dropped, but she nodded.

"Show me," I said softly.

*   *   *

Hesitantly at first, and then more surely as she finally let herself relive the past, Corrie picked up the dolls and worked her way back to that dreadful evening.

Darlene must have been drinking heavily, for the little bear and the schoolgirl doll both begged her not to drink any more.

"Just shut up, you two. I'm getting sick and tired of everybody telling me what to do. Get to bed!"

"Aw, cool off, babe." It was a creditable imitation of a masculine voice.

"You shut up, too."

"Aw, whatcha getting so steamed up about?"

"Shove it, Ray! One lousy window in this god-awful sweatbox and you can't get the damn thing open."

"I'll get the fucking window open. Give me another drink and quit yapping."

Maneuvering the G.I. Joe figure, Corrie leaned over and, for the first time, picked up the toy hammer. "Oops!" she said in the Ray voice.

The obscenities that poured from Corrie's lips then would have startled me if earlier sessions hadn't prepared me for Darlene's foul mouth.

"Shut up, shut up, *shut up!*" screamed the Ray voice and suddenly Corrie had the G.I. Joe pounding the Barbie doll with the toy hammer.

"Stop it!" cried the schoolgirl doll. "Oh, please, stop!"

The hammer fell to the floor.

"Oh, Jesus!" said the Ray voice.

Corrie pushed the G.I. Joe off the hassock and her voice was her own again as she quavered, "Ray ran away and Mommy just laid there and Tonnie tried to make her get up and she wouldn't and Tonnie said she was dead and she called the police and told them Ray killed our mommy—and—"

She dissolved in a flood of tears and I pulled her close to me and let her cry out all the grief she'd been holding in for so long.

Part of me was still absorbed in the traumatic scene the child had witnessed, but the other part exulted because my baby doll games had paid off. Corrie had finally unblocked and now a healthy integrated healing could begin.

[It really had been a textbook case, one I'd enjoy presenting to the conference, I thought smugly. I couldn't resist a triumphant smile toward the one-way window where I hoped A. H.'s cameras had captured some of the drama.

Okay, maybe I was thinking of myself a little right then as I held the sobbing child, imagining how Mrs. Harald's magazine article would help get my private practice off to a flying start; but I swear to God I was also thinking how great it was that I could end up my stint w/ Social Services by giving the Berkowitzes such a happily-ever-after ending.

A moment later, Corrie pulled away & turned the Barbie doll over. "Oh, my head," she moaned in a wobbly imitation of her mother's voice, & the ground slid out from under me as the schoolgirl doll lifted the toy hammer & pounded her back into silence.]

ABOUT THE AUTHOR

MARGARET MARON lives on the family farm in North Carolina. *Baby Doll Games* is the fifth in the Sigrid Harald series.